THE FALL OUT

FRIENDS MAKE THE BEST ENEMIES

THE DARK HEARTS SERIES

MARIA FRANKLAND

AUTONOMY
PRESS

First published by Autonomy Press 2023

This novel is entirely a work of fiction. The names, characters and incidents portrayed in it are the work of the author's imagination. Any resemblance to actual persons, living or dead, events or localities is entirely coincidental.

Maria Frankland asserts the moral right to be identified as the author of this work.

First edition

For Jane Browne, my writerly soulmate
and wonderful friend

JOIN MY 'KEEP IN TOUCH LIST'

If you'd like to be kept in the loop about new books and special offers, join my 'keep in touch list' by visiting www. mariafrankland.co.uk

You will receive a free novella as a thank you for joining!

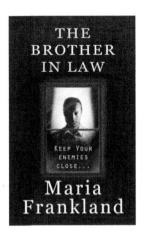

PROLOGUE

HER SCREAM RIPS through the darkness, only silenced as she hits the water. Though *hits* is too gentle a word. On impact from the eleventh deck, maybe *smacks* or *smashes* might cover it. Then the cold. If the moment of landing didn't kill her, the shock of the March temperature will have done.

Me, I'm just frozen with shock.

As I close my eyes, I can only hope it was quick, that her terror was fleeting, and she will now find peace and release. My thoughts surprise me. So calm and considered, even in these circumstances.

I wait for sirens. Panic. Commotion. *Someone* must have heard her scream. Or her subsequent crash into the water. The sounds are playing within me on a loop. I'll probably hear them for the rest of my life. Out to sea, all is inky black. I twist my head left, then right, my eyes aching in the reflection of lights. The laughter and distant music heighten my sense of being suddenly alone. Everything has changed. And yet, nothing has changed.

Eventually, I steel myself to peer *right* over the balcony. Perhaps flailing arms or white foam at the site of her landing will be visible. But there's nothing. It's as though she never existed.

Still the ship keeps moving, cutting its relentless path through the waves. I should raise the alarm, increase any chance of her being rescued. The odds of surviving a midnight plunge of that magnitude are slim, perhaps? But still possible. After all, she didn't collide with the ship on the way down like she could have done. But how long could someone stay alive down there?

I continue to stare for what feels like an eternity. Not that there's anything to see. Not a thing. She's gone.

Claimed by the North Sea. And what was left of her conscience.

PART I

HELEN

CHAPTER 1

"Ugh. Coco. Ger'off." If there's anything worse than waking up feeling like there's a drill inside your skull, it's waking up with not only that drill, but also a dog slobbering all over your face.

Pushing her off, I haul myself to my elbows. The doorbell *is* ringing. Again. And again. I wasn't dreaming it as I first thought.

"Alright." The room spins as I sit right up and swing my legs to the floor. "Give me a minute." Not that whoever it is will be able to hear me from up here.

Grappling on my bedside table for my phone, I squint at the clock. *Shit!* It's nearly nine. As I ram my arms into the sleeves of my dressing gown, I'm already on my way down the stairs. It's that bloody blackout blind. I keep thinking it's still the middle of the night when I should be up and moving. Of course my oversleeping this morning is absolutely nothing to do with the four bottles of wine I shared with Liz last night. *At least four.* I lost count after the fifth glass.

.   .   .

"Thank goodness for that. Penny thought she'd been abandoned." Jenna thrusts the lead at me. "I'm going to have to fly sis, or I'll be late." She turns on the heel of her boot, but must have second thoughts. She pauses. Then peers at me. "Are you alright Helen? You're a very funny colour."

"I will be. Don't worry. You just get yourself to work."

"You don't look good at all. Something you ate?"

"It's self-inflicted."

"Ah right. I withdraw my sympathy then." She laughs. "Good night, was it?" By that, she means who, where, when, how and why?

"Just drinks with a friend."

"Excellent." She nods with what could be approval. "I'm glad to hear you've been sociable for a change. Who?"

"Just the next door neighbour." She's got the when and the who.

"That one?" Jenna jerks her head to the right. To the house that's become notorious, for many reasons. "Really? Are you mad?"

I nod. And brace myself.

"After how she used to bully you? And all the history between you both? You're a damn sight more forgiving than I could ever be." She pulls a face. "She made your life an utter misery - I can't believe you could give her the time of day. Oh never mind what I can or can't believe. If I don't get a move on, I'll miss the bus. I'll have to speak to you about this some other time."

"Whatever. You'd better get gone then. Besides, there's a coffee with my name on it inside."

Her face relaxes into a smile. "Thanks again. I really appreciate you taking the dog like this."

"What are sisters for?"

"I promise I'll start paying you as soon as I get on my feet." She bangs the gate and looks back over it.

"It's not a problem. Honestly." I'm lying, but she doesn't need to know the extent of how broke I am. "One more dog won't be too much extra work. Come on then Penny. Let's have you."

Coco's dancing around by the back door as I head into the kitchen, making me feel guilty for not letting her out sooner. Flicking the kettle on as I pass, I rifle through the clutter on the kitchen counter to find the key. They both dart into the garden like they've never seen the outside world before.

I watch through the window, whilst forcing some paracetamol down. One starts to dissolve in my mouth. The bitter taste makes me want to throw up. Ugh. Never, ever again. It's only ever when I'm with Liz that I get into this state. And it's just not worth it the morning after. It's alright for her, a self-proclaimed lady of leisure, who doesn't have to get up and do any work. She has money coming out of her ears, though I don't ask questions. I kind of know anyway. It funds a life consisting of Netflix, the gym, umpteen spa treatments and frequent holidays. But she's never happy. Far from it, in fact. It was only last night she was moaning about her *lack of purpose* and *feeling lonely*. She can hardly blame anyone else for that.

I told her that she should try having ten dogs on her books, then she'd know about lacking human company. I've got another dog that I should have picked up by now, and three more for lunchtime walks. And today's a quiet day. It's a good job as I don't trust myself to venture outdoors just yet. I hardly want to be barfing in public.

I fill a glass with water, trying to steady my nausea as I continue to stare across the garden. It's one of those days where it doesn't look as though it'll get properly light. I'm not a fan of January at all. What I'd give to be like Liz, to be able to bugger off at a moment's notice. Away from this grey drizzle. Away from dogs, no matter how much I might love them all. And away from *myself.* That's the main reason. Amongst everything else, I'm fed up of being humdrum Helen. Jeans, wellies, anorak, straggly hair that I can never get a brush through. People pleasing, introvert yet lonely, and eternally single. At least since Liz moved in, I've had some company. Even if there were many times when the prospect of her living next door would have struck fear into the core of my being. I'm more relaxed about it now, after all, the past is in the past. Plus she doesn't know what she doesn't know. Only now, we've got more than just the past that binds us.

The dogs roll around together. What I'd give for an ounce of that energy. They start chasing up and down the garden. Running far too close to the pond. One of them will end up in it, the way they're going after each other. Suddenly they stop. Both of them. Coco's sniffing around the rockery at the perimeter. Penny's digging beside the pond for all she's worth. She's a swine for digging. I rush to the door. "Penny. Coco. Get here. Now." Without looking up, they continue sniffing and digging.

It's only when I dart towards them, dangling two slices of ham, that they come running. I must get that pond fenced off. And it's not just to prevent dogs from falling in.

DEAR DIARY

A new girl started at our school today. Liz Welsh. Mr Smith told us about her in registration. The whole class. *We have to be kind*, he said. *Look out for her.* She's been taken into care as her mum's gone away. I don't know if that means a children's home or a foster home - he didn't say, but he did say she's the only person in our school in the care of the local authority.

I wonder what he meant by *her mum's gone away*...Died? Run off? I've heard two rumours today. One is that she's been sent to prison for something to do with drugs, and the other is that she died from a drugs overdose. I wonder which one it is?

As the only person in class with a spare seat beside me. I hoped to get a new friend in this girl who needed *looking out for.* I got a glimpse of Liz through the classroom door, standing with an official-looking woman. She isn't what I'd expect *someone in care* to look like. She's tall, almost wiry, with bulging eyes. The way Mr Smith was talking, I'd already formed a picture of someone, small and terrified looking. She must have given her permission for him to be honest with us about who she is. After all, we'd find out about her background sooner or later.

She didn't *act* like a new girl. Instead, she sauntered in as though she'd been at the school her whole life. Mr Smith even told her to get rid of her chewing gum. I was shocked when she grinned as she spat it into her hand. Then he told her to make sure she got herself some proper school shoes instead of trainers. I couldn't help but feel jealous at her Nike Airs.

"Alright." It was the cockiest tone I've ever heard anyone use with a teacher. "Just let me get through the door, will you?"

By afternoon registration, she'd persuaded someone to swap places with her. So I found myself sitting next to the class swot, Jeremy, or Jez as he's known to those wanting to pick his brains. He's plastered in acne and emits the permanent stench of body odour. I want to sit on my own again - I can't believe I've ended up next to him of all people. He'd probably rather not be next to me either. He hasn't spoken to me, not even once.

After registration, we got Miss Taylor for Maths, Jez didn't even talk to me when she said *discuss the equation with the person next to you.* He just wrote something and covered it over so I couldn't see. Then there was a load of whispering behind me. And laughing. Something hit my shoulder. Then my neck. Then my ear. I reached for it. Globs of paper. As I turned, Liz hid something under her desk. Meanwhile sly Sally who she was sitting next to, had the barrel of a biro in her hand. I saw her spit something small and white into her hand. She grinned at me and pretended to write, whilst giggling with Liz the whole time.

"Would someone like to tell me what's so funny about these equations?" Miss Taylor swung around and glared at me. "Helen. Clearly it's *you* causing this mayhem. Would you like to tell me why you've gotten umpteen bits of paper stuck into your hair?"

I scrunched at my hair which has earned me many a derogatory nickname over the years - everything from bird's nest to hair monster. I could feel the spit-soaked lumps as I ran my fingers through it. Or at least, tried to. It wasn't long since I'd sat alone in the dining hall, forcing globs of pink custard down my throat. My stomach heaved at the thought of my hair soaked in someone's spit and phlegm.

"Go to the toilets and sort it out immediately." She pointed from me, to the door. "Then you can work on your own in the corridor until you learn how to conduct yourself in my lessons."

"But it was them." I swung around and pointed at Liz and Sally. "It should be them you're sending out."

"Are you deaf? I said out of my classroom."

No one likes me. Not even the teachers. And I was picking globs of paper from my hair for the rest of the day.

CHAPTER 2

I SHIVER as I slide my arms from my dressing gown. There's a ground frost this morning, but I only ever put the central heating on at night. Making a few sacrifices is the only way I can afford to stay in this house, whilst continuing to be self-employed. I bought it at the right time, as they say, but having remortgaged twice, I'm now up to my neck in repayments. But I couldn't work in an office or a shop. Besides, despite sometimes feeling isolated, I like dogs far, far better than people. Though I'm now two hours late to collect Honey, the labrador I'm paid to pick up at eight and drop back off at six. I hope the owners don't find out. That would be just my luck. A coffee and some toast has taken the edge off the nausea. A shower will cure it completely, fingers crossed. And then I'll go for Honey.

As I point my feet into jeans, last night's conversation comes flooding back. Liz was acting strange. *Really* strange. Going on and on about dying. I couldn't get her to shut up about it. Even asking me how I'd feel if *she* died. *Would I cry? Would I miss her?* It's all off its head really, considering how she used to be with me at school. She said other stuff besides that, but it's all a haze this morning. I keep telling myself that her being so maudlin was probably just the drink talking. The last thing I want to be discussing, or even *thinking* about with her is anything to do with dying. Especially not whilst sitting in what was Lou's lounge. And Darren's. I always feel weird going around there after everything that's happened. It feels as if Lou can somehow hear us.

A true friend will help you hide a body. Gosh. Did she really say that, or did I imagine it? I need to stop drinking so much. It does me no favours whatsoever. Apart from putting me to sleep, which is always a blessed relief. But Liz needs to stop drinking completely. As she's admitted several times, all it does is loosen her tongue. One day, I fear, it will loosen it too much. And I don't want dragging any further into her mire, than I already have been.

Last night was the first time I'd been around there in a while. It's funny really, as when Lou was alive, I yearned to be invited inside for a cuppa. Her life looked perfect to me, as an eternal outsider, and I couldn't help but eavesdrop on her conversations from my side of the fence. She had a mum I'd have given my right arm for, not to mention the boyfriend and the daughter. It just goes to show, no matter how perfect someone's life appears from the outside, they still never know what, or in her case, who, is around the corner.

I was in the public gallery when Donna was sentenced. She stood in that dock like butter wouldn't melt, and to be fair, it was hard to equate the wide eyes and demure appearance with someone capable of bludgeoning her best friend to death with a hammer. I really couldn't believe it when they found her guilty. At first I thought I was hearing things. Liz was sitting with Darren two rows in front of me and clapped her hands together when the jury spokesperson uttered that single word. According to news reports, Donna's going to appeal it. Though that remains to be seen.

After the brutal death Lou suffered in her garden and everything that's happened since, I prefer Liz to come here, to my house, when she wants some company. Being in that house chills me to the bone. Though it's not as if my house doesn't harbour secrets of its own. Not now. But last night, when Liz said she'd just lit a fire, I was enticed. It was a toss up between her cosy, comfy lounge, or my chilly, cluttered one. Plus, I didn't fancy spending yet another evening alone. It's not like I get any invitations, apart from the occasional one from Jenna when she's not too busy with her new job.

It's taken until now to stop feeling like I'm on the verge of puking. But two hours of hauling myself to the top end of the park, then back again with five dogs in tow, seems to have sorted me out at last. Coupled with the best morning-after cure of all. Tea and a bacon butty. But the hangover has given way to exhaustion now. I don't think it was sleep that found me when I hit the pillow last night. It was more that I slumped into an alcohol-fuelled coma. Still, it was preferable to the insomnia that's been plaguing me of late.

I curl up on the sofa with my fleece and my journal. Coco jumps up and lays across my feet. I'm grateful for her warmth. And her company. Without dogs, my life would not have been worth living at times. When my first ever dog had to be put to sleep, I was ten times more devastated than when Mum rang to say Dad had passed away. The difference being, Mabel was in my life every single day, whilst Dad was only *ever* on the outskirts of my life. I never felt as though I even knew him.

Because they already had Jenna, Mum once told me that they'd hoped for a boy when she was expecting me. Then, she'd had such a hard time having me, that to try for a third child was out of the question. I was obviously a poor replacement for the son they'd craved. Dumpy, unpopular, introvert. And a girl.

I reach for my journal. It's exactly where I abandoned it yesterday. I should hide it more carefully, not that I get many visitors who might spot it. I scan through what I managed to write yesterday afternoon before my pen went off kilter as I fell asleep. I can't imagine today being any different. I'm knackered. I'll try though - the page has always been my best friend, helping me to make sense of things. Like the conversation last night. It's not as if I can talk to anyone else about what was said between us. Someone who could help me unpick the bits I remember. I can't even talk to Jenna. She's unable to understand why I give Liz the time of day in the first place.

Who needs an alarm clock when you've got a doorbell? I wake with a start in the fading light, the doorbell reverberating around my brain. I pause, just in case I've dreamt it. When the doorbell used to go mid afternoon, it usually only meant one thing. But those days are over. Still, I jump as a shadow looms in front of the lounge window. Then Liz appears, cupping her eyes as she peers through the glass. She looks almost ethereal in the glow of the street lamp.

"Come on Helen. Open up, will you?" Steam curls from her lips. "It's bloody freezing out here."

I stagger to the door, whilst rubbing crusts of sleep from my eyes. I'd have probably slept until midnight on that sofa if she hadn't appeared. Honey would be late being dropped off as well as being picked up. It's a good job I only have dog owners to answer to instead of a tyrannical boss.

"You look exactly how I feel." Liz laughs as she pushes past me into the hallway. I quickly close the door before the dogs have a chance to make a bolt for it. They could do with going out again, but I really haven't got the energy. "Are you putting the kettle on?"

To an observer, Liz and I could be run-of-the-mill next door neighbours. Friends who live side by side, enjoying ready-made company to fill the void both of us have frequently known. The neighbours might eye Liz curiously, given where she's choosing to live, despite what happened there. It's also common knowledge that she married Lou's ex. But no one knows anything of the history Liz and I share. Only my sister. And luckily she doesn't know *everything*.

"I'd better sit down before I fall down." Liz slides her cup onto the coffee table as she lowers herself to the sofa. I'm glad it's semi-dark in here. At least she won't be able to see dog hair all over the place. I can't even remember when I last vacuumed. Nor can she see the muddy marks everywhere, when really, many people wouldn't let their dogs anyway near the furniture. But it's so tatty, that I'm past caring. Then before I realise I've left it out, she reaches for my diary, still open at the page I was writing before I dropped off to sleep. "What's this then?"

Shit. I was so startled when she came to the window that I didn't think to hide it. "Just a diary." I reach for it.

"A diary eh? Am I in it?" She laughs as she turns a page over. "I bet this would make for interesting reading."

I pluck the book from her grasp, sharpish. "Of course not. It's just for business and stuff." She's probably being sarcastic too. My life is far from interesting as we both very well know.

"Ah right. So it's not one about feelings and full of angst and all that shit then?"

"Erm no. I haven't kept one like that since I was in my teens."

"I bet I was in that one." She laughs even louder. Like her treatment of me when we were teenagers is anything to laugh about.

I glare at her, though my expression is probably lost in the fading light. "I don't want to think about those days." I try to keep my voice steady. Even though she's softened and even changed as an adult, Liz still has all the sensitivity of one of those rocks which border my pond. I'm unsure at times if she realises the extent of the misery she caused me. There were literally times when I could have ended it all. And she'd have been completely to blame if I had.

Liz must hear the wobble in my voice. "Look, I know I've said it a million times but I really am sorry about the past Helen. I can't change it, can I? I can't change anything."

I sit facing her and flick the lamp on, squinting as my eyes adjust. "If only." As the light illuminates her face, I detect genuine remorse in it.

"If only - what?"

"I don't know. I'm just having one of those days, I guess. I saw my sister this morning."

"Jenna, you mean?"

"Yeah. I've only got the one sister, haven't I? Anyway, she couldn't believe I was friends with you. Not after everything that went on between us."

"What else did you tell her?" Liz's eyes narrow, reminding me of the Liz I used to know. On some level she still terrifies me, and I'm always guarded in what I say, even though we're now 'friends.' Still, I can't afford to be choosy. It's not as if I have hordes of potential friends queueing outside my door.

"Nothing. Don't worry." I sip at my coffee, the nausea returning. I really am never drinking wine again. "She was just dropping the dog off and was in a rush to get to her new job." I nod towards Penny.

"Anyway, I just want to go forward now." Liz reaches for Penny who shrinks from her reach and lands at my feet. Penny can be funny with people, but they do say dogs can be an astute judge of character.

"Me too," I say. "But before we do, what was last night all about?"

"I'm surprised you can remember anything to be honest." Liz tucks her legs under herself.

She sounds as though she's half asking me a question, so I just shrug in response.

"Do you know how much wine we put away between us?" She laughs, though it's forced.

"I'm certainly feeling it today. But yes. You were going on about death. Big time."

"I know. I can get a bit morbid with a few drinks inside me. Take no notice."

"You didn't mean anything by it then?"

"By what?" She looks almost worried now.

"You were going on, you know, saying things like, *am I scared of dying* and all that. Then you got onto, what was it, *true friends helping to hide a body.* Of all the topics you could have brought up after everything that's happened round there."

Liz pulls a face. "I was drunk, wasn't I?"

"There are some things that shouldn't be talked about. Ever. Lines that shouldn't be crossed." It's not very often that I speak up in front of Liz, but this needs to be said.

"That works both ways." She seems to be peering at me

more closely. "Do you remember anything else I said? It's all a blur."

"Bits and pieces. It's the same for me to be honest."

"Well let's just forget it, shall we? Call it a blow out. Perhaps we needed it."

I nod and sip my coffee, not convinced.

"I do appreciate everything you've done for me," she continues. "I know we don't have a conventional friendship but..."

"That's an understatement." I force a laugh now.

"But... if you stop interrupting and listen. I want to do something for you. Something that will give me the chance to really make up for all the horrible times I've put you through."

At least she's admitting to them. In fact, last night was the first time she's offered any proper acknowledgement about the past. Distant *or* recent. "I'm listening."

"How do you fancy getting away from all this?"

"What do you mean?"

"Let me treat you." She tucks her hair behind one ear as she looks at me. Her eyes look more bulgy than usual when she's not wearing makeup. Like a fish's. "When was the last time you went away?"

"Well, I stayed with my sister before she moved back up from Birmingham."

"I mean *properly* away. Somewhere more exotic than *Birmingham*. She grins though it's a sarcastic sort of grin. "Like to another country?"

"I've never been to another country." It's true. I've never been able to afford it. Nor would it be much fun, going on my own. Now Jenna's started a new job, she won't be able to go on holiday for ages, assuming she'd even want to go with me. That's if I could afford it in the first place.

"Bloody hell. How on earth do you get to nearly forty

without going abroad?" Liz shakes her head. "I can't understand it."

It's alright for you, I want to say. With the home and whatever income she's managed to secure for herself from Darren, it's little wonder she can do what she wants, when she wants. But she's just mentioned *treating me,* so I stay quiet. No one ever *treats* me to anything. They never have.

"I've been looking at cruises," she continues.

Something in me lights up with excitement. *A cruise?*

"And I don't really want to go on my own."

"You mean...?"

"We'd have to share a cabin to keep costs down. But hey, think about it Helen. Imagine all the different places you'd be able to see over a couple of weeks."

I hesitate. It sounds absolutely amazing on the face of it. But with Liz? Firstly, I don't really want her paying for me. I don't like the idea of being beholden to her. But I wouldn't have a prayer of paying my own way. Not with a measly ten pound an hour, per dog, per day. And not getting paid at all from Jenna. I'd have to board ten dogs all year round, seven days a week to be able to afford to pay for my own cruise. Secondly, after everything that's gone before.

"Call it an apology if you like. And a thank you." She must be able to sense the cogs whirring inside my mind. "I say we do this, and then draw a line under everything, once and for all. Treating you to a cruise can be my way of wiping the slate clean."

If only it were that simple.

DEAR DIARY

Today was the most embarrassing day of my whole life. For a million reasons. I want to hide under my bedcovers and never come out again.

I already know how abnormal I am. After all, who gets to fourteen-and-a-half with a completely flat chest and no sign of their periods starting? And that's aside from the fact that I've no proper friends, I've never had a boyfriend and I get called every name under the sun at school. Then the teachers wonder why I don't want to do PE?

Miss Richardson was taking the register before we were all supposed to get changed.

"Helen Atkins." She stopped when she got to my name. My stomach lurched as she looked at me over the top of her glasses. "I think it's time you made an appointment with your doctor."

Everybody, and I mean *everybody,* in that PE hall twisted around to look at me. I was sitting at the back. As always.

I didn't reply. What would be the point? And nothing

could prevent the heat rising up my neck. I knew what was coming.

"It would appear from your mother's notes..." She waved my carefully crafted letter in the air, "that you've been on your period for the last five weeks. That, by anyone's standards, requires medical intervention."

A snigger went up amongst everyone as they continued to stare at me.

"Is that correct?"

"Erm, yes, I..."

"So if I was to check with your mother that this is the truth, and that this is also her signature, she'd back you up, would she?"

I stared at the parquet flooring. I wasn't going to get what I'd looked forward to all morning. The whole PE lesson in the school library. Being able to escape my daily reality by diving into a story. I might not have experienced it first hand but I've read about period pain. It doesn't go well with cross country running. But if Miss Richardson is going to double check with Mum, I could no longer get out of it.

"You can get changed with the others Helen." She pointed towards the changing room. "There's no way you've been on your period for half a term. And don't think you've heard the last of this."

"But..." I turned to the floor length windows in the PE hall. It had been trying to snow for the last couple of days. The prospect of cross country running made me want to cry.

"No buts. Five weeks of missing PE is quite enough. Right. Let's get you all into teams." Miss Richardson snapped the register shut. "Liz, you can pick a team, Sally, you can as well." Then she chose two other team leaders. In all my years at this school, Miss Richardson has *never* chosen me to be a team leader. She probably never will.

As always, I was the last girl to be picked. Even then I

wasn't actually picked. Instead, at the end, I remained, cross legged on the floor, listening to hushed voices saying things like *we don't want her* or *I'm not waiting for her*. Eventually, Miss Richardson said, "you can join Liz's team, Helen. Hurry up."

Things got worse when I got to my peg in the cloakroom.

"Where's my PE kit?" I combed every square inch of the floor before scanning faces to see who might have hidden it. *Everyone* looked amused. Therefore, it was impossible to pick one person out. I sank to the bench. "Well I can't do it then, can I?" The only person who probably heard my voice was myself.

Miss Richardson marched in and straight over to me. "Why aren't you getting changed Helen?"

"Someone's got my PE kit. It was right there." I pointed at the peg.

"You really will do anything to get out of cross country won't you?" Her voice was even more shrill than it had been in the hall. As if it wasn't bad enough with other kids picking on me, without the teachers doing it too.

Then I noticed Liz and Sally sniggering in the corner as they watched. "It'll be them." I pointed. "Look. They'll have hidden it somewhere."

"Girls? Have you got Helen's PE kit?" She used a completely different tone as she spoke to them.

"No, Miss."

"Can everyone check around where they're changing for Helen Atkin's PE kit?"

There was a collective shuffling, then a sea of nonchalant faces and much shrugging.

"Get in there, and borrow some gym knickers and an airtex top from lost property." Miss Richardson pointed at the door, to the side of the changing room.

"But everyone will laugh - I can't go out there just wearing gym knickers."

Everyone laughed again. Including Miss Richardson. I wanted to tell her to piss off. I badly wanted to. But Dad would have knocked me into next week if reports of that nature had gone home about me.

"You might think twice next week about remembering your PE kit then."

"But I'll freeze out there."

"Good. It will make you run for a change."

Everyone looked snug in their classrooms as we ran past the English block. By the time we got out onto the lane, Liz's team ran off, leaving me behind. Not that I was bothered. It was better than being punched or laughed at. I killed time in the graveyard, making stories up about people in the graves. No way was I running around the village wearing navy blue gym knickers.

By the time I got back to school, my legs were blotchy and purple with the cold. Miss Richardson made me strip off and shower with everyone else in spite of the letter I'd tried to give her. I turned my back, fighting tears when I overheard the comments Liz and Sally were making about my flat chest.

Tomorrow, I'm not going to school. And if Mum tries to make me, I'm running away from home.

CHAPTER 3

BANG. Bang. Bang. Bang. Bang. Something claws at my chest. Cold dread. Only the police would thump on someone's door like that at ten o'clock in the morning. What the hell's happened? I dare not answer it, that's for sure. Instead, I peer from the bay window, taking care not to move the net curtains. There's no police car anywhere. Even though they were a familiar sight around here not all that long ago. Nor can I hear the beep and crackle of police radios. It's just me being paranoid. Stupid, jumpy, paranoid Helen.

Why would the police call anyway? Everything that went on next door eighteen months ago got dealt with. Lou was laid to rest. Eventually. That was such a strange day. I was torn between a compulsion to be a part of it all, and the realisation I had no place there. Donna got sent down. Scott, the boyfriend, slunk away with his tail between his legs after giving evidence. It all came out at the trial what he'd been up to with Donna. To think I was once jealous of the friendship I thought Lou and Donna had. She practically lived at Lou's and they looked to be as close as sisters. Yet, she'd had it away with Lou's boyfriend. It goes to show how deceptive appearances can be. Only Darren is unaccounted for now. As far as anyone knows, he's working away. No one knows when he's coming back. Hopefully, that's how things will stay. And nobody other than Charlie seems to be looking for him.

"Open this door now." Thump. Thump. Thump. "Right now." The banging's not even at *my* door, it's at Liz's. But it's bloody loud. And I recognise the voice.

It belongs to Charlie. It's several weeks since she was last here so I thought she'd given up. She last turned up on Christmas Day, and was really carrying on at Liz's door. Well, *her* door, really. *I just want to see my Dad,* she'd wailed. *Please!* Other neighbouring curtains were twitching, but no one seemed to want to get involved. Not on Christmas Day. Not even for a poor kid in agony and wanting her dad. I'd felt like absolute shit, listening to her out there.

Liz was definitely in the house. I saw her returning from her run literally minutes before I heard Charlie banging and shouting. When I'd asked Liz about it later, her reply was, *I don't have to have anything to do with that girl. Not anymore.* Not that she ever really had, as far as I could gather.

I wondered where Charlie's grandmother would be. Lou's Mum. Especially on Christmas Day. Did she know where Charlie was? Finally, when she'd started throwing herself against the door, I decided to intervene. Someone had to.

Which is what I feel compelled to do now.

"Liz must have gone out," I tell Charlie as I approach the fence. She's taller than I remember. Even in just a few weeks, she's shot up. She's always been pretty and looks like a young woman now. I can hardly bear to look at her. Amongst the rest of it, she's everything I wasn't at that age. They described her as a fourteen-year-old in court, so she'll be fifteen now. And she's the image of her mother. It's almost spooky. It must kill Lou's mum every time she looks at her granddaughter.

"Yeah. Like hell she has." Charlie looks at me with fire in

her eyes. "Why are *you* covering for her? Surely you can tell what a bitch she is. And I know she's in there."

"I'm not covering for anyone. I just came out because you sound upset."

"To have a nosy, more like. Mum was bang right about you. She always called you the *nosy neighbour.*"

"I'm only trying to help." Something within me plummets. I'm pig-sick of being called names. Though what Charlie's saying doesn't really come as a shock. Lou never wanted to know me. I was good enough to keep a spare key for their house, in case Charlie lost hers but that was it. After she gave it to me, I tried to use it as an 'in,' so went to her door with my key. It was well after she'd split with Darren so I figured we were equals. We were, by then, both on our own and each with a failed relationship, admittedly in very different circumstances. But she knew nothing about my 'relationship.' No one did, apart from my sister. It wasn't exactly one to shout from the rooftops about. I know I never will.

"One good turn deserves another." I'd thrust my own spare door key in front of Lou when she opened the door to me.

"Oh," she replied. "But you only ever seem to go out with your dogs. And it's not as if you have a scatter-brained teenager, like I have."

It felt like she was rubbing things in. On both counts. " Well, it's always handy to have a neighbour with a key, isn't it? Just in case I ever lose mine."

Lou eventually took it. Extremely reluctantly. "OK. I'll hang it on the hook then. *Just in case* you ever lose yours."

I loitered. Stared at her. Waited. Would she ask me in? There's a first time for everything.

"Was there anything else?"

I shook my head and shuffled away. She could have invited me in for a coffee.

A couple of months before she died, I let myself in when they were away overnight. I'd signed for a parcel delivery on Lou's behalf, so dropping the parcel into her house was a good chance to have a poke around. I'd often wondered what it was like inside. I wanted to see if their house married up to their over-the-fence portrayal of packed and vibrant lives being led. There was no chance of Lou and Charlie returning. Of them catching me in there. I'd overheard their weekend plans whilst I'd been weeding the garden.

I wandered from room to room, running my hands over crisp cotton sheets and fleecy cushions. Their home was homely, yet orderly, feminine, and welcoming. I wondered if it had been as nice when Darren lived there or whether she'd put her own stamp on it since becoming single. Whatever the answer, it was everything my home isn't. Not just because I have no sense of style, but because my dog-walking money barely gives me enough to live on, let alone to buy fancy cushions with. My envy had reached fever pitch by the time I let myself back out. I'm unsure whether I was jealous of their home, their lives, or an existence they wouldn't allow me to be involved with. Other than keeping a spare key for them.

I went back in a couple more times, through the day after that, knowing Lou would be at work and Charlie at school. I yearned to be more like Lou. It wasn't just her home that offered everything mine didn't, it was every aspect of her existence. It was probably a good thing that Donna asked me for the key for herself shortly after that. It prevented me from continuing to torment myself.

. . .

"Look I'm sorry." Charlie steps away from the door and towards the fence. "You're right. I'm just upset. And I shouldn't be taking it out on you."

"It's OK. I do understand you know." Here I go again. *Doormat Helen.* People speak to me however they want, and I just seem to let them.

"I only want to see my dad. Why the hell won't Liz answer the door to me? Why won't she tell me where he is?" She kicks the fence now. Perhaps I should tell her off, but I can't really blame her.

It's pointless me asking about her own door key as I know full well Liz changed the locks on all the external doors months ago. But she looks freezing. And so depressed. I know what it's like to spend your teens being utterly miserable. I can't imagine she's as friendless as I was, but certainly as parentless. Nor does she have a sister like I've always had.

"I can't answer that Charlie. All I can do is let her know you were here."

She doesn't move. Just stares at me. With eyes like Darren's. The only part about her that isn't her mother. She knows as well as I do that Liz is in there. In the house her parents bought. The house she grew up in. The house, by virtue of marriage, that Liz has managed to acquire. Even I know it's not right. But there's not a lot I can do. Especially now.

"Look do you want to come in Charlie? Get warmed up a bit? I'll make you a hot drink." I regret the words as soon as they leave me. I really shouldn't get involved with her. Not with what's happened since. And as usual, I haven't got the heating on, plus my house is in its perpetual state of disarray. I should have a spring clean. But it's not spring yet.

"No, it's alright. But thanks." She shakes her head vehemently as she speaks. "I didn't tell my grandma I was coming here. She thinks my dad's a waste of space even more than she did before. And she reckons I should leave him to it. He obviously doesn't want to know me."

"Do you want to let her know where you are?"

She shakes her head. "It'll only make things worse. She's been put on tablets. She's really depressed. Cos of my mum, obviously. And she's having a more awful day than normal today. It would have been Mum's birthday."

"I'm sorry. It must be really hard for you both." I mean that. I really do feel sorry for Charlie. I used to think she was an entitled brat when I saw her coming and going, laughing with her friends and her trendy clothes, her expensive trainers and brand new bikes every Christmas. But who couldn't feel sorry for a young lass who lost her mum in the way she did?

"My grandma's right though, isn't she? About my dad being a *waste of space*. I mean, what sort of decent dad vanishes into thin air like he has?"

"When did you last see him?" I already know the answer to this. However, she looks like she needs to talk about him.

"Last August. Before Liz dumped all my stuff at my Grandma's."

"Have you tried calling him?"

'Of course I have." Her tone changes. As if to say *how stupid can you be*. "It just goes straight to voicemail. It's the only time I can hear his voice."

I grew up with enough of my own shit, but this is heartbreaking. Whatever the circumstances. A young lass, ringing her dad's number, just to hear a recording of his voice. Liz really is heartless.

"There wasn't even a message over Christmas from him," she continues. "Nothing for my birthday. Yet it's my poor mum who died back there." She jerks her head towards the back garden gate. "It should have been *him*, not her."

Her bottom lip wobbles. For all her bravado, there's

clearly still a little girl in there. The same one I've watched running around their garden, and coming and going with her mother all those years. Charlie's life certainly seems to have changed beyond recognition. And in the few times I've talked to her, she seems like a decent enough kid. I can't understand why Liz has never been able to get along with her. But it's worse than that. She won't even give her the time of day.

"I saw you talking to Charlie before." There's no *hello* as I throw the door open to Liz.

"So you *were* in the house then? I thought as much. I think Charlie knew as well."

"I don't care. But what I do want to know is why did you bother to come out?" Liz glances behind, down the drive, as though to check who might be listening. "She'd have just buggered off without *you* interfering."

"I felt sorry for her, that's all. Look, why don't you come in." I hold the door wider. "We're letting all the heat out here."

"Why would you feel *sorry* for her? She's always been an over-privileged, sullen, self-entitled little bitch." Liz enunciates every word as she reels off her list.

"She's a teenager." I say over my shoulder as Liz follows me along the hallway. I try not to wince at her calling Charlie a bitch. "And we know better than anyone how horrible teenagers can be." I give her a knowing look as I pull two cups from the cupboard.

"You never miss an opportunity to remind me, do you?" Liz lifts a pile of towels from the chair and stacks them on top of a pile of books. "Gosh, do you ever put things away Helen?" She lets her gaze roam around. "It's getting worse in here. I don't know how you live like this."

"Coffee or tea?" I give her my sweetest smile. But I'm glad to steer the conversation well away from Charlie *and* Darren.

We skated close enough to the edge the other night when we were drinking. It's probably better that we talk about the state of my house.

"Tea please. Look. I know I was a bitch to you when I was younger." Liz sits at the table.

"An *absolute* bitch." I force a laugh. Though it's not remotely funny. Sometimes I wonder if she can truly remember the extent of how she treated me. But she *has* changed. And it is nice to have a friend of sorts to have a drink with. No matter what my sister thinks.

"I had my reasons for being that way, didn't I?" Her face clouds over. "What with my mother dropping dead. Even before that, her drug addiction was always more important to her than me." As she continues, her voice becomes angrier. "You don't know what things were like for me Helen. And then to top it all, I got dumped in a children's home. I had every right to be bitter."

"I'll still never know why you chose *me* to take the brunt of that, I really don't. And sometimes, I can hardly believe we're even friends now."

"Well, I'm glad we are."

It's not like Liz to say something so heartfelt, so I allow her to continue. Even if her tone suggests she's being sarcastic. She often is. But we rarely talk about the past, and I need all the help I can get to exorcise the teenage demons that still haunt me.

"When I first bumped into you that time at the checkout, it was like fate had stepped in."

It's *also* not like Liz to be so poetic either. I glance at her, wondering if she's had a personality transplant.

"I recognised you straight away. I was hardly likely to forget *your* face." I drop tea bags into the cups. Twenty years had elapsed since I'd last seen her. When she'd said *Helen, is that you?* I was terrified at first. Some part of me must have feared she would beat me up, right there, at the supermarket checkout even at the ripe old age of thirty-eight.

"Why? What's wrong with my face? It's not that bad, is it?" At least her bitter expression has relaxed slightly.

As we talked at the checkout, Liz asked me where I lived. Because my brain never works fast enough to come up with a lie, I ended up divulging the actual street. I was kicking myself afterwards. *What if she turned up at my door?* When she told me she was married to Darren of all people, my jaw must have hit the floor.

"When I found out it was *you* Darren had married after Lou, I couldn't believe it." I pour hot water into the cups.

"Small world, as I said back then."

"Though I did think to myself that you must be nicer now, for someone to have wanted to marry you, that is." *Even Darren,* but I don't say this. I walk to the table with the cups, nearly tripping over the dogs. "In your baskets," I tell them both.

"Erm thanks. I think." She smiles and sips her drink.

Darren had been unfaithful to Lou time and time again, including with *me.* However, I couldn't believe that one of the notches on his bedpost was Liz. And that he'd married her. How could I not have known? Not that Darren and I ever did any meaningful talking whenever he turned up here. It was clear what he wanted, and being the only man that had ever expressed an interest in me that way, I was only too happy to give it to him. I was however, terrified that Liz might find out that I was another of his notches. As well as Donna. If she had, my life probably wouldn't be worth living. At least he's taken our dirty secret with him. Nobody other than Jenna knows. And I'd trust her with my life.

"Look, Helen, we all make mistakes." For a moment, I wonder if Liz can read my mind. "But I was pleased you gave me a chance that day. You'd have been well within your rights to have told me to piss off."

"I think I was scared to start with." I might as well be honest.

"I can't deny it was useful to be able to keep tabs on the likes of that slag Donna, as well as what Darren might be up to." She jerks her head in the direction of next door.

"It's like they say about school reunions." I steer the conversation. I don't want to talk about Darren. Or Donna. "People revert back to the people they once were."

"I don't want to be that person anymore." Liz's voice is quiet. "I want to change. Really I do."

DEAR DIARY

Today, Liz told me she wanted to make friends with me. She'd made me jump out of my skin when she slid her lunch tray in front of mine.

"I know I've been a cow." She peeled her banana, not taking her eyes off me.

After two years of being constantly bullied by her and everyone in school who looked up to her, I just stared back. It was probably the first time I'd *really* looked into her face. Until today, she'd terrified me so much that I'd always avoided direct eye contact.

You've been a cow. I wanted to say, *that's putting it mildly,* but I kept quiet. Obviously. She did seem different though. Calmer. Quieter. I looked around. Were the others watching, laughing? But none of her usual gang were around. Not even Sally who she was normally conjoined with. But that didn't mean I could trust her.

"What do you say Helen? Do you want to be my friend, or what?" She bit into her banana. As if she was actually sitting across the table from me, inviting me to be her friend. *As if.* No, there had to be a catch.

"Straight up. I'm sorry. I want to be friends with you. I want you to invite me to your house. To sit together in lessons. Partners in PE. Help with homework. All that."

Now I really didn't trust her. *Help with homework.* Liz never, ever, handed any homework in. She once told a teacher that it wasn't cool to do homework when you live in a children's home. The teacher made her stay in at lunchtime for a week to do it after that. For me, it was a week of not having to look over my shoulder quite so much. Her gang were not as evil to me when she wasn't in the middle of it, egging everyone on. Even Sally.

"You've gone from making fun of me and hitting me, or getting others to hit me, to wanting to come to my house?" Not that I'd ever invite *anyone* to my house. Out of the four of us living here, there's only really me and Jenna that have a proper conversation. Mum barely speaks to us, let alone anyone else.

"Yeah. Like I said. Straight up."

I pushed a carrot around my tray. I hated being on free school meals. Having to queue up for dinner tickets on a Monday because my dad didn't earn enough. Another thing which made me a target for the bullies. Same as the hand-me-downs from Jenna.

"What about your friends? Will they start to leave me alone?" For the first time since Liz sat down, I allowed hope to bubble up. If she meant what she was saying, maybe I could start to enjoy school again, after all, it used to be my sanctuary. Before she came along and joined forces with Sally. But then anywhere was preferable to being at home.

As she chewed on her banana, I noticed her grinning at someone over my shoulder. I twisted in my seat. Sally was mouthing something through the window, whilst manically gesturing. She stopped as soon as I turned and spotted her.

"What's going on?" I turned back to Liz, who was also grinning.

"Bet won." She beckoned to Sally. I turned again, my appetite completely vanishing as I watched the rest of Liz's cronies striding towards my table as if they owned the place. What did she mean, *bet won?* Were they on their way over to make friends with me too? Or something else?

I froze as four of them slid into the seats. Two either side of me, two either side of Liz. I was completely boxed in.

"Friends." One of the girls still standing said the word in a mock-sweet voice and giggled into her hand.

"I win." Liz looked around at them all. "Five minutes, we said. Come on then. Pay up."

I watched as one-by-one, they slid coins across the table towards Liz.

"That's the hardest money I've ever had to make." She dropped the coins into her top pocket as she smirked at me.

"What do you mean?" Tears of fear were burning behind my eyes. I wanted to run. Get away from them. But I couldn't move.

"Having to sit with *you.*"

They all laughed so loudly that everyone else in the dining hall turned to look at our table.

"Do you really think I'd *ever* choose to sit with *you?*" She laughed harder.

"But I thought..."

"I'd rather eat my own vomit than eat lunch with you." With that, she rose sharply and pushed my lunch tray into my lap. As gravy and custard trickled down my legs, I continued to fight the urge to cry. I wouldn't give them the satisfaction.

They didn't even look back as they walked away. I spent the afternoon in a lost property skirt, knowing I'd get told off from Mum when I got home. And I did.

CHAPTER 4

"Right, this is what I was thinking."

"I can't afford that." I slump in my seat as Liz scrolls down the page. "No way. Paying the mortgage on this place takes every last penny."

I used to contemplate putting it on the market. I bought this house when prices were cheap and the area wasn't as sought after as it is now. But it's not as if I can leave it. Not now. Not ever.

"Just look at that swimming pool." She points at the screen. "How blue it is. And the cabins. Wow."

"Yeah, lovely." I drain my tea and rise from the table. I'll do the dishes whilst she lives in cloud cuckoo land. It's alright for her. Though she's never admitted it directly, she can only be using the money Darren's been given access to for bringing Charlie up. Only he's not bringing her up anymore. I don't know how Liz is getting away with it. There's a chance Charlie's completely unaware of Lou's will, having only been thirteen when she died. And from what she told me, her Grandma doesn't sound to be in the right frame of mind to consider things such as money.

"I'll pay for you."

I have to ask. I have to know. "Is it even your money to be offering to pay for me with?"

'What the hell's that supposed to mean?" She frowns and her eyes darken in the way I've always feared.

This is uncomfortable territory. But I have to know if she's throwing money that's meant for Charlie around. To pay for me to go on a cruise of all things. I can't think where else Liz would get the money. After all, she doesn't do a stroke of work anymore. Before Lou's death, I got the impression that Darren wasn't exactly well off either. I overheard all kinds of arguments between him and Lou at her door, as well as when she was on the phone to him. She was possibly trying to shield Charlie from their arguments by taking the calls into the garden. I used to spend a lot of time in mine and heard the lot. On a quiet day, if I was right up to the fence, I could even catch his replies. Especially if he was shouting back at her. Money was clearly a huge bone of contention between them.

Darren, as Charlie's new guardian, will have probably received things like Lou's life insurance, pension - the lot. Maybe some of it's in trust for when Charlie gets older. Perhaps when she's sixteen or eighteen, she'll get her own access to her mum's money. I really hope this is the case, otherwise there's the potential for there to be nothing left. And I do have a conscience about it.

"I'm waiting Helen. I want to know what you meant by *is it even your money?*"

"Exactly what I said." I busy myself in rinsing cups to avoid her eye. "Is it the money in *Darren's* account that you'd be using for the cruise?"

"It's *my* money in an account he gave *me* access to. I'm Darren's wife. And he's not here anymore, is he, as we very well know?"

"But is it..."

"My money is *my* business Helen." I don't need to look at her to tell the effect my question has had. "Do you know what, I can't bloody believe this. Here I am, giving you an amazing invitation, yet you've literally thrown it back in my face."

"I'm sorry. I really didn't mean..."

"Let's just forget I ever mentioned it, shall we?" I wince as she slams the lid of my laptop. If she busts that, I can't afford to replace it.

"You've been really strange since we got together the other night." She pushes the laptop away and gets to her feet. "What's up with you?"

"Nothing."

"Are you sure? Is there something you want to say to me?

"No. Look - I'm sorry."

"I'd better be getting home. I'll see you later."

"Liz. Please. I was only asking. The last thing I want is to fall out about this."

"I can't be friends with someone who doesn't *trust* me. Like I said, I'm off."

I thrust my hands deeper into the soap suds, listening as her footsteps die away along the hallway before the front door bangs behind her.

I sigh so hard that the suds wobble beneath the force of my breath. One minute she's inviting me on a cruise, the next she's storming out of the door. I stare out at the garden, at the sun reflecting off the surface of the pond. I used to love my pond. One of my few things of beauty. I would sit out with Coco and a glass of wine, or a coffee, right next to the water fountain. I've always been lulled by the sound of water. Now the very sight of that pond makes me feel ill.

I pour another drink and return to the kitchen table to check she's not damaged my laptop screen. It's still on the page she wanted to show me. *Nordic Cruises.* Admittedly, it looks amazing. Clear seas, blue skies, even bluer swimming pools. I scroll down. There's plates of what they're calling *the finest cuisine,* there's spas, clubs, bars, gyms, restaurants. Plural *everything.* It looks like a floating small town. Without meaning to, I compare the ensuite cabin on the screen to my cluttered and damp bedroom, badly in need of redecoration and a new carpet. I *could* do with getting away. And I *do* trust Liz now. Don't I? I *should* let her pay for me, shouldn't I? After all, she said she wants to make amends for everything she put me through. I don't think ten cruises could cover it, so I should jump at the invitation to go on *one.*

Coco nudges at my elbow.

"I know girl. Time to go out."

I do need to get out with Coco and Penny. And I've my lunchtime dogs to collect. After all that with Liz, a walk might clear my head.

I knock on Liz's door with similar trepidation to what I'd have experienced when Lou was still here. After the words we had earlier, maybe there's as much likelihood of her letting me in as there was with Lou. I've always found it so hard to make friends, and even harder to *keep* them. When you're ignored and unwanted by even your own mother, it's bound to negatively colour all other female relationships. Over the years, it's manifested in all sorts of ways, from not trusting people, to feeling inferior around other women. I really do. Kind of dumpy, plain and totally uncool. I'm also incapable of dealing with more than one friend at a time. Any more than one and I feel left out. I even feel jealous of my sister's friends. So really, I should hang onto my friendship with Liz. It's certainly better than the alternative.

There's a thud of a door being closed. I know she's in there. Then footsteps. Why isn't she coming to the door? This is how Charlie must feel when her visits are ignored. However, I'm sure, eventually, Charlie will get back in here. She'll have the law on her side. Perhaps when she's old enough to live alone. But knowing Liz like I do, I can imagine Charlie having a fight on her hands for the house. Whatever happens, there's no way Liz will just hand it over. She's more likely to argue about how it was once Darren's house, giving her rights too.

I knock again, harder this time. And again.

"Alright. Alright." Her voice is muffled behind it but close enough to make me wonder if she's watching through the spy hole.. Then a rattle of keys.

Finally, the door swings open. "What do you want?"

I clear my throat. "I want to apologise about before. You're right. Where your money comes from is none of my business."

"I do have money of my own. I sold *my* house, didn't I? The one I owned prior to meeting Darren."

She's right. I relax and decide that's what I'll keep reminding myself. I have to stop feeling guilty about everything. It keeps me awake on many a night, especially these days. That's unless I knock myself out with wine first. "Are you going to invite me in? Or do I have to stand here, freezing on your doorstep?" I smile at her, hoping it's the former option. It really is bitter out here. Which I can't lie, makes the prospect of sunshine and luxury appeal even more.

She holds the door wider. I follow her through the hallway. Every square inch of the place has been repainted. Not that it needed it, but I do understand Liz wanting to put her own stamp on the house. Who wants to live with a dead woman's decor? I'd love to see what she's done with Charlie's bedroom since she shifted all her stuff out. I've only ever been upstairs once. The final time I let myself in. It will have completely changed upstairs since then.

On the rare occasions I come in here, I usually use the downstairs toilet. But if I need to go at the same time as Liz, whilst she's in the downstairs one, I can sneak a look upstairs. Just so I know. After all, it's me that has to intercept Charlie whenever she turns up here in a distressed state. And technically it's still her home. I'd like to think her bedroom will still be there for her.

Gosh, what a day it's been so far. It's barely mid-afternoon and I'm exhausted. I'll certainly have lots to write about later in my diary.

"I've made a pot of coffee. Want one?"

I nod as Liz reaches for the jug. I probably shouldn't be drinking filter coffee in the afternoon, but I don't want to be any trouble by asking for tea. I'll just have to have an extra glass of wine this evening to help me sleep. I walk around with perpetual shadows around my eyes, not to mention the shadows that follow me around.

I glance at the closed laptop on her kitchen table. "I had a look at the cruise," I tell her. "After you'd gone. It does look gorgeous."

"You've changed your tune." She gestures at the table. "Have a seat, if you want."

I sit, my gaze inadvertently travelling over the garden. Then I quickly look away. I can *never* unsee that night, much as I'd give anything to change things. At least it was dark as I watched them covering poor Lou with a tent. Thank God Charlie never saw her body, that's all I can say.

"Here we go." Liz sits facing me and passes a cup across the table. Then turns the laptop towards herself and opens the lid. "Since you've stopped being ridiculous, let's have another look, shall we?"

"Right you are." I *am* excited at the prospect of going on holiday. Getting out of the UK too. It's crazy that at my age, I've seen nothing of the world. I haven't lived at all really. I've never married, never had kids, never done anything other than survive. My stomach flips at the prospect of finally changing this, even if it is with Liz.

"Right. Look. Here's what I'm thinking. Ten nights. All inclusive. Sharing a cabin, like I said."

"Sharing?" I don't know if I like the sound of that. Liz and I do get along nowadays, but ten days and nights in such close proximity? I'd hesitate even at sharing a cabin with Jenna for that long. As I've got older, I've become more of an introvert, and I do prefer my own space.

"Yeah. But look at the size of the cabin. It's not like we're sharing a bed." She laughs. "Besides, we'll hardly be in there."

"What if I get seasick? I've never been on a boat."

"*Really?* Well, according to what I've read, we can get a cabin in the middle of the ship. There's less swaying about there."

"Won't it be noisy all the time? The engines, the bars."

"I might have known you'd say that." She rolls her eyes. "We'll be in those bars ourselves, you know. But we can ask for a cabin where it might be quieter, if you want. I know what you're like."

I feel a strange sense of belonging at her words. *I know what you're like.* It's actually nice to hear. Like someone takes notice of me, even Liz. But like she said herself, she wants to change. And everyone deserves a second chance.

"I say we just do it." She squints at the screen as she continues to scroll.

"But like I said, I can't..."

"I'll cover it, like *I* said. All you need to do is get a passport sorted out. I take it you don't already have one?"

I shake my head.

"Well, get one applied for today. It shouldn't take long to come at this time of year. And I'll book for, say, four weeks today? The twenty-fifth of February?"

"Wow. That soon?"

"If we leave it any later, we've less chance of seeing the Northern Lights."

New excitement bubbles in me. *The Northern Lights.* Then it's replaced by a thud of guilt at the thought of the others. People who will *never* see the Northern Lights. Namely Lou. And Darren. But if I voiced these thoughts, Liz would go completely berserk.

"Shall I book it then? Can you get time off from the dogs?"

"I should imagine so. I *never* take time off. I'm too busy looking after dogs when *other* people go away. It's about time someone returned the favour." I do a mental reckoning of who might take Coco for me. Jenna probably will. She works during the day, but perhaps I can employ a different walker to take both our dogs for a lunchtime walk. It'll be worth the extra expense to get away. "Look Liz, are you really sure about this?"

"I said so, didn't I?" She plucks her purse from her handbag.

"But why? Why are you doing this? For me? It'll cost a fortune."

"I'm not just doing it for *you.* I want to go too. And after our conversation the other night, I've been thinking." She looks at me over the top of the screen. "I've put a hell of a lot on you. Not many people would do anything near what you've done for me."

"What do you mean? Done for you?"

"Everything. And after how I treated you in the past, I'm lucky you've forgiven me." She laughs. "However, you've certainly been much more use to me as a friend than you were as an enemy."

"The past is the past, like you've said, it's time to move forward. Starting with ordering my passport." I pull an excited face to disguise my puzzlement over her last comment. *More use to her as a friend than as an enemy?* Wow.

"I do appreciate it you know. And I think you'd have spoken out by now if you intended to tell anyone."

"About Darren, you mean?"

She nods. "And the other thing. You know, what I told you when we were drunk?"

"What other thing?"

"You must be able to remember."

"No?" I wonder if she's going to enlighten me. I knew there was something. It's been needling at me, but I've been totally unable to remember the details.

"That's good then. If you can't remember what I said, it doesn't matter."

I rack my brains. If she's brought whatever it is into our conversation, it must be something important. At least, it must have been when she mentioned it. "The two things that stick out the most were when you were going on about dying, and then saying something along the lines of *a true friend will help you hide a body.*"

"And that's it? That's really all you recall me saying the other night?"

She's got a weird look on her face, like she's searching me for something.

"Yeah. I think so. Why?"

"No reason." She laughs again, though it has a nervous edge. "It's all a bit of a blur, isn't it? Wine, eh? Anyway, like I said, I wasn't good to you in the past - this cruise can be my way of properly making up for my behaviour, can't it?"

If anyone had told me twenty-two years ago that I'd be sitting with Liz in her kitchen, as her next door neighbour, drinking coffee, and on the verge of booking a cruise with her, I'd have told them they were deranged.

DEAR DIARY

Today was one of the worst days of my life. Yet, it started as one of the best. Finally, after saving and saving, I managed to buy the roller boots Mum has said no to for as long as I can remember. Even better, they'll be too small for Jenna to pinch from me. It's me who gets her outgrown stuff, rather than the other way around. So why should she get my boots? After all, it's me who's been dragging myself out of bed at half past six every day, breaking my back with the heavy bag, pushing newspapers through letterboxes, morning after miserable morning for thirty-five days since my fourteenth birthday.

It's hard to write today. Even my *hand* is bruised after what Liz and her friends did to me. When I spotted her across the park, I thought I'd be able to get away from her quickly on my new wheels. But she was on her bike. As was Sally and the two other lasses who looked as rotten to the seed as Liz and Sally are.

Everywhere I go I'm on 'Liz and Sally watch.' Mum doesn't even try to understand. She still forces me to go out, *to get out from under her feet.* Even though I'm petrified. Even when I beg her to let me stay at home where I'm safe. I've thought of talking to Dad about it. But all he's interested in is his work, the pub and watching the telly. I can't remember the last time I had a proper conversation with him. I don't know that I ever have.

Jenna doesn't understand either. She just tells me to hit Liz back. Or hit her before she gets the chance to hit me. She would say that. After all, she's never needed to fight anyone.

"That'll stop her, she won't come near you again," she always says. But I can't hit her. Nor do I think that anything will stop her. It's actually rare for her to hit me. It's the name calling and ignoring that's the hardest thing, not just from Liz, but from everyone. I don't know why Liz Welsh hates me so much. She's hated me since the day she started at our school. She's the only person in our school who lives in a children's home, so everyone thinks she's cool. I think she's the most awful person I've ever known. If her mum hadn't died, if she hadn't been taken into care in our area, our paths would never have crossed. And she's *everywhere*. It's as though she follows me. And because everyone feels sorry for her, she gets invited to their houses which means I bump into her, even out of school, all the time. Meanwhile, I'm on my own with no real friends. Only my dog and my sister. I'd give anything for Liz to have gone to live somewhere else. She's already turned everyone else against me more than they already were.

I was in the snicket leading from the park back to the road.

"What do you think you look like?"

Her other friends laughed as everyone's gaze travelled to my boots. So what if I was wearing leg warmers as well. It was cold. Liz blocked my path with her bike whilst Sally got behind me. Like a PacMan with the ghosts either side of it, I was cornered. And another two ghosts were circling nearby.

"Get out of my way."

Liz laughed again, whilst rolling her front wheel right up to my boot. "Or what?"

"I want to get past."

"What do you think?" She nodded at her friends, dressed similarly to her. Tight pinstriped jeans. As skinny as she is. It's funny what you notice when you're cornered. "Shall I let her go?"

"Nah." One of them said. "She's too fat to fit through anyway."

"I don't know how them wheels are taking the strain." Sally pointed at my feet.

"Just leave me alone." Yes, I was a bit plump, and yes, I would be digging into the Neapolitan ice-cream in the freezer the minute I got home. But it would only be to make me feel better. Especially after this.

Ice-cream is the only thing I want to eat after what happened. I've got a fat lip and a bruised eye. That's the last time I listen to my sister. Following her advice, I elbowed one of the girls as she squared up to me.

"Is that the best you've got?" Liz had thrown her bike down.

What happened next is a blur. I remember being dragged to the ground. Kicked and kicked and kicked. I curled up in a ball. Nobody helped me. And one of them took my roller boots so I had to walk home in my socks.

CHAPTER 5

I'M glad to be catching the last of the daylight with the dogs. I can just about pick their shapes out as they jump about after each other.

Well, it looks like I'm going on a ten-day cruise. Liz has actually booked it. She's even *paid* for it, *in full,* with it being so close. Four weeks. If it's possible to feel excitement and dread all at the same time, that's me right now.

I'm still puzzling over what she asked me. The *other* thing she supposedly told me about. She had such a weird look on her face as she checked what I could recall her saying. The truth is, we talked about so many things and drank so much wine, that it's all a complete haze. Even when I told her I couldn't remember, she looked as though she didn't believe me. Perhaps if I stop *trying* to remember, then whatever she said will come back. I *want* it to come back, then hopefully I can set both of our minds at rest. As well as my curiosity. It must be important for her to keep quizzing me about it.

I can't stop thinking about what else she informed me of

earlier either. Me *being far more use to her as a friend than as an enemy.* She keeps going on and on about last year. I've repeatedly told her that I'd rather not talk about what happened. It's bad enough having to live with what I helped her with.

A true friend will help you hide a body. After all that's gone before, I still struggle to think of Liz as a *true* friend. No doubt I'll always be guarded around her, apart from, of course, when we get drinking together. Perhaps, when we get on the cruise, we should curb our alcohol intake.

I slide my numb fingers into gloves. I wish it were a hot and exotic cruise we were going on - I'm unlikely to be any warmer on board a Nordic cruise than here in this park. I can't exactly grumble. I'm going to be seeing places I've only ever dreamt of; far-flung, picture-perfect lands, clear skies, hopefully full of the Northern Lights, hot lagoons and sleds when we leave the ship, and everything from shows to being pampered whilst we're on it. Really, I can't wait. For once in my life, maybe I can consider myself lucky.

As we all head deeper into the park, I throw a ball for Coco then another for Penny. I tighten the scarf around my neck as I stand dead still. Suddenly, I'm chilled all over. And it's not just because of the January murk.

The other matter Liz spoke of when we were drunk has just slammed back into my mind.

It's nearly half past two in the morning. I've long ago given up trying to sleep. There's nothing more soul destroying than lying awake whilst staring into the void of the night. My mind is rotating like a washing machine on a doubly fast spin cycle. I'm getting to a point where I won't be able to cope with it for much longer. Finally, when I've all but driven myself demented, I get up. I can't lie here like this for another moment.

Shivering, I tie my dressing gown and head down the stairs to make a chamomile tea. Coco looks at me curiously as she curls up beside me on the sofa.

"Yes, I know it's the middle of the night." I tuck my feet under her, nestling them into her warmth. If someone had told me I'd still be single at the age of thirty-eight, I'd have been horrified. I never planned to be a lonely, old spinster with only dogs for company. At least the only time they ever cause any hurt is when they pass away at the end of their all-too-short lives.

I open the book I started last night. Reading has always been my escape, but I don't think *anything* could rescue me tonight. It's a good thing I'm self employed - if I had to clock in anywhere in the morning, I'd be screwed. My insomnia is bad at the best of times, but tonight I'll be lucky to get even a whisper of sleep.

Even pouring what I remembered into my diary, instead of pouring a glass of wine hasn't helped me deal with it. Whilst I was actually writing, it felt like it was helping, but as soon as I put my pen down, a wave of panic washed over me. Then another one of guilt. As the night has drawn on, these waves are threatening to drown me. I know, deep down, I *really* know, that I should be pouring everything that's happened into a statement to the police, never mind my diary. It's no wonder Liz didn't want me to remember what she'd told me.

She killed Lou.

Bludgeoned her to death with a hammer.

Donna is serving Liz's time after being expertly framed for it. What an absolute nightmare. Yet what can I do? I stretch out on the sofa, manoeuvring my legs around Coco. I reach for a throw I keep on the back of the sofa, still unable to stop shivering. And it's not just the cold that's causing it.

My newly-gained knowledge is crushing me. I can hardly breathe under the weight of it. I really should tell someone. Perhaps I've got a responsibility towards Charlie for the truth to come out. I found out at Donna's trial that she's Charlie's Godmother. The trial painted Donna as a pretty appalling friend for Lou to have chosen, but it seems she's not the murderer they showed her to be. I should do the right thing. I really should.

But how could I do that to Liz? After all she's done for me in more recent times? I'm desperate not to return to having *no one* ever calling here, apart from those dropping their dogs off, or delivering something. Even my sister would hardly call at my house without her dog in tow.

I busy myself with my book again. Read and re-read the same paragraph three times. It's no good. Visualising Lou lying in a pool of her own blood by her shed won't leave me. It was haunting enough before, but now I know what *really* happened, the image is dominating my mind. I don't know exactly how Liz managed to frame Donna for it, but she's clearly cleverer than I gave her credit for. And then the same with Darren. It's all coming back to me now. He knew what she'd done. She told him she'd killed Lou. Then she killed him. At the time she'd said it was self defence. They'd rowed about Charlie. It had got massively out of hand and he'd threatened her with a hammer. It was going to be his grave we dug out there, but it could have just as easily been hers. That's what she told me.

She'd called for me over the back fence. Asked for my help. If only I'd been away somewhere. Or out for the evening. But no. She knew better than anyone that sad and lonely Helen doesn't go anywhere much.

Apparently she'd been agonising for several hours over

what to do. I said no at first. Told her to call the police. I'd offered to call the police for her. I offered any other avenue of help other than what she was demanding. She ramped up the terror she's always inflicted on me and made a veiled threat of what might happen if I didn't do as she asked. Like an utter idiot, I felt as though I couldn't say no. And I didn't even notice how blood-splattered she was until I was in her house, under the light.

An hour has passed since I came downstairs. I can't stand being so cold any more. I'll have to give in to the central heating. Whilst I'm at it, I'll top up this tea. I'm exhausted, yet wired. I don't know how to get beyond this. It's not as though there's *anything* I can do to make what has happened go away. And I can never, *ever* move house in an attempt to escape what I've allowed myself to get involved with. Bones in the ground decompose eventually. But not entirely.

I thought something of Darren once. Enough to keep allowing him into my bed. Sometimes, he'd turn up two or three times in a week. At other times I wouldn't see him for months. I didn't know at first that he was sleeping with Donna as well. Not until I heard Lou and her mum discussing it in the garden. She was devastated and rightly so. Her husband and her best friend. Then, as it came out in court, Donna and Lou's boyfriend, Scott, had been at it. I'd thought he looked too good to be true. Donna, turned out to be the worst sort of best friend anyone could have. And I turned out to be the worst sort of next door neighbour. Guilt has often shadowed me; it did back then, and continues to do so. Sometimes it leaves me in peace, but not for very long. More often than not it sits beside me, nudging me if I forget things for a moment. It lies beside me when I try to sleep, and thumps away inside me at every opportunity in between. What will it take to force it to leave? Doing what I know is right perhaps? But where will that get me? Exchanging places with Donna, most likely.

Darren is the only man I've ever had a serious relationship with. Well it was serious as far as I was concerned. To him, it was just sex. He'd be lovely before we went upstairs and then as cold as ice afterwards. I shiver. Perhaps it's fitting that he's where he is now. In the cold. In the ice.

Afterwards he'd return to Lou. He couldn't get out of my bed and out of my house fast enough. I'd have to check the coast was clear for him first. He'd walk in the opposite direction to his house along the street, before looping around and back. Back to his unsuspecting wife and daughter.

There were a couple of years where I only saw him the odd time, coming and going from the house. Then they split up so I only saw him in passing on the odd occasion when he turned up for Charlie. By then, I'd long since resigned myself to my passionless existence.

He'd married for the second time when he eventually returned to my door. His wife was away for the night and he was bored. He also told me they didn't generally get on very well together. I still can't believe I let him back into my bed. I suppose I'd been bored and needy too. At this point I had no idea who he was married to - he never mentioned her name. And I didn't ask. I'd often hoped after he broke up with Lou, and they got divorced, that he might come to me permanently. But what he got from me, was just sex. Then he disappeared again. I can now track his absences back to when he was sleeping with Donna.

By the time me and Liz got talking in the supermarket, it had been months since I'd slept with Darren. Then I'd only slept with him once more after I found out she was his new wife. The night before Lou died. In my head, I justified it because Liz had thrown Darren out. But if she'd got wind of me, of all people, sleeping with her husband, it might well have been me at the mercy of one of her hammer attacks. She can *never* find out.

As I wait for the kettle, I twist the blinds. Normally, I keep them all closed at the back of the house, especially at night. It was eerie enough out there even before my garden became Darren's final resting place. Sometimes, through the day, I'm compelled to look. I need to make sure everything's as it should be. Liz has assured me that where we dug beneath the pond liner is deep enough for Darren not to be disturbed by foxes and the like. And by now, according to research I've done, there should no longer be the smell of decomposition to attract any attention.

DEAR DIARY

I hate being a teenager. Going to school. Doing what Mum tells me. As well as putting up with being bullied. And no one gives a toss. Not even my sister. It's alright for her, with her slim figure and long blonde hair. And always too busy with college, discos and her boyfriend to take any notice of me. We used to be close, but now we're older I'm just her pain-in-the-neck little sister. She never bothers with me anymore. She's hardly ever at home these days.

I'd love to have a boyfriend. But I don't think I'll ever, ever get one. Most of the boys at school call me names. I'm too fat. Too ugly, especially with my glasses and braces on my teeth. Too unlikable. My own parents don't even seem to like me. Same with most of my teachers.

I've been given tons of homework to do but I don't see the point anymore. Who's bothered if I get good grades? Who's bothered what I want to do when I leave school? No one. Certainly not my parents. They think that feeding us, clothing us and putting a roof over our heads is being a parent. No wonder Jenna's never at home.

I managed to keep well out of Liz's way today. But it shouldn't have to be like this. Hiding in shadows, not daring to go into the dinner hall, spending my whole lunch break in the library. I didn't even have anything to eat today. At least I can escape into stories there. Right now, stories are the only friends I have.

I often wonder why I'm alive. Why I was even born. What's the point? Thinking about all this is keeping me awake at night. If the only point of me being here is to be bullied, laughed at and ignored, then I may as well not be.

I. Have. Had. Enough.

CHAPTER 6

IT's BEEN two weeks since Liz booked the tickets for our cruise. I want to go, and I don't want to go all at the same time. I haven't told a soul about it yet, not even my sister. Though with only two weeks to go, I need to decide what I'm doing. After all, there's my dogs to think of. I can't just disappear.

Really, I should be jumping at this. The cruise sounds amazing. An absolute dream for someone like me. But sharing a cabin with a double murderer for ten nights is well out of my comfort zone. Until sixteen days ago, I firmly believed *Donna* had killed Lou with that hammer. I also believed Liz had acted in self-defence when she gave Darren the same treatment. The fact they'd been killed in exactly the same way should have rung alarm bells. I'd never have got involved if I'd known the truth. At least I say I wouldn't. Really, if I'm honest, that terrified fifteen-year-old lives on inside me. I'll always fear Liz. Especially now.

Night time is the worst. I've had sixteen nights of being unable to sleep. Sixteen nights since I remembered what she admitted to. At times it threatens to overwhelm me. But what can I do? I've managed to get myself involved up to my neck in it. If I was to tell anyone the truth, I'd be on my way down to the cells too.

As I sip my tea, Coco sighs from her basket. I'd love to be able to sleep so peacefully. To have the troubles and cares of a dog. Eat. Sleep. Play. Repeat. Oh God, I really don't know what to do. Sliding my laptop across the table, I raise the lid and stare at the webpage that's still open. I could probably recite the copy word for word in my sleep. If I was getting any. The photographs blur in my vision. What's in front of me is beyond anything I could ever imagine experiencing. If only it wasn't with Liz. And if we weren't sharing a cabin, it wouldn't be so bad. I wouldn't feel as though she was watching me, testing me. Why would she want to share a cabin with me anyway? I'll never forget her first day at my school when she refused to even share a desk with me.

It's my turn to sigh as I close the lid again and slump against the cushions.

I jump as the post drops onto the doormat. Coco rises and arches her back.

"Oh no you don't. The post is for me to read, not for you to eat." I pat her head as I pass. I can hear my boarding canine for this week, Russ, sniffing from behind the kitchen door. I'll have to get the morning run done soon. It'll do me good to get out of here.

"It's a dog's life for you two, isn't it?" I bend to scoop the post up, my breath catching as I feel a stiffer envelope amongst the pile. There can be no doubt as to what's inside that one.

I open it carefully, sitting on the stairs as I do. My passport.

I can't suppress the flutter of excitement in the pit of my gut. The picture of me is horrendous but who cares? It's my *first ever* passport. I can go anywhere I want. Except I can't. What I get paid for boarding and walking the dogs just about scratches a living, especially in the winter. It wouldn't get me to Scarborough right now, let alone anywhere requiring a shiny new passport.

I leaf through its pages. I *so* want to use it. Why shouldn't I see something of the world? Why not me? I'm sick of looking after every bugger else's dogs so they can go on holiday. But never me. I never hear the words, *have a lovely holiday,* or *did you have an amazing time?* asked of me.

Right, that's it. I'm going to make the most of it. I might have to *sleep* in Liz's vicinity at night, but for the rest of the time... well, from what I can see on the website, the cruise ship is enormous. There's plenty of opportunity for our own space.

In any case, it could be said that she owes me. After all, as she's so-rightly admitted, she made my school life hell. And not only did I help her conceal what I believed was her darkest secret, I'm now burdened with another which is darker still. The cruise might take my mind off it all, even though I'm nervous about leaving my garden unattended for any length of time. Whilst I'm here, I can make sure no one ever goes into it. I can keep an eye on wildlife or stray dogs getting in. Whilst I'm away, it's vulnerable. I hope I can stop thinking about it for long enough to be able to enjoy myself.

It's not very often I look in the mirror if I can help it. Nobody else is interested in looking at me so what's the point? I tug at my hair, trying to tease it into a bun like Liz often wears hers. Mine's as wiry and unmanageable as it was when I was young, so it really takes some tugging. But it does look better off my face. I just need to buy myself some clips to keep it there.

This new attention to my appearance should probably be combined with a clothes shop. I leaf through my wardrobe, unable to recall the last time I bought something new. Then my fingers pause over the black dress I bought for Lou's funeral. I don't often buy dresses but it had been half price. At the time I'd decided it was cheaper to buy one thing, a dress, rather than two things, a top and trousers. By the time it had come around to her funeral, it had been almost the end of September, seven weeks after she'd died. They would have had all sorts of investigations to do. Other than the dress, all I've got in here are skirts and blouses from the days I was trapped in an office. Skirts and blouses which don't fit me anymore. And a copious amount of dog walking clothes. But most of what I own is navy or grey. The only other colour I've bought myself is white. However, over the years, because I shove *everything* into the wash rather than separating it out, anything that was once white is now grey anyway.

I do a mental reckoning about how much money I can raise to buy some new clothes. Certainly not enough to last me for *ten* days. I wonder if cruise ships have launderettes. Or perhaps I'll have to resort to washing clothes out in the sink.

I can probably raise a couple of hundred pounds for clothes. At the most. And that's if I eat beans and start walking instead of driving until we go. It's not as if I can ask Jenna for help. Since her divorce and her move back up to Yorkshire, she's struggling enough herself.

I stare at myself in the mirror. I'm still the bird's nest. Still with the same sallow skin and pudgy body. Perhaps I could use this as a turning point. Sort myself out once and for all. Lou is the ultimate proof that life is not promised. And Darren, but I can't let myself think about that. One thing is for sure. I certainly haven't been living. Just existing.

. . .

"You need me to look after her for *how long?*"

"Well, it'll be more like twelve nights by the time we've got down to Southampton and back."

"*Southampton?*"

"Yes. I think we're going to fly down from Leeds Bradford."

"*Fly down?*"

"Is there any reason why you keep repeating me Jenna? Or have you turned into a parrot?"

She frowns. "I just can't believe you're going on a cruise. How the hell are you paying for it? You're as broke as I am."

"Liz. She offered. She wants to make up for things, she said."

"As in next-door Liz?" Jenna's voice rises as she throws herself in the armchair opposite me. A cloud of dust rises in the streaks of late afternoon sunshine. "You'd be as well staying away from anything to do with her *next door*. Not that you should need *me* to tell you."

I nod. "Look it's all fine now. Really. I've told you a million times. We've reached an understanding."

"I don't know how you can give her the time of day after what she did to you."

"That was all years ago. She's changed."

"Like hell. You seem to forget it was me who used to listen to you weeping and wailing every night. You've got a very short memory Helen."

"I *want* to get along with her. She's my next door neighbour."

"It's one thing *getting along,* but quite another going on bloody holiday together. Are you mad?"

"I've never been on a proper holiday, have I?"

"Honestly, I don't get it. Why would Liz pay to take *you* on holiday?" She looks as baffled as I probably was when Liz first suggested it.

"Why wouldn't she? Am I that awful? Is that what you're saying?" I squint against the setting sun. It's hitting my face from the top of the window.

"Of course not. I just don't trust her. I saw what she did to you. I remember the nights of having to talk you out of taking a load of tablets."

"Like I really want reminding about that. I only asked if you'd take care of Coco for me." I stride over to the window and pull the curtain across.

"But what am I supposed to do with her and Penny through the day?"

"I'll get someone to come to your house and take them out every lunch time."

"Like who?" She crosses one trousered leg over the other and I notice her new boots. She must have been paid. I make a mental note to speak to her about paying me to look after Penny. Maybe when I get back from the cruise.

"Like another dog walker."

"Maybe I don't want a complete stranger coming to my house." She pouts, making me wonder if she's jealous. "Why can't they just come here?" She gestures around my lounge.

"Don't be daft. Besides, they've got insurance." I can't tell her that over my dead body do I want anyone coming inside this house. Especially when I'm not here.

"If you're hellbent on going away, why don't I just stay here? I've just got a new carpet. It's hard enough keeping it clean with one dog, let alone two."

"So it's fine for your dog to muck up my floors but not the other way around, is that it?"

"Helen, I'm not being funny but..." She gestures to the floor, whilst pulling a face.

"You're calling my house mucky now as well?"

"Not mucky, but you could do with a new carpet."

"Jenna. I'm asking you to take my dog for me *at your house* while I'm away. I can't afford to put her into kennels any more than you've been able to afford to pay me to look after your dog whilst you've been starting a new job." Hopefully, talking about her inability to pay me in the past tense is sending out a clear message that this favour is only temporary.

"Fair point well made." She sniffs. "I don't see why I can't stay here though. It's more geared up for the dogs. I haven't even got a garden."

"Because I don't want you to. I want to be able to lock up and go away. Have everything the same when I get back. Not run up bills and an even bigger mess than it is already." My voice is rising higher and higher. No way can she stop here. I wouldn't get a moment's rest for worrying about it.

"Alright, alright. Have it all your way. Whatever. Though I'll never understand why you've agreed to go on holiday with *Liz* of all people."

"Look Jenna. Can we just change the subject? Are you going to take Coco, or not?"

"It doesn't sound as though I have much choice in the matter."

We sit in silence for a few moments. It looks like I'm going on the cruise. It's paid for, my passport has arrived. Jenna is taking Coco. I can lock the house up. I just need to buy a bigger and even stronger bolt for the gate into the back garden. I wish I could afford to fence the pond off now but it's going to have to wait.

"Mum rang earlier." Jenna fiddles with her phone as though avoiding having to look at me.

"It's always *you* she rings. Never me. I haven't heard from her since I went up on Christmas night. And then all I got was comments about how I smell of dogs." Not that I can recall an occasion when my mother has ever said anything complimentary to me.

"Charming." Jenna smiles and I'm relieved. It's not very often we disagree about things. "Well if it's any consolation to you, she was only ringing to grill me."

"About what?" I notice Jenna's had her nails done too. I glance down at my own, brittle and discoloured.

"What am I doing living back up here? Why have Tim and I split? What I'm doing? Why haven't I told her? You know." She reels the list off as she taps her fingers one at a time.

"So suddenly she's trying to act like she cares?"

"I know. Mother of the year."

"Perhaps it's because she's getting old. After all, it's up to us what care home she'll end up in."

Jenna pulls a face. "A saucer of milk for Helen. She actually asked after you if you must know."

"Really? Or are you just saying that?"

She means well, but Jenna's often saying things to try and make me feel better. Even when they're not strictly true.

I'm usually glad of her company but I'm relieved when she leaves. I heave a sigh of relief as I lock the door after her. It's not so bad through the week. She needs to be straight off for her new job. But it's a different story at other times. I only hope she's not going to make a habit of sitting her judgmental self on my admittedly grubby sofa and trying to take control of my life. But our relationship has always been this way, so she's only reverting to type. Running to her all the time as a child has clearly shaped our relationship as adults. And because she's only just moved back up here after her divorce, she's lost touch with many of her old friends, and seems perfectly content to settle her focus on me.

Really I should have always saved my angst and woes for my diary. I've definitely over divulged to my sister throughout the years and she knows way too much. At least the written word can never judge me. Nor does it repeat anything I say. The page is my secret sanctuary.

I stride back to the lounge. Slide my diary out from where I thrust it under the chair when Jenna arrived. I have to write. I need to. One thing is for certain. I can't take this diary on the cruise. Thoughts and feelings whilst I'm there will have to be got down and locked up in the notes on my phone. I can copy them into my diary when I get back.

No one, not even my sister, has ever read any of my diaries. And I plan for it to stay that way.

DEAR DIARY

My sister saved my life today. At least she thinks she did. Just because I had sixty-four paracetamol tablets tipped out onto my bed doesn't mean I'd have actually taken them.

I got them from the bathroom cabinet. Two boxes of thirty-two which mum had been prescribed. Probably for the constant state of headache she moans about. Usually that I've given her, she says.

I pressed the tablets from their foil onto my bed and was busy lining them up against the pattern on my duvet when Jenna burst in.

"Oh my God. What are you doing?" She darted towards the bed, her ponytail swinging behind her.

"Don't you ever knock?"

"Answer me Helen. Now."

"Nothing." I grabbed my pillow and buried the tablets beneath it. "I was just messing about."

She sat on the other side of the bed facing me and reached for my hand. "Please sis, I want to help. Tell me what's happened."

"The usual. Same old. Same old." I wiped at my tears. The

worry on her face was real. But she was about the only person in the world who'd care if I took those tablets. If I'd taken every one of them, it would probably be tomorrow morning before Mum even thought to check on me. And that would only be to get me up for school so she could have the house to herself.

"Same crowd?"

"Yep.' I wiped traces of powder from my fingers onto my jeans. Jeans that used to be Jenna's. Like every other item of clothing I own. Mum doesn't think me worthy enough to even choose my own clothes.

"What happened this time?" Jenna let my hand go.

"I'm sick of it. Absolutely sick of it." I collected some of the tablets in cupped hands before letting them trickle back through my fingers onto my duvet.

"Sick of what?"

"Being alone. Being called names. Being laughed at. Hit at all the time. Stolen from. I can't take it any more."

"So you thought you'd take tablets instead?" Her face hardened. "And what about me?"

"No one would care if I died. I might as well not be here."

"I care." She swiped at the tablets, scooping up a handful.

"You're the only one."

"Am I not enough?"

"It's alright for you with all your friends, and your job, and your boyfriend. You don't know what it's like for me."

"I know now. And I want to help you."

I leaned forwards then. Dropped my head into my hands. "How can you help? Nobody can help. I just don't want to be here anymore."

I'd watched as she scooped the rest of the tablets into my bin. She promised to replace them without telling Mum. And promised to help me.

I don't think I'd have taken those tablets if I'm honest. Even if Jenna hadn't come in. Once I had them in my hands, I was terrified. Yes, I could have swallowed them. One after the other, after the other until I found oblivion. But I'm scared of dying. Of *really* being nothing and no one anymore. At least if I'm alive, I've got a chance. As Jenna pointed out, I won't be at school forever. I can leave it behind, move out of this house in the not too distant future, and start a brand new life. Away from my parents and away from the awful people at my awful school. Especially Liz Welsh.

CHAPTER 7

"I'VE BEEN KNOCKING on this door for ages." Liz barges past me into the hallway without invitation, her high heels clicking against the wooden floor.

"Sorry. I must have dropped off on the sofa." I check my watch. Shit. I've so much I need to do.

"But it's not even the afternoon! How depressing. You're acting like an old woman."

"I'm knackered. I've not been sleeping properly." I face her in the hallway which she fills with the scent of whatever perfume she's doused herself with. Though I have to admit, it smells better than damp washing and dogs. I don't really want her here right now. I'm not in the mood. I'm really dreading leaving my house and need to give myself a pep talk. I'm terrified of something being found whilst I'm not here. There's no reason why anyone should come poking about, but the way my luck goes... The way it's always gone...

"How come?"

"It just goes like that sometimes, doesn't it? Insomnia, I mean."

"You were yawning your head off when I was round here last night."

"Because I was tired. That doesn't mean I can sleep. Especially not..." My voice trails off.

"What?" She takes a step closer.

"Nothing."

"Is it because of me?"

"No. Why would it be?"

"I can read you like a book."

"Look, it doesn't matter Liz." *It doesn't matter.* What planet am I on. I've remembered her confession to bludgeoning Lou to death with a hammer and I'm too spineless to do anything about it.

"Come on. Out with it. You've remembered, haven't you?"

"Remembered what?" I turn from her. She really *can* read me like a book.

She grabs for my arm and turns me back to face her.

"Our conversation. That night when we were drinking?"

She isn't taking her eyes off me.

"Bits and pieces." I can imagine that's a reply she doesn't want to hear.

"I was hoping you'd forgotten what I said."

"I wish." My voice rises, then lowers again. "Look Liz, I'm not sure this cruise is a good idea."

Her fingers are still on my arm, beginning to bore into my flesh. "It's a bit late for that, don't you think? The taxi's booked. It's coming in." She checks her watch. "Less than two hours."

I don't know how she can keep her face so straight and her voice so level given the subject behind our conversation. We're skirting around it but we both know the magnitude.

"It's the house Liz." I need to change the subject. "I'm scared of leaving it. In case, you know." I daren't even say the words out loud. Sometimes I worry that our conversations can be tracked. Through our phones, or something. This is how paranoid I've become. Especially over the past couple of weeks.

"What the hell are you on about?"

"The garden. What if foxes, or badgers, or something, start digging? Round the pond I mean? They could dig him up and if I'm not here, I wouldn't be able to stop them."

"He'll have rotted away by now. It's been five months."

I stare at her. She's blasé beyond belief. "Not necessarily. I've Googled it. His bones could stay buried there for another twenty years."

I can't imagine living with this secret for that long. I really can't. When it first happened, I tried to justify it to myself, but the longer this goes on, with Liz getting away with it, the more I can't cope with what I know.

"You've done *what*? You've Googled it? You might as well send the police an invitation to a garden party." She cocks her head towards the back of the house. Her face is a cross between fury and anxiety. "What the hell else have you been Googling?"

"Nothing much. In any case, I've done it all incognito."

"That means nothing. Your searches can still be tracked. You absolute idiot." She glares at me. "You're not taking me down with you Helen. No way."

Her expression reminds me of the Liz of our teens. "I'm sorry." My voice sounds like the Helen of my teens too.

"I just can't believe it. It's like you *want* us to be caught." She stands with her hand on one hip.

"It wasn't *me* who actually did anything though, was it? It was *you*." I'm shaking as I stand up to her, but I don't like this *us* reference. " I had no idea what you were doing until you'd already done it. In either case. Lou *or* Darren."

"Have you done any Googling about that as well? What happened to Lou?"

She makes it sounds as though Lou had an accident or something. *What happened.* "Of course not."

"You better bloody not have done." We continue to face each other across the hallway like opponents on a chess board. Except I'm a pawn and she's always been the queen.

I want to say, *or else?* I would if I was speaking to Jenna. But I'm safe with her. Liz looks like she hates me right now. How the hell am I supposed to go on holiday with her? *In two hours?* I'm scared. After all, she's smashed the skulls in of two people with a hammer. If they aren't cold-blooded killings, I don't know what is. I don't want to be number three. She could take a hammer to me and then easily make it look like a robbery if she really wanted to. There's probably only my sister that would ever notice my absence. I'm best off reverting to type. I can't win. I never will. "Look Liz, I really am sorry." Here I am, behaving like a wet lettuce. As usual. "But I really think it's for the best if I don't come on the cruise with you."

"You have GOT to be joking." I jump as she shouts the word *got*. Her face is crimson with fury. I remember that about her as well from when we were younger. When Liz is angry, she colours up. "You bloody well are coming. It's all paid for. You watched me book it!"

"It's because you're mad with me like this, I don't want to go with you. Who would?"

She glances around the hallway. "Have you even packed yet?" Her voice lowers. Thank goodness.

"A bit. I fell asleep." I just can't seem to muster any enthusiasm. The truth is I haven't packed a stitch. I'm not going to tell her that. As if I ever agreed to this cruise in the first place. I'm an advertiser's dream, wowed by pictures and a promise. Even when Liz is the presenter of them. When she first invited me, it sounded better than it feels now. I don't want to leave my garden unattended. I'm terrified of leaving my garden unattended. "Where's the dog?" She never refers to

Coco by name. It's always *the dog*. Her jaw hardens and she strides towards the kitchen as if she owns the place. She acts like she owns me as well, and in some ways, she does. We're bound together by the darkest of secrets. Our whole friendship, if it can even be classed as a *friendship*, is built on a foundation of fear and the threat of loneliness. As my sister was only too happy to remind me when she collected Coco earlier this morning. She was even more incredulous I was still going than when I first mentioned it to her. And she doesn't know the half of it.

"Coco's with my sister. She picked her up earlier."

"That's something then. Right. Get your packing done. Now. I'll pour us a drink."

As though nothing's happened. Just like that.

"But..."

"No buts. Now. And no more bloody dodgy internet searches." Her voice softens. "Unless you want to give me a heart attack." She smiles. This is the thing. I never know whether I'm coming or going with Liz. Her mood changes direction more often than a weather vane. "Right. We'll forget about all that's gone on. Let's just get out of here."

"OK." I'm beat. I'm going whether I like it or not. And I can't blame anybody but myself. The word no doesn't ever seem to have been part of my vocabulary.

"We'll have an amazing time. So go and get packed."

There's no argument to be had. I'll have to try to enjoy it. However, when I get back home in a couple of weeks, things are going to change. I can't go on like I have been. And if that means coming clean, telling the truth, and facing up to my part in things, then maybe that's the way forward. Like I wrote in my diary last night, I'll just do it. I certainly won't be letting

Liz know what I'm planning beforehand. There's no way she'd allow me to live long enough to go through with it.

One thing I've learned about Liz over the years is she has no conscience whatsoever. She's got all the traits of a psychopath. Perhaps she can live with what she's done to Lou and Darren for the rest of her life, but I certainly can't.

For my sake, for Donna's sake, but most of all, for Charlie's sake, I've got to do something. I'm so weighed down with guilt I could drown in it.

DEAR DIARY

I've been delivering papers along my round for nearly a year. Along with the babysitting, I bet I earn as much money as I would get if I had decent parents, especially after the Christmas tips some of the people on my round have given me. When I've listened to conversations amongst some of the girls at school, they all seem not only to get pocket money, but a clothing allowance. Liz gets the most and she's in a children's home. Sally's *sooo* jealous of that. I sit in front of her and Liz in Maths and recently overheard her saying, oooh, *I wish I could come and live with you there.* I would rather die than live in the same place as Liz.

There are literally five more terms until I can leave school. And home. I can leave at sixteen.

My life at home is rubbish but at least I've got my sister. Since she found me with the tablets, she's been spending loads of time with me. Sometimes she even lets me tag along with her friends, like today, and they're all nice to me. My sister is the best. I know I'm just one *part* of her world. But to me, Jenna's my entire world.

The bullies, even Liz, have left me alone for a few days. I

hope this carries on when we go back to school after the holidays. Someone must have had a word with them.

Today was a miles better day than most. I went into town with Jenna and two of her friends. I had my baby-sitting money to spend, but didn't find anything I wanted. At least I managed to get a few ideas of things my sister might like. I still had my baby-sitting money on me when I did my paper round. How I wish I'd taken it home where it was safe.

As I delivered the papers, everyone was coming out of their houses. Thrusting notes at me. Coins. Chocolate. Christmas cards. Words of thanks. It felt am-ay-zing. Like for once, everything was going right. People were acting as though they liked me.

After I'd posted the final newspaper, I found a bench near the shops. I was so excited to count up what I'd been given. Enough to get my sister something really cool for Christmas, I hoped. After all, there was one more day left for me to go back into town. I gasped when I realised I had nearly forty quid. People thought enough of me on my paper round to say thank you in this way. Tears stung my eyes. Happy tears. An alien feeling.

Then suddenly my bench was surrounded.

"Well look at Miss Money Bags here." Liz sat at one side of me, Sally at the other. A shadow loomed over my head from behind. A hand came down and plucked the notes from me. Then they all ran off, shrieking with laughter. As if I'd counted my money out in public. What an idiot. What an absolute idiot.

I can't get my sister anything for Christmas. Nor are there any paracetamol left in the bathroom cabinet. No matter how much I want to die, I can't.

CHAPTER 8

I WHEEL my borrowed suitcase from my door to the taxi. Liz is standing by the open boot, grinning as I walk towards her. She must have forgiven my earlier reluctance.

"Excited?" She says as the driver helps me load it into the car. She smells as though she's sprayed even more perfume on. Drowned herself in the stuff. Someone should tell her that less is more.

"I guess so." My voice is too high-pitched to be authentic. I'm really trying to be excited, but no matter what I do, I can't quell this dreadful sense of foreboding. Maybe when we board the ship, that will change. I hope so.

Liz's grin fades. "Well bloody get excited." She ushers me around the side of the taxi, clip-clopping on even higher heels than those she was wearing earlier. She's wearing a jumpsuit that I'd give my right arm to wear. "This is the trip of a lifetime. Let's leave all the shit right here and enjoy ourselves for a change." She points back at the house.

She actually sounds genuine. Maybe I can enjoy myself with her. Maybe she's right and I'll feel differently once we're away from here. I have to try. I just wish it was Jenna I was going with rather than Liz. We haven't been on holiday together since I was sixteen. I can relax with Jenna. Be myself. Or at least I used to be able to. She has no idea who I am or what I know these days.

"Leeds Bradford Airport." Liz climbs into the passenger seat. I sit behind her, hoping she'll talk to the driver, rather than to me, as we make the ten minute journey. I've gone more and more into myself in the six months since we did what we did. Especially now I know the entire story. It was bad enough before.

I miss Coco already, the only soul who truly cares for me other than my sister. Jenna said she'd have dropped me off at the airport under normal circumstances, rather than me having to get a taxi, but that she wouldn't be able to stomach having Liz in her car. *Not even for one minute, let alone ten,* she said. I don't know how I've managed to keep them apart since Jenna moved home to Yorkshire, but I've done a good job of it. So far, so good. I know for a fact she wouldn't be able to stay quiet about everything Liz put me through in the past. After all, it was always Jenna who picked me up and put me back together. Or tried to.

She hasn't got a clue about Lou or Darren. Or any of it really. I wonder how she'd react if she knew the truth. If I could tell her one day? Would she cut all ties with me if she knew her only sister was capable of helping to drag the body of a former neighbour across my garden? A married man I'd even allowed into my bed?

Would she still want to be my sister if she knew I'd then spent four hours throughout the night taking it in turns with Liz to dig my pond deeper and deeper? Would she ever speak to me again if she knew I'd then helped Liz manoeuvre and tip his dead weight into the hole, before covering it back over with soil and re-laying the pond liner? No. I doubt my sister could ever look me in the eye again if she'd known what I'd been capable of that night. Even though she knows I was sleeping with Darren, and how shabbily he's treated me over the years, I reckon she'd be frogmarching me to the police if she were to uncover my darkest of secrets. Knowing Jenna as I do, she'd put the blame squarely on Liz for involving me. Hell, I'd never have believed I could be capable of what happened that night either. It happened so easily, so fast, it was almost as though Liz had planned it. Maybe she had. She's always maintained it was self defence. *Him or her*, she told me.

"Are you going anywhere nice?" The driver jolts me from my spinning thoughts. He glances sideways at Liz then into his mirror at me. There it goes, the question that I've so often longed to be asked. *Are you going anywhere nice?* I actually am. It's really *my* turn to go on holiday at last. After all the years of replying with *lovely* when I've taken in boarding dogs. Their owners drop them off, say they'll be back in a week, two weeks, whatever, and tell me of far-flung locations I've never heard of. I deserve this.

"We're flying down to Southampton, then boarding a cruise there," Liz replies, as though it's all run-of-the-mill for her. I suppose it is with the finance she's acquired. "For ten nights."

"That's fantastic. I bet you can't wait. Which one have you booked?"

She tells him the name of the company, and reels off the countries we're docking at. For the remainder of the drive, he waxes lyrical about his own cruising experiences. Where he's been. Which companies he's sailed with. How entertainers are swapped on and off the ship by helicopter. If I could get a word in edgeways, I'd remark how huge the cruise ships appear on the website, but not so big they can accommodate a helipad. He tells us we'll have a paper delivered every morning detailing what's on and when, and that we'll be waited on hand and foot. It does sound exciting. If only I didn't have to share a cabin with Liz.

I'm glad I decided to leave my diary at home. It's the only place I'm free to tell my truth. I nearly packed it today but took it back out. It's far too much of a risk. If Liz were ever to come across it I'd be in so much shit. And if anyone else were to find it, we both would. It's safely tucked into its usual place in the sofa lining. Not that I really need to hide it so carefully; it's not as though anyone can get into my house while I'm away. The only spare key I've got is the one I once gave Lou. I've asked Liz for it back, but she reckons not to have come across it in the time she's lived in the house. I really should change the locks, but it's always been an extra expense I can't stretch to. I've managed to put off Jenna's requests for a key so far. Since she's moved back, she's occasionally asked for one, but as I've told her, it's not as though she needs one. I never go anywhere, apart from out with the dogs. I don't even go shopping these days. For the last six months I feel as though I can't hold my head up anymore. Something's got to give. I can't carry on living like this. I haven't really been living, more existing.

It's the first time I've ever flown. Liz knows this. She doesn't say anything, but I can feel her watching me intently. It's a short flight in the scheme of things, but I still grip the seat as the plane takes off. Not that it takes a great deal to evoke my anxiety these days. The entire thing just feels so weird, right down to the genuine smile Liz gives me, as if she's enjoying being the one who's facilitating my brand new experience. I can't get my head around the fact that my first trip abroad is being taken with the girl who mercilessly bullied me throughout my secondary school years. Mercilessly. The girl who made my life an utter misery. The girl who grew up to become a double murderess. No one would know it to look at her.

As our passports and tickets are checked, I feel dowdy and shabby beside Liz, who as always, has gone to maximum effort with how she looks. Her hair is curled and her nails are shaped and polished. And she's wearing enough makeup for both of us.

Having not even packed anything until the last minute, I'm still wearing the clothes I walked Coco in this morning and I'm not even sure if I've washed my face today. I really do need to get myself sorted out. It will take a lot more than new clothes, manicures and a hairstylist to make me feel any better about myself. The longer I live with the awful truth about what happened to Lou and Darren, the lower I'm going to sink, no matter how hard I try to fight. Yes, I'm away from it all, yes, I'm travelling even further away from it all. But it makes no difference how many miles away from home I am, I can never, ever, escape myself.

DEAR DIARY

If anyone would be stupid enough to fall for the same trick a second time, that someone will always be me.

"Get into pairs."

I glared at Miss Richardson. My hatred for her has grown after what she did to me last term. The gym knickers episode will haunt me forever.

I loitered at the back, knowing no one would ever choose me to be their partner. The only person who would ever choose me for *anything* would be Jenna. And even then, she didn't actively *choose* me to be sisters with. Rather I was forced on her.

"Hey. I'll walk with you." I turned to a voice at the side of me. The voice of Joanne Carr. A mousy girl who everyone copies their answers from. Popular, yet not popular, if that's possible. *Why would she offer to walk with me?*

I stared at her. "Why?"

"Because I want to." She smiled and something gave way inside me. Perhaps after walking with me, she'd want to be my friend. I've always behaved like this. If someone shows me the tiniest amount of interest, I latch on to them. But it would be amazing to have someone to walk to school with everyday, someone to sit with at lunchtime, someone to spend breaks with. Instead of just hanging around, and killing time, alone.

I smiled back then. "Great." My voice was probably too high-pitched with enthusiasm. A cackle of laughter erupted from somewhere amongst where Liz and Sally were standing in line in front of us. I hoped Joanne wasn't going to cop it.

As we walked, Liz and Sally kept looking back at us. They kept whispering to each other. The girls around them were looking back at us too. All nudging each other. I don't know what was so interesting about Joanne choosing to walk with me. If she was aware of them all staring and gossiping, she pretended not to notice. It was mainly me making all the conversation - I asked her about her favourite music, whether she was allowed into town on her own, and whether she had her own room. All I got back were one-word answers. Eventually, I wondered why she was walking with me in the first place.

Thankfully, I was already wearing my swimming costume beneath my uniform. Therefore, I would only have to endure the comments about my pancake chest, as they all called it, in the showers afterward. Joanne hung her bag next to me in the changing room. This prompted even more laughter amongst the school bitches. It was such a nice surprise, so I carried on trying to talk to her. Perhaps I'd even have a pool partner if Miss Richardson wanted us to get into pairs again. I'm so desperate to have a friend. I know I've got my sister, but it's not the same as having a friend at school. Not only had Joanne walked to the pool with me, she was also getting changed right beside me. I've read in a magazine somewhere that people like to talk about themselves. So I tried to ask her some more questions... what was her favourite food? Did she have any brothers or sisters? What films did she like? But again, one-word answers.

The pool was freezing. I can't understand why anyone enjoys swimming or would even *pay* to go. I was forced to swim a length of the pool when I was eleven, and I've never been a good swimmer. I detest the smell of the chlorine and it's so strong in this pool that I can still smell it on my skin even now, hours later, as I write this.

Miss Richardson ordered us to warm up by swimming two lengths of breast stroke.

"What if you've got no breasts?" Sally shouted out, pointing at me. Cow. Everyone burst into raucous laughter, especially Liz. I was shocked when Miss Richardson made Sally stand in the corner for what she'd said, however she looked like she was stifling a smile too.

Meanwhile, I had to stay afloat for two lengths. Torture. I was on my way back up the pool when someone grabbed my foot from beneath me. I was already well out of breath, but when I swallowed a lungful of water instead of oxygen, it felt as though something in my throat was going to explode. I've never tried to scream underwater before, and it came out as a gurgle. I tried to fight back as I was tugged further beneath the surface, kicking out with the foot being held, trying to free it, whilst feeling for the bottom of the pool with my other foot. But it was no good. I was still in the deep end, and I was going to die.

My chest felt as though it might burst, and I was swiftly running out of fight.

I'm not sure how long I was struggling, trying to wrestle my foot from whoever had hold of it, but it felt like forever. Time seemed to slow; even the light filtering from the surface of the water above was fading. Then a sound... as though something was cracking inside my head.

I was really going to die.

Suddenly, strong hands gripped my armpits and there was a rush of water in my ears as I was hauled to the surface. The silence of the water gave way to frantic voices.

"I. Need. To. Get. Out." I gasped each word to the lifeguard who steered me to the edge and onto the side. I thought I was going to be sick. Luckily, after a minute or so, I managed to get a grip of myself. I'd have never lived it down if I'd have puked right there in front of everyone.

"What on earth happened?" He crouched beside me, concern knitted into his eyebrows.

"She..." I pointed towards Liz, still unable to get my breath. There couldn't be anyone else who would do something like that to me.

"I haven't a clue what you're talking about." Liz was wide-eyed with innocence. "I dropped my goggles Miss," she looked towards Miss Richardson. "So I didn't see what happened. But I never went anywhere near her."

Glancing through the crowd, I noticed Joanne standing with Sally, pointing at me and laughing. She hadn't wanted to be my friend after all. She'd probably done it for a bet. Just like Liz had done.

I felt lucky to still be alive. Or unlucky, given the state of my miserable life. "I just want to go home." Tears were cascading down my cheeks. "Can you call my mum?" I wasn't sure whether she'd even come for me but I figured it was worth a try. I suddenly longed for the sanctuary of my bedroom, and my diary. At least I'd be able to pour out everything that had happened today.

But it's only now, hours later, that I've stopped crying enough to feel able to write about it.

At least the lifeguard was kind to me. He wrapped a towel around my shoulders and said he'd ring Mum from the first aid room. He'd have to fill out a form, he told me, and he wanted to get the other lifeguard to check me over - to make sure I was definitely OK. At least someone cared.

The woman in the first aid room was kind as well. I was left on my own for ten minutes, to recover, she said, while she rang Mum. Wrapped in the towel beside a heater whilst laid on the first aid couch, I felt cocooned. And safe. Voices and laughter drifted in from the changing room. But they felt far enough away, as though they couldn't hurt me anymore today.

The rest of the class had set off back to school when the female lifeguard eventually suggested I went for a shower. Mum had reluctantly agreed to leave work early and collect me. From the look on the lifeguard's face, it was obvious Mum wasn't going to be happy when she got to the pool.

A note had been left in the spot where I'd stripped down to my swimsuit when I arrived.

*As if I would ever want
to be friends with you!*

I shredded it into tiny pieces and washed it down the plughole of the shower. I will never trust anyone again.

I was right about Mum not being happy. I've had many years of being able to read her moods and tiptoe around them. But at least I knew what to expect.

CHAPTER 9

"Wow! Just look at this place. Which bed do you want?" Without waiting for an answer, Liz dumps her hand luggage on the bed nearest the balcony door. The cabin is every bit as impressive as it appeared on the website. I can hardly believe I'm here. *Me* in a place like *this*.

"Are you going to cheer up now Helen?" Liz unzips her case. "You've been a right misery since we set off."

"I'm sorry. I'm OK. I will perk up, I promise." I sink to the other bed. I need to pep myself up. Right now I could just curl up and fall asleep for the rest of the day. I can only hope the sea air goes some way to cure my insomnia. I've a feeling Liz will get seriously pissed off with me being up and down all night like I am at home. And she'll probably moan about the light from my phone if I read or journal whilst she's trying to sleep. I wish for the millionth time I had my own cabin. If only I could have afforded to pay the difference in cost.

"I thought we were going lower though." I point at the balcony door. "So it would be less noisy."

"Yes, but we wouldn't have had a balcony if we'd been

lower down would we? You're not complaining, are you?" She fixes me with a hard stare.

"Sorry. No, of course not." As usual, she hasn't listened to me.

"What are we doing then?" She sits on her bed whilst still looking around. "I wouldn't mind going for a drink or three."

"I need to shower and spruce myself up."

She gives me a look as if to say, *blimey, not even a ten-strong team of beauty therapists could spruce you up.* She's not wrong either. What I need to do is get away from her for a while. I've been in her company nearly all day and I'm beginning to struggle with it.

"Then I'm off to explore," I add. I'm eager not to spend too much time stuck in this cabin or anywhere else with her. I'm grateful she's paid for this trip, of course I am, but that doesn't mean I want us to be acting like we're married or something. No way.

"I'll come with you."

Great. That's quashed my hopes of a break from her. I hop from foot to foot, wondering what I can say to get a breather on my own.

"Go on then." She points at the ensuite door. "I'll unpack my stuff and call room service for some coffee while you're in there." She moves towards the telephone on the dresser. I'm surprised she'd not raiding the mini bar yet.

I pick up the towel from my bed, lily-white and fluffy - not like the threadbare grey things I have at home that hardly look like towels anymore. I slip my shoes off and reach for my phone.

She's got her back to me but is watching me through the mirror. "What are you taking that into the shower for? You planning on calling someone?"

"Erm no. But my sister might text. Or call. To check I've got here OK."

She swings to face me, one hand on her hip. "Oh, I get it Helen. You don't trust me enough to even leave your phone lying around, do you?" That look. Again.

"Don't be daft. It's just, you know, habit, I guess." We've only just got here. I don't want us to be falling out. And it's not as if Liz can get into my phone without my thumbprint anyway. I've got to stop being so paranoid. I'm making myself ill.

"Go on then. I'm not waiting around all day." Liz flicks a finger towards the en suite door in a similar way to how a teacher would if they were saying *run along then*. "If your sister calls, I can always answer it, can't I?"

I reckon Jenna would probably hang up if Liz answered. I don't fancy dealing with that scenario, so I flick the phone onto silent before dropping it onto the bed. Liz doesn't seem to have noticed.

"And off we go." She throws the patio doors open and steps out onto the balcony. I'm hit by a blast of freezing air. It will be even colder as we head further North, no doubt. But according to my searches, we're more likely to see the Northern Lights if the sky stays clear. I'm obsessed with seeing them. That, and so many other things. There's so much living I haven't done and am unlikely to do. Without a miracle anyway. There's so much to do. So much to see.

A horn blares out from the front of the ship followed by music striking up. Dropping my towel back on the bed, I join Liz on the balcony, watching as we cast off. I'm relieved to leave all my troubles there, albeit only for ten days. I lean over the rail, watching as the hull slices through the waves like a fillet knife through a fish. I've missed the smell of the sea. It's been so long since I've been anywhere near it. Too busy merely existing, surviving, and accepting the meagre crumbs life keeps offering me.

As we leave the harbour behind, it hardly feels as though

we're moving. But we must be: the buildings and the waving crowd gathered on the pier are becoming smaller and smaller. Maybe I didn't need to worry about seasickness. I hope not because I couldn't afford the tablets. Perhaps I'll be absolutely fine.

I wander around the ship with Liz, in and out of the spa area, the gym, restaurants, lounges and shops, just taking it all in. The portion of the ship we cover in thirty minutes is barely a fraction of it. We might as well be in another world. One full of vibrancy and colour, music and enjoyment. This must be what living *really* is. Everywhere, people are smiling, laughing and relaxing. I can't imagine that ease, though I yearn for it. Instead, I'm on the outskirts, much as I always have been, teetering between survival and falling into a sea of depression.

As I follow Liz like a sheep, listening to her *ooohs* and *aaahs,* it dawns on me that people around us might think we're a couple. I don't want that. Maybe I could get my hair done, like Liz has. And my nails. A new top. I've got some space on my credit card, I think. There *must* be some single men around. Meeting someone would be the only thing that could possibly take my mind off my crappy life. This is something that only seems to happen for others. The best I've done so far is bloody Darren, and only to scratch his itch when he wasn't getting it from whichever woman he happened to be with. I know I don't get out of my house a great deal, but the fact that he's the only man to ever come anywhere near me is shameful. Sometimes I wonder if I've done something in a previous life to warrant my existence being such an utter struggle. Perhaps, deep within me, there's something really hideous, something so deeply ingrained that I deserve the endless misery.

Liz picks up a pair of jeans. Then a dress. I haven't worn a dress since I was a child, apart from at Lou's funeral. I'm not pretty enough and as everyone used to tell me at school, Liz included, I look more like a boy than a girl.

As my paranoia kicks in even more, I worry everyone can see right through Liz and me. Who we really are and what we're actually capable of. Every time I begin to enjoy myself or relax, even just slightly, it's as though a hammer of its own kind comes thudding down onto my skull. It reminds me, *who the hell do you think you are? You don't get to enjoy yourself. Not after what you've done.* The guilt will pursue me for the rest of my life if I don't do something about it soon. *The rest of my life.* Poor Lou didn't even make it to forty.

Finally we settle in one of the upstairs bars. Liz swipes her card for a bottle of champagne that costs what I'd spend on a weekly shop. I'm ready for a drink, but not one costing this much. She leads me to a table by the window. Not that there's anything to see anymore. It's so dark out there, it's difficult to tell where the sea meets the sky. The ten days aboard this cruise will probably consist of me trailing after Liz, as she calls the shots and makes all the decisions about where we go and what we do. Just because she holds the pursestrings.

"Cheers." She holds her glass aloft and nods towards mine.

I clink mine against hers. "Here's to a really great ten days." I attempt to load my voice with a joviality that's a million miles away from how I'm really feeling. "Thank you," I say to a waiter who passes our table with canapés. I'm hungry, ready for some dinner, but Liz insisted on having a drink first.

I place the canapé I've just accepted onto the table. It's probably all Lou's money we're spending here. My appetite abruptly departs. Lou can't eat again, can she? Neither can Darren. How can we be doing this?

"What the *hell's* up with you now." At least Liz isn't shouting at me, it's more of a hiss across the table. She bangs her glass down, not taking her eyes off me. I can't keep up this charade, no matter how hard I try. Jenna's said from when we were kids that my face gives the game away - I can never mask what I'm truly feeling. But at least I'm safe from Liz out here - away from the cabin and amongst people. Amidst the roulette tables and tinkle of glasses and pleasant conversation. She can't touch me.

I can't bear to imagine how she'd react if I were to enlighten her about the plan that's formulating itself in my head. As soon as we get back. How I've decided that being punished is preferable to this. Even being sent to prison would be less painful than living with this heaviness. If being locked up sets me free from the burden of guilt, it's a price I'm prepared to pay. However, I want to be the one who leads the police to Darren; the prospect of him being *found* by other means doesn't bear thinking about. It would make things even worse than they already are. I want to *jump before I am pushed,* as the saying goes.

Before I found out it was *Liz* who'd murdered Lou, rather than Donna, I could cope with my regular attacks of conscience over Darren. They'd come, they'd go, and I would get through them. Especially since he used me so badly when he was alive. But the truth about Lou has tipped me over. Completely over. I look back at Liz. At her long dark hair curled around her shoulders and her lipsticked mouth. Yes, she looks as though she's got a mean streak running through her, but a *murderer?* An extremely cold-blooded one at that, from what I heard about the state Lou was in. However,

Donna looked even less like a murderer as she stood cuffed to a guard in the dock. The jury, who almost unanimously found her guilty, clearly didn't take appearances into account. I'd wondered why Liz looked so happy at the time. Now, I know.

"I'll get us another bottle." Liz scowls as she throws her chair back with a scrape. "And when I get back to this table, you're bloody well going to talk to me. I want to know what the hell's going on in that miserable head of yours."

Whilst she's at the bar, I glance around the room. The couple at the next table are staring at me, evidently having observed our brief altercation. Realising I've clocked them watching, they turn back to each other. Another couple, two tables away, are all loved up. The woman's inspecting her ring finger and waggling it about, as though they've just got either engaged or married. I decide, with a pang, that's unlikely to ever be me. Especially not if I end up in a prison cell.

What could be a mother and daughter are dressed up like dog's dinners at the table on the other side of me. Another scenario that will never be mine. My mother is so distant, she might as well live in Australia. It used to really get to me. Jenna and I have spoken many times about it and her theory is Mum's hostility towards me stems from looking like our father, and me reminding her of him. And not in a good way. I'll never know why they stayed together. Death was probably a relief for him. I can certainly identify with that.

Raucous laughter erupts from a card game in the corner, followed by a cheer from the poker table. The sound of those enjoying themselves causes me to feel even more removed from reality than I already do. I want to be part of the laughter and the cheers. I want to belong. Maybe I never will.

I peel my cardigan off. The warmth and soft lighting will be a ploy to keep people spending at the tables. To say it's so cold out there, I'm surprised at how many people are outside on the deck. Either wandering up and down under the stars, many hand in hand, or just gazing out to sea. I turn back to my champagne. To say it cost so much, I'm struggling to get it down. I must try. I don't want to irritate Liz even further. And perhaps drunken oblivion is the way forward tonight, despite my 'never again' promises. Anything to help me to sleep. I stare into the bubbles as though they might offer some much-needed answers. Is it really possible to be around so many people and yet feel so alone? Is what I've decided really the right thing to do?

After all, if I go through with this, I've no choice other than to take Liz down with me.

DEAR DIARY

The *only* good thing about being on holiday is the week off school. No Liz. No Sally. No bullies. I doubt anyone will even notice I'm not there apart from when they're looking for someone to laugh at. Or pick on.

Mum and Dad aren't speaking to each other again. Jenna and I are tiptoeing around them in the chalet so as not to make things worse. I don't think we'd ever come on holiday if it wasn't for Grandma living down here. At least she's in a decent mood, unlike my stupid parents. Even Jenna's doing my head in this week, moaning about being forced to come when she's got her A Levels coming up. She's been dumped by some lad, so is wallowing in her own misery and not bothered about me.

So far this week, I've been getting away from the lot of them by going for long walks on the beach. For the fourth day in a row, it was so warm that the sand looked hazy. However, I felt as dark inside as the dreariest of December days. Mum was yelling at me this morning, taking her bad mood out on me, like she always does. I felt like wading into the water and never looking back. But I'd probably chicken out. It's not that long ago when I got a taste of drowning, after all. If I were to go to the top of the cliff and just throw myself in, there'd be no going back from that. I wondered how long it would be before anyone noticed. I'm hated by everyone at school. And I feel just as hated by everyone at home right now. It would probably be days before Mum would even report me missing.

I dropped onto the sand. All around me, couples were strolling hand in hand. Kids threw balls and frisbees to each other. Everywhere, people were together and happy. I can't imagine what it must be to genuinely smile or find something funny. I was the only person on my own. Perhaps that's how I'll always be. On my own.

CHAPTER 10

I'VE COME BACK to the cabin. Left Liz to it. She went on and on at me when she came back to the table, demanded to know why I'm struggling to raise a smile. She wouldn't believe that I'm just tired. It's *partly* true. Too tired to even eat, not that I could have faced a meal sitting across a table from Liz. I've just forced a banana down - that will do me until tomorrow. I don't deserve nice food anyway. Not after what I've done. And with what I'm carrying on my conscience.

Liz might be content to sit at that table drowning herself in expensive champagne, but I couldn't have stayed for a moment longer. I need to be on my own. I need to think. When she finally comes back, I'll pretend to be asleep, even if I'm not.

I unlock the patio door and step onto the balcony, the air hitting me with such a slap, it's hard to breathe. The sky is sheet-ice clear, enabling me to pick out the formations of the plough. And the bear. Within minutes my hands and face are numb. But I don't care. Just as I don't deserve nice food, I don't deserve to be warm either. Darren isn't exactly warm where he is, buried beneath my garden pond. I lean over the rail, mesmerised by the white spray generated as the ship parts the sea. Eventually, watching the waves causes me to feel disorientated. I stagger back and try to regain a sense of grounding by looking outwards. I've not been too bad so far with seasickness. I don't want to kick it off now. But whichever way I look, there is only inky blackness. Both inwardly and outwardly.

I. Just. Need. To. Stop. Thinking. Perhaps after some sleep, I'll feel more positive.

I sink to the bed, wishing I could talk to Jenna. I want to tell her the truth about what I'm going through. She'd give me some advice. Some assurance that what I'm going to do is the right thing. But as always, I can only speak my thoughts in writing. However I need to let it out right now. I'll go mad if I don't. I tug my phone from my bag. As soon as I start typing, it all comes pouring out.

Night one of the Cruise.
 So I'm here. I didn't want to come. I don't belong. Amongst all these happy people having a wonderful time. They deserve to be here. They never slept with someone else's husband over and over again. They haven't got a body buried in their garden. They don't have the secrets I have.
 And Liz deserves to be here even less than me. I don't know how she can even look in the mirror. I've tried everything to change how I feel, but I HATE HER. I really, really hate her. She's done nothing but ruin my life, not just once, but over and over again. Usually, I'd be able to write all this in my diary, but I couldn't even bring that with me because of HER. How little I trust her not to go through my things. I don't know how I'm going to survive this cruise. Ten

days! Why on earth did I ever agree to it? One thing's for certain, I can't go on like this.

All I can do is come clean about what I've done and what I know. From what I've read, they'll go easier on me if I tell the truth. So as soon as I get home I'm going to the police. Nothing, and no one is going to change my mind.

I feel slightly better. Perhaps I'll even sleep, though it's still fairly early. Only just ten o'clock. Today seems to have lasted forever. Probably because I've been in Liz's company since eleven o clock this morning.

The beat of the music and people's chatter and laughter is as loud as I feared it would be. It's a good job I've drunk some champagne. That should help me drop off. But I need to make sure. I glance towards the minibar. If Liz has got enough money to fill her gullet with expensive champagne, she can pay to put me to sleep. I wrench a miniature gin from it, then gag as the liquid hits the back of my throat, before burning all the way down to my stomach. Then I do the same with a vodka. I *will* sleep. I need to sleep. And I want to be asleep by the time Liz gets back here. I can't cope with being around her any more today. I shuffle towards her bed, before lowering myself to sit and stare out at the blackness beyond the patio doors. I'm at one with it. Bloody hell, I thought at first that agreeing to this cruise might help me escape myself but things seem even worse now I'm here. I lay back and close my eyes. I've. Really. Had. Enough.

"What the hell are you doing?" Liz looms over me. For a moment I wonder where I am. What I'm doing here, not in my own bed, surrounded by peeling wallpaper and looking up at a polystyrene ceiling rose. I rub at my eyes.

"That's your bed, over there. Surely you're not that drunk." I sit up, feel for my phone. It's at the side of me, the screen still illuminated. I must have dropped off whilst trying to read on my Kindle app. I vaguely recall deciding to read. To tire my eyes out. Why didn't I move back over. The combination of champagne, gin and vodka clearly worked. Evidently whose bed I was sitting on whilst reading didn't occur to me. I can only blame the concoction of alcohol I drank before lying down.

"Move it."

I swing my legs over the edge of the bed.

"Now." She shoves me.

I stagger to my feet in the darkness and start towards my own bed. I'm just about able to pick out shapes with the help of the faint light filtering through the patio doors from the upper decks. I'm not sure why Liz hasn't switched any light on - she's not usually the type who would show any consideration for someone sleeping. I tilt my phone towards me. It's only just gone eleven. I've barely been asleep for five minutes. No wonder I'm disorientated.

"Not there either." She says as I'm about to sink to my own bed.

"Leave it out Liz. I'm knackered."

"I said move it." She's pointing towards the balcony.

"What are you on about?" I lean towards the lamp but she knocks my arm sideways before I get to it. "What's up with you?"

"You are."

"I need to wee." I suddenly feel nauseous, a combination of being suddenly woken combined with the alcohol. Plus I've hardly eaten today.

"Get out there."

"What do you mean?"

She's still pointing towards the balcony. She can't be serious. What's got into her?

"Don't be stupid. It's freezing outside."

"I want to talk to you."

"We can talk in here, can't we?" I step towards the overhead light switch and turn it on. Liz swiftly turns it off again at the switch above her bed. I've no idea why she insists that whatever conversation she wants to have has to take place in the dark. "Have you gone mad, or what?"

Nevertheless, I tie my dressing gown around my waist and follow her to the door. Perhaps she wants a cigarette. I'm not sure if smoking's allowed, even on the balcony, but who's to know? As she said herself when we first got here, there's no cameras out there. As far as I know, Liz only smokes when she's seriously drunk. Which judging by her behaviour, she is. Though I'm confused - her speech seems more wired than slurred.

"You see all this." She gestures beyond the balcony, out to sea. Then she waves her hands up towards the deck. "You wouldn't be here if it wasn't for me." She spins on her heel and looks at me, the whites of her cosmetically-treated teeth luminous in the moonlight. I wonder who paid for them.

"I know. And I'm grateful."

"You're not though. Are you? You've had a face like a smacked arse since we set off. *Before* we set off."

"Is that what all this is about?" I'm relieved if the truth be known. I thought she was mad about something else. She'd have to be a mind reader though to have anything else on me.

"You're a liar Helen. *Tired.* You just want to pull me down to where you are, don't you?" Her fists are curled at her sides. I wonder if I'm going to get the brunt of them. "You've always been the same."

"What do you mean?" I continue to face her in the

darkness, my eyes beginning to adjust to it. "Is *this* why you've dragged me out of bed? Just to have a go at me?" I should have trusted my gut. I should have stayed at home. What an idiot I am.

"I've tried with you Helen." She shakes her head. "I've really tried to put the past behind us."

"What have *you* got to try about? It was you who made my life hell, remember?" My teeth are chattering with the cold. She hasn't lit a cigarette. Why the hell couldn't we have done this inside?

"It was *you* who was sleeping with my husband though, wasn't it?"

Shit. Shit. Shit. I swallow rising bile. How the hell does she know about that? And more to the point, why hasn't she said anything before? Whilst Darren was married to Lou, he generally only came to me when his and Donna's on/off relationship was off. I never knew it was Liz he'd married. Only that very last time when I let him in... How could I have been so stupid? Not to mention desperate.

"Cat got your tongue Helen?"

"How do you know about me and Darren?"

"*Me and Darren!* Have you heard yourself? I make it my mission to know about *everything.* Especially slags like you that go after other people's husbands."

"I didn't know you..."

"I bet you didn't."

"I actually got the shock of my life when I found out he was married to you." I look down at my bare feet. I certainly can't feel them anymore. My voice is a mumble. "I didn't go anywhere near him after that. I promise you." I can't exactly say, *I only slept with him once after I found out he was married to you.*

But I was so lonely. Yes he was paralytic that last night. He only turned up at my door because he had no where else to go but still... when you're in my position, chances have to be taken wherever they present themselves.

"You're just as bad as Donna. An absolute slag. Not to mention, a liar. Even though you're cornered, you're still lying about when you slept with him."

"I'm not. I promise."

"I saw him coming out of your house. Well after me and you had first met up again."

"Look Liz, I'm sorry. I'm not proud of myself. For that. For any of it." I look at her again. That bit's true. I'm far from proud of myself. If I could turn the clock back, I'd do it in a heartbeat.

"Donna got what was coming to her. And now it's your turn."

The whites of her eyes glint at me in the faint moonlight. I don't know how I ever saw friendship in them. All I see now is pure evil. I want to tell her that she's going to get what's coming to her too. But I'm in a precarious position here. Instead, I'm going to try and reason with her. It's the only way. "Do you know something Liz, we could use this conversation as a turning point." I wrap my arms around myself in attempt to warm up. "Now it's all out in the open. The rest of both our lives doesn't have to be like it has been so far... we can..."

"Shut the fuck up will you." Her voice is a snarl. "Don't you think I heard enough of your whining, bleating voice when we were at school?"

Tears prickle at my eyes. "But..."

"I said shut up. I don't want to hear your do-gooding crap Helen. But like I said before, you've definitely been more use as a *friend*." She draws air quotes as she says the word *friend*, "than as an enemy. Only you've served your purpose now."

"What do you mean? What purpose?"

"Do you really think our meeting in the supermarket that

time was an *accident?* Do you really think I could ever want to be *friends* with you?"

"You're deranged, you are." I step backwards, hearing an echo of my school days. I need to get back inside. I'll ask for a transfer to another room. Then I'll get off this ship the moment it's possible. Somehow I'll get myself back home. I have to get away from this woman. It will be worth maxing my credit card out to end this, to end it right now. Or I'll have to come clean to Jenna. She'll help me. God, if she could see me now. If she knew the full story...

"*You're* the one who's deranged." Just as I've got one foot back in the cabin, Liz grabs my arm and yanks me back over the threshold. "If you think you can get in my way..."

"Let me go." I try to tug my arm from her vice-like grip. I bruise easily so it's going to come up like a peach. "I want to go."

"There's only one place you're going." She tightens her grip. "I haven't planned all this for nothing, you know."

"What do you mean?" I stop struggling. It's pointless. I've never been any match for her. I'll let her rant. Let her fall asleep. Then I'll leave.

"Bringing you here. Do you *really* think you're worth spending money on for a luxury cruise?" She throws her head back and laughs. "Really? I mean, look at you." She points at me. "You're not fit for a long weekend in Skeggy. You're an absolute disgrace. You always have been."

"I don't understand why you've pretended to be friends with me. You've told me things." I choke back a sob. This is the story of my life. "You asked for my help. Why? If you still can't stand me?"

"You were useful, like I said. Eyes and ears." She loosens her hold on me slightly. I'm ready to run the moment I can. "Letting me know if Darren was sneaking around to see Donna. Two-faced hypocrite that you are. Whilst you were sleeping with him yourself. I couldn't believe it when I found out."

"Please Liz, I would never..." She still hasn't said how she found out. Not that it really matters.

"But now you're not useful anymore."

"Why have you never liked me?" I edge away as I speak. It looks as though I'll be forced to tear through the ship in my dressing gown to get away from her. "What did I ever do so badly to you?"

"Like you've said yourself, even your own mother doesn't like you." She steps into my path, blocking any chance of running. What the hell have I got myself into here?

"In fact, you'd be best off climbing that railing and chucking yourself over." She shoves me backwards.

Even in the darkness, I catch something terrifying in her eyes. Over the years I've come to expect the worst from her. I know better than anyone what she's capable of. *Anything.*

"Go on then."

Our faces are so close, I can smell her sour breath. I turn my face, not daring to reply. She's right about my mother, of course. She's also right about the fact that I'm not fit to be somewhere like this. I've never had friends, I've never even really had a proper boyfriend. Only a man who was using me for sex when his wife at the time wasn't putting out. His words. Not mine. But her suggestion that I end it all... Surely she doesn't mean it.

"Right now."

Only she does.

"You'll be doing us all a favour." She pushes me closer to the railing. "Especially yourself." I've got to get away from her. I knew she was unhinged, but...

Gasping, I glance into the dark void beneath us. Nearly two hours ago, I was contemplating leaping into it. I'd had thoughts such as, *how long would it take to reach the sea from here? Would I have a heart attack as I fell? Would it be the shock of the cold, or the impact if I made it still alive, into the sea? Would anyone try to save me? Would anyone even care?* But now, self preservation is kicking in. I don't want to die. I might not want to live as I have been. But I really don't want to die.

"We can do this the easy way or the hard way." It's not so long since she said these exact words to me. In different, but just as dark circumstances. She's as close to me now as she was then. Right in my face. But her voice sounds faraway. I've gone light-headed again. I clutch at the railings. I'm certainly in far more danger now than I was then.

"Please Liz. I need to go inside. I don't feel too good."

"That won't matter where you're going." She gets hold of me again. This time, at the back of my neck. The sudden pain brings me back into the moment.

"Owwww! No! Please Liz. *Please*. Let me go. We can talk about this. We can sort this out." I really am in trouble. Surely someone in another cabin can hear all this?

"The only thing you've got to sort out is whether you go willingly. Or whether I *make* you." She pushes my head forward as she says the word *make*.

"Go where? What do you mean?" Though I know exactly what she means. And as she's proven twice already, she's perfectly capable of carrying out her threats. I squirm in her grasp, trying to break free. However, she just grips harder. I'm going to be covered in bruises. That's if I ever see the light of day again.

"What's it to be? Jump... or be pushed? Lots of people book cruises purely for this reason." She shoves me right up against the rails. She's pressed so closely behind me that her breath's hot on the side of my neck and I can feel the shape of her breasts in my back. Bile rises again and I swallow it down. She means it. She really means it.

"What reason?" The words wheeze from me.

"Suicide. Way to go Helen."

She's mental. She always has been. "Please." Being sandwiched between her and the railing has forced all breath from me. I can hardly breathe, let alone speak. I want to scream now. But I can't.

"Jumping would be so much simpler, obviously. Than me having to chuck you in there."

I twist myself this way and that. I can get away. I've got to. In an instant, she releases my neck but then her hands are in my armpits. I suddenly remember the lifeguard pulling me out of the swimming pool in my teens.

"It's not as if anyone would miss you. Far from it."

She's trying to hoik me upwards. It's time to fight. She's going to throw me in there. She's really going to do it. I swing around. Try to knock her off balance. But her endless hours in the gym are evident in my inability to break free.

"Please Liz. Please. Just let me go,"

Then a searing pain. One I've never felt in my life as she brings her knee up, square and sharp, right between my legs. As I scrunch in response to her knee bone slamming my pubic bone, she's fisting me in the back. Now I really can't breathe. Her hand returns to the back of my neck. She's squeezing, pushing, grunting with her exertion over me. I'm bent over the railing, wheezing. Terrified. Then she lets go and drops to the deck. Just when I think I might have a split second to run, she goes for my legs, rugby-tackle-style, toppling me. As I go over the rail, my nails scrape against it, in a final attempt to save myself.

The last thing that flashes through my vision as the waves rush up to meet me is the face of my lovely sister.

PART II

LIZ

CHAPTER 11

I AM the very definition of the words *frozen to the spot*. Has that *really* just happened? Have I really just done that? I mean, *really*?

I expected her to float on the surface for at least a few seconds, minutes even, but she's vanished. Swallowed by the jaws of the North Sea. If there's a good way to go, that could be it. Better than Lou or Darren's final moments. I doubt she'd have felt much.

I look to the right. The ship's still moving, slicing its dark path in two. Perhaps she's ended up beneath it, sucked into the propellors that continue to drive the ship, blended like bone into broth. I glance back. In daylight, perhaps there'd be a pool of blood left behind and bits of mashed limbs. Nothing's visible in the white foam trail as we proceed. No one knows, and like I said before I sent her on her merry way, no one cares either. Good riddance.

I turn my attention from the sea and stare at the spot where Helen stood, just moments ago. Shock seems to be replacing my anger. I've become sick and shaky. Like I do every time. I prefer the anger. Thankfully, it won't be long before it returns. Helen deserved to die even more than the others did. She's been a thorn in my side for as long as I can remember. I never have to put up with her bleating voice and piggy eyes again. It was only a matter of time before she drowned in her own self pity. Literally.

I don't know how much time passes as I stand here, watching, waiting. There's certainly nothing to see, and I'm not sure what I'm waiting for. Voices maybe? Sirens? Alarms? Somebody knowing *something*. But there's nothing. Nobody knows she's gone overboard. Nobody apart from me. It's like she never existed. Music still fills the night air. When will the music stop? When will the ship stop? Or is it possible that I have just got away with murder? Again?

Eventually, I return inside, pulling the door behind me, swapping the faraway clinking of glasses and laughter, for being swathed in silence. I let out a jagged breath. The sudden heat of the cabin is like being lowered into a warm bath. I didn't realise how cold I was out there. I flick the light switch, my eyes struggling to adjust to the sudden glare. As feeling begins to return to my hands and feet, I stare at the patio door, half expecting Helen to suddenly reappear at the other side. Instead, I look into the eyes of my own reflection, the night beyond it appearing darker than ever. Daylight is at least eight hours away. We can get a long way in eight hours.

I march to the fridge, pull out what's left in there. She'd obviously been at it. I kick the bin where she's chucked her empties. As the cold continues to wear off, I have to anaesthetise myself with *something*. I'll go mad otherwise. After Lou, there was lots to do. I had Donna to set up for a kick off. I had to be in her house quick, then I had to be out as soon as I'd done what was needed. First, with the clothes, then ensuring that traces of Lou's blood would be found around Donna's shower. With Darren, there was the added problem of his body to dispose of. That night's probably the only time Helen's served any worthwhile purpose.

There's nothing to be done with Helen's body. She's just gone. Like she's disappeared into thin air. In a sense, she has. If anyone asks, I'll tell them she's sick. Perhaps they'll check passengers off, one by one, at the end of the cruise but I've plenty of time between now and then to think something up. What I'm trying to avoid is them realising *now* that's she's overboard. There's no chance of survival, of course. None whatsoever, but what I can't risk is a postmortem - something which may enable the screws to be tightened on me. Whilst there's no body, there's no proof of what happened.

My fingers are so numb, I can barely open the bottle. And I can't stop shaking. She's gone. She's really gone. I've ended another life.

I snatch up my phone, wanting to type in *how many people does someone have to kill to be classed as a serial killer,* but then remember how incensed I was at hearing about Helen searching online for information about rotting bodies and how long bones take to disintegrate in the ground. I'd wanted to kill her there and then, but I managed to calm myself. I'd already half decided what I was going to do.

It was only after reading her diary when I knew she needed to go once and for all. I'd let myself into her house whilst she was out with the dogs. Even I could see it was only a matter of time before her conscience would get the better of her.

DEAR DIARY

HELEN

I'm sitting here, on my crappy plastic garden furniture. The neighbours all around me are having a wonderful Sunday afternoon. Listening is like picking at a scab. I know it will make me bleed but it itches like hell. Therefore, I can't help myself. It's not even four in the afternoon but I've just poured myself a double gin - anything to feel better. The house to one side of me is having a barbecue. There must be ten people over there, plus a load of kids. They tear up and down the garden, yelling and screaming, whilst a dog yaps alongside them. Every so often Coco pricks her ears up, looking as though she'd quite like to join them. The longing in her eyes makes me feel even worse. I know how she feels.

To the other side, Lou sounds as though she's having some kind of dinner party. Charlie's there - I've heard her's and Lou's mum's voices. Donna and then Lou's new bloke arrived a short time ago too. Scott. I listened as Lou introduced him to everyone. So now she's officially with someone else. And so is Darren. I heard Lou talking to her mum in the garden several months ago. I can't believe I've had to find out he's remarried this way. By eavesdropping on a conversation from my garden.

Clearly he didn't have the guts or courtesy to tell me himself. The woman he's gone off with apparently can't stand Charlie. As if he'd put up with someone like that. I don't know what the woman's problem is - Charlie's a pleasant enough kid who always says hello to me - I'd be happy enough to have her as *my* stepdaughter.

I was fuming when I heard Darren had gotten married. I didn't even know he was that serious with someone - he was still coming around here from time to time and never mentioned a thing. Then again, he didn't exactly turn up for the conversation. For a while I'd been hoping that perhaps he'd consider making a go of things with *me*. He was clearly attracted to *something* in me to keep coming back for more. Whilst I'd lived in this ridiculous cloud-cuckoo-land, I'd contemplated for the first time in my life, having a 'proper' relationship at last. I wasn't, I figured, too old to have kids. Fair enough, there'd be an age gap between 'it' and Charlie, but these things can be worked out. The last few times I slept with Darren, I didn't mention that I hadn't taken my contraceptive pill. If I were to get pregnant, I'd have happily gone it alone if he didn't want to know. But he doesn't want to know. Full stop. Me, that is. It's been ages since I've heard from him.

As I listen to laughter echoing all around me, the tinkle of glasses, cutlery and pleasant conversation, it dawns on me that this is how Sundays should be spent. Not alone with a double gin and tonic. I bend forward. Pat Coco on the head.

"I'm sorry girl," I whisper. "Sorry you've only got me." The neighbouring children shriek with laughter as a jet of water fires up into the air.

"Watch where you're squirting that," an adult voice admonishes. There could be neighbours sitting out in their garden.

Neighbours. Their. Plural. I'll never be plural. It will only ever be me. The loneliness I'm feeling today is like a hole in the centre of my being. Right now, if it wasn't for Coco, I reckon I'd go in that house and just take a load of tablets.

And nobody would even notice I was gone.

CHAPTER 12

"Can I have your cabin number madam?"

"C251."

"Very good." The steward runs his finger down a list. "There's a table for two set by the window." He nods in its direction. "Is Miss Atkins joining you shortly?"

"Erm no. She's not too good, I'm afraid."

"Oh?" He looks at me inquisitively. Nosy git. "I'm sorry to pry, but we need to keep a check on passengers who fall ill. Partly as a duty of care, but also as you can probably understand, certain illnesses spread like the bubonic plague on a cruise ship." He smiles.

"She's seasick, that's all."

"Oh, I'm sorry to hear that. But at least it's not catching." He does a mock-up of mopping his brow, his starched clothes rustling with the movement. What an idiot.

"Can I go to my table now?"

"Of course. And I'll ask the duty nurse to pop along to see Miss Atkins when she gets a moment."

"No!"

The steward looks taken aback. I've probably reacted too

quickly. The occupants of several tables also crane their necks in our direction. Shit. I need to tone it down.

"Perhaps we'll be able to give her something to help," he says. "With the seasickness, I mean."

I lower my voice. "She's already got something to take. She doesn't want to be double dosing, does she?"

"Well, if she needs any help, be sure to let us know."

"I will." I flash what I hope is my most genuine smile. "Thank you."

Having not eaten last night, I'm ravenous. I make short work of the full English breakfast that's brought out and order some pancakes for dessert.

I'm always hungrier when I haven't slept. The alcohol and the day spent travelling to Southampton had made me weary enough yesterday. Then after my exertions on the balcony, I was well and truly wrung out. When I first lay down after I'd showered it all away, I assumed I'd drift straight off. Instead I quickly became wired again, and spent the entire night trying to tame my spinning-top mind. Insomnia's just the worst thing, especially as I usually sleep so well. One thing I don't do is guilt. Unlike some.

Though I can hardly believe I've ended so many lives. It could be said I've ended Donna's too. After all, her life is effectively over where she is. As it should be, after she slept with *my* husband. Over and over again. There's not a lot of 'living' that can go on inside Newton Prison. I imagine she'll be getting a hard time in there. With what she's serving time for, she'll be targeted. The other woman will have her down as some hard-knock from inner-city Leeds. Instead they're lumbered with some soft-arse who couldn't fight her way out of a bubble.

Having watched her closely over time, before she got arrested, I've seen her use her so-called looks to get whatever she wants. But she certainly doesn't have any brawn available.

That was evident when she allowed Lou to go out and deal with some loony tune she was seeing who was threatening her. Darren told me how Donna had cowered inside. That was a handy scenario though. The bloke apparently goes by a couple of different names, Ash, or Brad, but I just refer to him as the loony tune. He was the number one suspect at the start. Until they found what I'd planted at Donna's place. I'd suspected for a while that Darren was screwing someone else, which was why I'd engineered the friendship with Helen in the first place. I'd thought it must be Lou; I hadn't suspected her so-called best friend.

But, as I was to find out, when Donna wasn't available, either due to a supposed attack of conscience, or because she was getting it elsewhere, Darren went crawling around to Helen's instead. Talk about desperation. She's found out, to her detriment, what happens when you sleep with someone else's husband. Especially mine. Really, I don't know how she had the balls.

In a strange way, I'll miss Helen. I've always despised the victim she's made herself, but I'd got almost used to having someone next door. Someone open all hours. At times, any conversation is better than none, and it's always heartening, not to mention, convenient, to have a lap-dog at your beck and call. Someone who's still terrified of putting a foot wrong. I've had to scrap for everything in my life, ever since I ended up in that manky care home. Why shouldn't I have a bit of something decent in my life now? After going through all I went through when I was young, surely I deserve it?

I stare into my cup. The more I stare, the more I imagine seeing Helen's face in the surface of the liquid. Perhaps I'm going mad. She forgave my treatment of her in our teens, so she said. I was a bitch, but then I had to be. She said she understood that I was a product of firstly my mother's life, then death. And if I hadn't have ended up where I did after that, I wouldn't have had to become a bully to survive. As soon as I landed in that care home, I had to prove myself. I was different. The only person in the home who was there because of someone's else's behaviour - a victim, rather than an unruly teen. That's as far as anyone else knew. During my first night there, I vowed I would never accept the label of *victim*. I was also the only person at the school who was forced to live in a children's home. Even foster parents didn't want me. I was tried out with a couple of families for weekend visits. One sent me back early and the other refused to have me in their house ever again. Their own kids had been petrified of me. After a while, I got off on this. Having people fear me at the home and the school gave me some control over my life. Especially when they started asking questions about how my selfish bag-head of a mother had died.

I certainly didn't get all the trappings that came Charlie's way after Lou died. The life insurance, the trust fund, even the house I now live in belongs to *her*. But for now, as the wife of her father, I'm safe and secure there. I've never been able to bring myself to be known as her step-mum. But there's going to come a time she'll need dealing with. Whilst she's only fifteen, I can usually pretend she doesn't exist. On the rare occasions she turns up, I can swat her away like an insect. However, in the not-too-distant future, she might get serious. Or her grandmother, if she ever pulls herself together, might get involved. After all, Darren was only granted control of everything until Charlie gets to eighteen. Even though, there's enough money twenty times over to cover her until then -

there's a standing order going from that account into her Grandmother's, as well as one to our joint account.

Yet I'm unable to move any of it to a place where it can secure *my* future. I've looked everywhere to get proper access to the accounts, where I can set things up - but all I've got is Darren's debit card. And that expires next year. So I need to do everything I can to preserve the belief that he's working away and has buggered off indefinitely. As long as his death doesn't come out, I think I'll be OK. Secure for the time being, for the first time in my entire life.

Now Helen's gone, there's no reason why things shouldn't carry on as before. She was the only person on the planet who knows where Darren is. And the only person who knows what happened to Lou. Still, I'll relax more after the replacement card is sent. No questions have been asked from the bank so far - everything in the house continues to be paid. I can carry on living for free.

Another thing that pissed me off was all the crap I found in the house after I went looking through everything. Album after album of sodding Charlie at every stage of her life. Bags filled with pictures she'd drawn, clothes she'd worn, everything. I mean, what was Lou ever going to do with them? It was a bit freakish. They're in bin bags in the loft, but at some point in the not too distant future, I'm planning to take them to the tip. Maybe when I get back. Though to be honest, finding it all depressed me on another level. No one's ever loved me like Charlie and Lou loved each other. They had everything I should have had - yet my mother cared more for the shit she could inject into her arm than she did for me.

I've lived an entire life on my own, and since that's set to continue, I might as well spend it in a decent house with all the trappings. At times, I could pinch myself. How the tables have turned. From Lou threatening me on my doorstep the day before she died with the Child Support Agency, it's become my turn to call the shots. I'll never forget the self-entitled look on her face as she quizzed me over Darren's maintenance money for Charlie. Like I told her, it was *nothing* whatsoever to do with *me*. I'd grown pig sick of her lording it over us throughout the years... with her fancy house, car and holidays. They didn't do her any good in the long run though. It was when she confirmed my suspicions, that Darren *was* sleeping with another woman, her best friend, that I snapped. What made me even angrier was the smug trace of amusement I saw in her eyes as she waited for my reaction. So, as far as I'm concerned, Donna can rot in her prison cell. Whilst Lou, Darren and Helen rot in hell.

A waitress slides the plate of pancakes in front of me. She loiters as though waiting for thanks, but after a few moments, shuffles away. With her pudgy face and dropping shoulders, she reminds me of Helen. Everything reminds me of bloody Helen. Everywhere I look, I see her. This will fade in time - like it did with Lou and Darren. It's been over eight hours since she went overboard, and no one suspects a thing.

Part of me wonders whether I should have handled things differently last night. Perhaps goaded her for a bit longer. Until she couldn't take any more. If she'd have just jumped without putting up a struggle, it would have been far simpler. I've heard numerous tales over the years of how cruise ships are popular for people wanting to end it all. I'd have liked to have done an internet search on the exact number, but that would make me as stupid as Helen is. Was.

I did consider raising the alarm. Telling someone she'd jumped. But if I had, there was the slimmest chance of her being rescued. Or at least of her body being recovered from the water. After the struggle she put up to break free, she'd have bruises. The finger would be well and truly pointed at me. Especially if anyone had noticed us having words before she'd flounced back to the cabin. I couldn't risk that. However, nothing solves the problem of her being unaccounted for at mealtimes. It's a matter of time before they start noticing and possibly looking for her. So perhaps I can use her debit card to buy a round of drinks with later. Book us into the spa under her name so at least she's flagged up on the systems. Then, when we dock, I can pretend she's lost when I return to the ship at the end of the day. That should work. So long as they don't count people off as they leave. I've no idea how it works but somehow I'll sort it. I just need to keep the stewards and housekeeping people out of our cabin until after day four when the ship makes its first stop. It's only today and tomorrow. Surely I can manage that?

CHAPTER 13

HELEN'S PHONE buzzes inside my bag. I glance around, wondering if anyone can read the guilt probably written all over my face. It's not that I feel remorseful guilt, more like I-really-have-got-away-with-it-again guilt. Her phone's another thing that'll have to go overboard soon. I'm not even sure why I've hung onto it. Just in case, I suppose.

What happened last night wasn't meticulously planned, and wasn't supposed to happen on the first night. But seeing what she'd typed into her phone when I found her asleep on my bed sealed the deal. I'd held the phone against her thumb to open it up. It was almost too easy.

I knew there must be something in there after she'd tried to take the thing into the shower, and I'd had a hunch it would be along the lines of what I'd read in her diary a few weeks ago. I've tried to pass the diary off as a momentary wobble after what I told her about Lou. She'd been wetting herself enough about Darren. I can be such an idiot when I've had too much to drink and aren't really sure what came over me that night. I've never regretted talking about something more.

When I read what she'd typed into the notes on her phone, I couldn't just leave her sleeping. *As soon as I get home I'm going to the police. Nothing and no-one is going to stop me.* She didn't reckon on me finding out though, did she? And the fat bitch was as good an actress as I am. Going on about how much she hates me and how I deserve to be on this holiday even less than she does. She had it coming to her. Shit. There's her phone again? *Who the hell would want to be ringing her?* Finally I tug it from my bag. Jenna. The only person who'll notice her absence as far as I can tell. She's had five missed calls from her. The first part of a text is displayed on the home screen. *Call me sis. I'm sorry but Coco's gon-* That's it. I can't get into the phone anymore to read the rest. Something to do with her damn dog. Why didn't I think to alter the settings whilst I had the chance? If I could reply to this message, that would shut Jenna up. I can hardly use Helen's thumbprint when she's nestled at the bottom of the North Sea. What happens is something I *have* been able to research on a general science website. Dead bodies get eaten by sea-life fairly quickly, and what's left reaches putrefaction in just four days. Then the bones sink to the bottom. Result.

I've already hung the *do not disturb* sign on the cabin door to keep housekeeping out. I *can* hold my nerve and get through this. I've got away with it before. There's enough to keep me busy on here for a couple of days until I can report her missing for real. However, there's the question of what to do about Jenna. A real fly in the ointment.

"Is this seat taken?" A man, around my age, hovers opposite me with his plate. "I noticed you eating alone. I'm on my own too so I thought, hey, let's eat together."

He's so upbeat it's difficult not to smile back. "Go for it," I say, gesturing to where Helen would have been sitting. Even if the man looks so much like Darren it's unnerving. The floppy fringe, the height, even the slant of his eyes. I've never met Darren's brother. He emigrated well before I came along. Could it be?

"I'm Stephen." He puts his plate down and offers his hand. I'm sure Darren said his brother's name was Paul. So unless I've got it wrong, or he's using a middle name, it isn't.

"Liz. Nice to meet you." I offer my hand which he takes and kisses. A bit forward perhaps, but shows he's interested. And I would certainly welcome the distraction right now. I nod at the seat opposite which he slides into.

"I was going to talk to you last night but you disappeared before I got the chance."

"I was knackered," I tell him. "It had been a long day."

"Where are you from?" This is creepy. He really *is* like Darren. Maybe this is just my conscience haunting me, since I suddenly seem to be developing one.

"Yorkshire. How about you?"

"Norfolk." He stabs at a sausage. "Not a million miles from you."

"Lovely." It really is. Darren's brother's in abroad somewhere as far as I know. He tried getting in touch a couple of months ago but I managed to fob him off. "Are you here on your own?" He must be. Married men don't go seeking out women on their own to eat breakfast with. Not in view of the whole world.

He points at his mouth as though saying, *hang on.* I like that. A man with manners. "Yep. Having a much-needed break from work."

"What do you do?"

"I own a haulage company."

"Right." I keep my voice nonchalant, as though I'm not impressed. But looking at his huge wristwatch and the shine of his shoes, I thought he looked well-off the moment he approached me.

"How about you?"

"I've just left my job actually. I'm setting up on my own too."

"Interesting. Doing what?"

"I'm exploring a few options at the moment. Anyway what are we talking about work for? Are you here with anyone?" I can't believe I'm asking him almost the same question twice. But I can do without some irate wife turning up and drawing attention to me.

"Nope." He grins. "I've been married to my company for far too long. Which is why I'm here. All the eligible ladies take cruises, so I'm told. How about you?"

Now I really *am interested.* Not only is he single, but he's on the lookout. I should snap him up before someone else does.

"Separated," I reply, curling up my fingers. I'm not sure if he's noticed my ring. I'd like to take them off really, but that hardly ties in with my story of *Darren working away.*

"Is your husband still around?"

"He's working away. I've come on this cruise for a bit of reset. Then I'm starting divorce proceedings when I get back."

"Oh right. Sounds messy."

"Not really. I just need to find out where he is to serve the papers." Now I'm getting carried away. I need to change the subject.

"You don't know where he is?"

"I'm here with my friend, Helen actually. But she's not well so she's holed up in our cabin." I load regret into my voice.

"That's a shame. May I?" He points at my teapot. "It can't be much fun for either of you. Her poorly and you on your own."

"Hopefully she'll feel better soon." I smile, all thoughts of where she is and what I've done escaping me.

"Well until she does." He winks at me. "I'd love to get to know you better."

DEAR DIARY
HELEN

Today started off well. I certainly felt better at the beginning of the day than I did at the end of it. Jenna rang me this morning from Birmingham. We were on the phone for ages. It's not until I speak to her that I realise how much I miss her and can't wait for her to move back, once she's worked her notice out. Next the post came with a cheque from Inland Revenue. Over four hundred pounds. I still can't believe my luck. It's all going to have to go on bills, but still...

When the doorbell rang this evening, I told myself that good things always come in threes. But when I opened the door, I wasn't sure whether the person standing on my doorstep was a good thing, or not. Now I know *who* he's married to, probably not.

The last time I saw Darren, he'd vowed it would be the *last time*. I reminded him of what he'd said as soon as I saw him.

"Ah you know," he replied, his words slurred. Very slurred. "It was just an attack of the guilts. Especially now I'm married again."

"Are you drunk?" I stared at him.

"A bit. Not much. Are you going to invite me in or what?" He looked back into the street then across at next door. No matter how drunk he was, he clearly didn't want anybody to spot him coming into my house.

"You can't just turn up after all this time and expect me to welcome you with open arms." I resisted the urge to say *legs*. How crass would that have sounded? Nevertheless, I widened the door. He always knew I would never turn him away. Everything inside me was screaming *idiot! Idiot!*

"Perhaps in the not too distant future..." He began as he checked back over his shoulder once more. Then he stepped over the threshold bringing the whiff of whatever he'd been drinking with him. He looked disheveled. Angry even. As though he was trying to rein something in.

"What?" I closed the door after him, already enjoying this sense of having a man inside my house, whatever the circumstances. It was the first time Darren had been here at night. Usually, he turned up during the day. A quickie to fit in between whatever else he happened to be doing.

"Nothing. It doesn't matter."

"It *does* matter. What did you mean, *in the not too distant future?*"

"Just that, you might be able to see more of me. The way things are looking."

"Really? You mean..."

"Things couldn't be any worse between me and Liz."

"You wouldn't think you'd only been married for five minutes." I beckoned toward the kitchen. "Isn't the first couple of years supposed to be the *honeymoon period?* I'll put the kettle on, shall I?" I started towards the kitchen but stopped when he didn't follow. "There isn't any chance of her knowing you've come round *here*, is there?"

Even at the age of thirty-eight, I'm still scared of Liz Welsh.

No matter how friendly and apologetic she's seemed at times when we've bumped into each other lately. It's been weird. I haven't seen her for years, and then in the last couple of weeks, she first came up in the supermarket, then the post office, and then only a week ago she was running in the park where I was walking Coco.

"And as if I haven't got enough going on with *her*, Lou's gone and found out about bloody Donna. That's where I've come from." He leaned against the banister, evidently struggling to stand up straight. "Getting it well and truly in the neck."

"What, *even now*? After all this time? How did she know?"

"Donna went and confessed to her. I've no idea what she hoped to gain from it."

I used to see Donna sneaking into the house when Darren and Lou were still married... when Lou's car wasn't there. And I've gathered from things he's come out with in recent months that even though he got married again, he and Donna are *still* off and on. Literally. He clearly doesn't need anything from me when he's got *her*. There's nothing I could ever do with my clothes or appearance to measure up to Donna. My hair will always be coarse and wiry, my skin sallow, and I'll always be, no matter how far I seem to walk with the dogs - chubby.

"Sounds messy."

"Yep. Sod's law really. Especially since me and Lou have moved on with our lives. I'm surprised she's as bothered as she is, really."

"What about Liz? Does she know?"

"Oh yes." His jaw hardened. "Lou went round and told her this afternoon. God knows why. Anyway, she's thrown me out."

"So *that's* what you're doing here."

"I've been walking round for a bit actually. After rowing

with her I mean." He jerked his head towards Lou's house. "Then I thought I'd come here for a bit. I had no where else to go, had I?"

"I'm your last resort then! Charming."

"Sorry. I didn't mean..."

He looked so weary, I felt for him then. "Do you want to actually *stay here*? For more than just tonight, I mean?"

I hoped he'd say yes. I'd donate my spleen to make a go of things with him. I hate living alone. Not that I'm ever likely to meet anyone between the park and the supermarket - the extent of my raging social life. But Liz could never find out. I'd be dicing with death. Even though I knew Darren long before she did.

"We'll just see what happens shall we?" It wasn't a *no*.

But I was terrified of Darren's presence here getting back to Liz. And if Lou was now in the business of blurting the truth out. "Where is she now? Lou I mean? Are you sure she didn't see you come in here?"

As usual, Lou's name in my mouth felt as comfortable as a dislodged filling. Perhaps if she'd made friends on the numerous times I'd reached out, I'd have thought better of sleeping with her husband, well ex-husband. Being friends with Lou certainly hasn't stopped Donna though - then, or now. I wonder what will become of Lou and Donna's friendship since her confession? The whole thing is certainly interesting - I'll be keeping my ear to the fence when I'm out in the garden. Perhaps Lou will forgive Donna since she's not married to Darren any more.

"Who's the bloke round there anyway?" Darren staggered after me into the kitchen. "He seems like a right dick."

"Scott, I think his name is, he's been coming and going for a few months. They seem happy together."

The bleep of Darren's phone echoed around the kitchen.

He pulled it out and stared at it as though he was struggling to focus on the screen.

"It's Liz. She wants to speak to me."

The sound of her name certainly pulled me up. I pulled a cup from the cupboard. "You'd better go then, hadn't you?" It was an effort to keep the sarcasm from my voice.

"Listen. I'm not bothered about drinking tea, if you know what I mean." He winked as I turned to face him. "I've still got twenty minutes spare if you have?"

"Twenty minutes?"

"We don't need more than that, do we?" Darren laughed as he slung his coat over the back of a chair.

I turned to face him then. "I don't understand what you're doing here Darren. If she was to find out you were with *me,* she'd-"

"I doubt *anyone* would believe I'd be sleeping with *you.*" The way he said *you* brought tears to my eyes. It nearly put me off going upstairs with him. Nearly. After all, it's not as if men are queueing along my garden path.

"Donna's with someone else, I take it?" Darren peeled his jeans off and I wondered if he picked up on the jealousy in my voice. "That's why you've come here tonight, instead of to *her.*"

"Yep. Some nutter, from what I've gathered on the grapevine. She certainly knows how to attract them."

"She attracted *you,* didn't she?"

"Me and Donna go way back. Anyway we're wasting time here."

"Do you think Donna's ever suspected anything about *me?* I mean, she was here a couple of weeks ago."

"Here? As in, at your house?"

"Yeah. She wanted Lou's key. If she knew I'd been sleeping with you, she never said."

He threw his head back and laughed. "No Helen. Of

course no one knows. Anyway, it's not as if we've ever had anything serious going on, is it?"

"You don't call sleeping together, serious?" I peered over the top of the duvet. I don't like him seeing me naked. It's not the prettiest vision. Unlike it probably is with *Donna.*

"It's just sex, isn't it?"

"Is it?"

Clearly, he took no notice of the look on my face as he continued. "Whereas with Donna, it was, well, let's just say...." He looked at me strangely then, but possibly realised what he was about to say wasn't a good idea. "How many men have you actually been with?"

"Enough." I felt my cheeks turn from cherry to crimson. Darren might as well have said, *have you looked in a mirror lately?* He's told me before that he's got an abnormally high sex drive. Once we argued when he was dressing to leave. He had the nerve to say he was doing me as worthwhile a 'service,' as I was offering him.

I've always accepted the crumbs he throws me. And now, even though I know full well who his wife is, I've *still* allowed him to slip into my bed again. It's as though I've got a death wish.

I never felt so cheap as when he slipped straight back out of my bed afterwards and reclaimed the jeans he'd so carefully folded on the chair. He even thanked me before he left. He might as well have left a fistful of tenners on the bedside table.

It won't happen again. I know I keep saying this, but it can't. He's married to Elizabeth Welsh for God's sake. That's reason enough to not go within spitting distance of him. And above all, no matter how shitty he claims his situation is, he doesn't give a toss about me. And he never will.

I'm so pissed off, that if it wasn't for the risk of Liz finding out, I'd go marching up to Lou's door and tell her what's been going on between me and her ex- husband, as well as Donna, for all these years. But like Darren's already said, she'd never have believed me. Instead, she'd probably have had me down as some deranged and deluded stalker.

CHAPTER 14

"Miss Atkins?" My stomach twists at the sudden knock. I've spent the last two nights in Stephen's cabin. Days *and* nights. I can hardly believe my luck. Although I had a definite agenda when I booked this cruise, hooking up with someone who is not only good company, loaded, and sex on legs was not an item on it. But chances have to be taken when they arrive.

"What?" I shout at the polished wooden door.

"Miss Helen Atkins?"

"Yes. Why?"

"My name's Phil, I'm one of the cabin crew. I'm just checking you're OK in there? I gather you haven't been well."

"I'd be fine if everyone would leave me alone."

"Can I come in please? Just for a moment."

"I'm ill. Like you've just said."

"We need to do a welfare check. It's procedure."

"I'm fine."

"That's good but we do need to see you. It's Captain's orders, I'm afraid."

Bloody *Captain's Orders.* "I'm getting into the shower," I call back. "I'm getting ready for when we dock."

"It's good that you're getting out of the cabin." I can hear the smile in his voice. They're all *nice,* these cabin and housekeeping staff. Always smiling, in their pressed uniforms. I don't do *nice.* At least I don't, usually. Spending so much time with Stephen has had a strange effect on me. An almost softening effect. "OK then. I'll leave you to get ready." His voice becomes louder as if he's stepped closer to the door. "Make sure you report to the service desk before you leave the ship, won't you?"

"Will do."

"Enjoy your day Miss Atkins. Andalsnes is great at this time of year. Well, *any time* of year."

I want to shout *piss off and leave me alone.* We're supposed to be grown ups, here on holiday, not school kids being counted into line. Instead, I step into the ensuite and switch the shower on. If he can hear it, hopefully he'll get the message.

He's still there. I sink to the bed, watching the gap at the foot of the door as his shadow moves side to side. What's his problem? Doesn't he believe me or something? He needs to clear off. We're docking soon. Hopefully, later today, I can get the ball rolling and raise concern about Helen's whereabouts. But without me at the centre of it. I've told Stephen I'm spending the day with her. He knows about her 'seasickness' and her 'desire to get onto dry land.' He's already queueing to disembark; apparently he knows someone who lives in Andalsnes. Which was part of the reason for him booking onto this particular cruise.

Eventually Phil's, or whatever his name was, footsteps die away along the corridor. I open the door onto the balcony, my eyes aching with the sudden glare of the sunshine. The air is so sharp it stabs at the back of my throat. Who'd have thought it? Me - on a holiday like this. As well as spending a delicious forty eight hours like I just have. That might be all I get for the foreseeable future. Today, the shit storm is going to erupt when Helen can't be accounted for. Despite my anxiety, I smile as I stare out to sea, the place where my dark secrets have reached their ultimate depths.

Only eighteen months ago, I barely had two pound coins to rub together. How things have changed. And how the mighty have fallen. First Lou with her threats and her smug triumph, then Darren with his po-faced judgment when I confessed to what I'd done to her. I honestly thought he already knew. He of all people should have approved. With Lou and Donna out of the way, not to mention Charlie being sidelined, I honestly thought me and Darren might have a chance of making a go of things. But the drink had made me talk too much, as usual, and I knew my confession was a mistake as soon as I'd made it.

I'll give Darren his dues - he put up a valiant fight to start with, and managed to hold me off for quite a while. But he knew by then what I was capable of with a hammer.

And I got it before he did.

I had a lot to lose. As it's happened, I've had everything to gain. I occasionally relive that feeling of power I exuded as I brought the hammer crashing down on his skull over and over again, even after he'd hit the floor. It was as though I'd gone into a trance. A strike for everyone who'd ever wronged me. Blood spurted from his head into every orifice of the kitchen. Me, I was covered in it too. I just couldn't stop. Again and again and again. His body would have been unidentifiable even through dental records. That's if, of course, anyone would have been given the chance to identify it.

. . .

Eventually my manic energy had given way to exhaustion. I'd slid to the ground. Surveyed my handiwork, unable to believe how the day had panned out. It certainly hadn't been planned. I hadn't got up that day, the first anniversary of stoving Lou's skull in too, thinking I'd confess all to Darren, before doing the same to him.

One thing I never experienced was panic or guilt. Even when staring at what I'd done. No one ever felt panicked or guilt for me when I was a kid, did they? As I watched my mother inject. Watched men come and go. Never having enough to eat or clean clothes to wear. I've scrapped for everything I've ever had. So no, I will not feel panic or guilt. Ever.

And now Helen. I gaze over the waves which yield to the movement of the ship as we cruise towards the Norwegian shoreline. Water has always soothed any errant stress levels for me. I stand for a few more moments, taking in the sunlight as it catches on the movement of each and every wave. It's one of those days to feel glad to be alive. And I'm looking forward to seeing Andalsnes. I've always wanted to see something of the world. Life's so short. And now I've also met Stephen. I've got to hold back with him. Not get too involved. It's something that could easily be over before it's begun. Or maybe not. He seems just as smitten with me as I'm trying not to be with him.

"Miss Atkins?"

Bloody hell. I swing around and peer through the cabin towards the door. *What now?* I keep quiet, hoping whoever it is will give up and piss off. It's a woman this time.

"My name's Michaela. I'm the second-in-charge of cabin crew. Are you in there Helen?"

"Yeah." I suppose I'd better answer her. She might just let

herself in if I don't. "But like I keep telling people, I've not been well. I want leaving alone, alright."

"I've got a message for you Helen." Her voice remains sickly sweet. "Can I come in please?"

"No - you can't. Just push it under the door."

"It's urgent. I have to deliver it in person."

"*What* message?" It's bound to be her bloody sister. I can't imagine it being anyone else.

"If you could just open the door, I can give it to you."

"Just tell me now."

"Miss Atkins. If you won't open up, I've been instructed to use the master keycard. Just to make sure you're alright."

I've no choice in the matter. I fling the door open and stand eye to eye with a woman who looks like a cross between an air hostess and bloody Donna of all people. She's not even dead, yet she's managing to haunt me too.

The woman peers at me closely. "Are you Miss Helen Atkins?"

I'm going to have to pretend, since I'm answering as though I am. It's only a few minutes since that other bloke was here and I lied to him too. I nod, but something in her face suggests she doesn't believe me.

"I'll need to see some identification please. Before I can give you this message."

She's gripping a slip of paper. I could do with knowing what it is really. And, if I'm going to avoid suspicion, I do need to become Helen now I've said I'm her. Shit. Shit. Shit. I seem to be digging myself in deeper here. The woman wants ID. Helen's passport, and maybe her driving licence will be in her bag somewhere. But there's the small matter of me looking nothing like her. Think. *Think.*

"I don't have any. My friend's got my bag. My passport's inside it."

"Your friend's got your bag?" Her voice gives away her incredulity, even though her smile doesn't waver.

"Erm yeah. Liz. She wanted one the same colour for her sister so she's taken it with her to the shops."

Her face darkens. "If you could bring some identification to reception when we dock at Andalsnes, we'll give you the message then."

As the door falls closed behind her, I know I've got some fast thinking to do.

CHAPTER 15

I STAND in line with the other passengers. We docked a while ago, so Stephen's probably long gone. I stare down the line as it starts moving again. As I feared, they're checking everyone off the boat one by one. In person. Which probably means they'll be checking us all back on. What I'll have to do is just get off for a couple of hours, then act dumb when I come back. Blame *the staff* for missing something when Helen doesn't return. They'll act all nice, as they do, and apologetic, but they won't be able to prove anything.

As I approach the front of the queue, I realise the crew are actually checking ID cards closely against each person - it's not just a case of them swiping them through a machine like I thought it would be. That's how we access different parts of the ship, Swipe your card and you're in. I wrap my fingers around Helen's card, shuffling from one foot to another as I deliberate what to do. I can't risk this. I don't look remotely like Helen. We're as alike as a daisy and a cowpat.

Nor am I going to get the chance to swipe two cards. I can't get caught for this. The whole thing just needs to blow over. Now that I've met Stephen, the stakes seem even higher. I like him. Really like him. I don't want him to find out what I've been capable of. I've even been wondering whether I can change. Put it all behind me and become a better person. Everyone deserves a second chance.

I step out of the line, trying to look inconspicuous. I'll go for a coffee, then I'll come back when the queue's gone. Maybe when it's completely disappeared, the staff will think everyone who wants to get off has gone, then perhaps they'll go for a break or something. Surely there won't be someone just standing here for the rest of the day? Not once everyone's got off? If I don't end up being able to swipe Helen's card, I'll tell them, that as far as I knew, Helen left the ship with the others this morning, and they must have just missed her.

I relax as I walk towards the entrance to the upper deck. Whatever happens, they can't prove a thing about what I've done. They can be suspicious, but that's it. With what's left of her body languishing at the bottom of the North Sea, and no CCTV on our balcony, there's no evidence. This regret thing is doing my head in though. I don't know what's come over me. But if I can only get away with it this one last time, I'll really try to sort my life out. Especially if Stephen still wants to see me when we get off the ship.

"Mrs Rhodes?" I've barely reached the back end of the queue when a man dressed in white uniform blocks my path. With the stripes on his arm, he clearly fancies himself as some sort of big shot around here. I hate being called *Mrs Rhodes*. I haven't mentioned the little detail of my being married to Darren. Well, widowed now. A status of my own making perhaps, but still my current status.

"Yes. Why?" I try to keep my voice steady, but low. I've

already tried to pass myself off as Miss Helen Atkins to two of the crew today. I need to be careful.

"Mrs Elizabeth Rhodes?" I glance around. One of two of the passengers still queuing are watching us, but that seems to be it.

"Yes. That's me. Why?"

"I'm Captain Devonshire. I'd like to see your cruise ID card please?"

How does he know who I am? Nevertheless, I tug the card from my pocket. As I bring it in front of me, I realise both cards, mine and Helen's, have stuck themselves together. I peel Helen's card from behind mine and stuff it back into my pocket, hoping he hasn't realised what it is.

"I'd like to see the other one as well if you don't mind?" Like the woman who came to my cabin, his smile doesn't waver either. A fixed plastic smile must be part of the job description to work here.

"That's not another one, erm, I mean - it's just a bank card." My hand flies to my coat pocket in a protective gesture.

"I saw it madam, it's one of our cards. And I'd like to see it please." Impatience creeps into his voice, though he's nothing if not polite.

I hate being called Madam. "If you'll excuse me, I was actually leaving the queue just now as I really need the toilet. Can we deal with this in a few minutes please?"

"No we cannot." His voice takes on a sudden sterner tone. "We'll deal with this right now." He glances at another staff member who's standing across the deck, next to the turnstile, watching us. I really thought I could swipe both our cards and get out of here. Still, like I keep telling myself, they can't prove a thing from Monday night.

"Are you going to hand the card over madam, or do I have to involve security?"

I reach back into my pocket. "Oh." I feign surprise. Helen's image stares out from her card. Her expression seems to say *what have you done to me*? "You're absolutely right. I've obviously picked up my friend's card thinking it was my bank card."

He plucks it from my fingers and turns it over. "So where is she then? Your friend?"

"I'm not sure to be honest." I look up at him, hoping I'm giving my best wide-eyed expression. "She must have got off the ship already. If you could give me a moment, I'll try to call her."

Am I going to get away with this? I look him straight in the eye. He's a weathered looking man with grey hair and a hint of a beard. He's much as I'd expect a ship's captain to look.

"She couldn't have left the ship without this." He waves the card in front of my face. "But we'll obviously scrutinise the CCTV footage to be on the safe side."

"OK." I stare at him, wondering what happens next. He sounds as though he's going to let me go.

"I'm going to have to ask you to remain here whilst we locate Miss Atkins." He points at some seats in front of the reception desk. "I'll see that you're looked after for however long it takes."

I do as instructed, watching as he talks to the man behind the desk. What choice have I got? I'm so, so glad, that Stephen will be long gone by now. Him seeing me getting singled out like this would have been beyond embarrassing. The person he's speaking to first shakes his head, then follows the captain's gaze towards me. He's got his back to me so I can't make out what's being said by lipreading, nor can I hear anything above the voices of the now-dwindling queue, and the irritating piped music. It occurs to me to wait until the queue's at its end, then have another go at getting off. Make a dash for it whilst the captain has his back to me. But, realistically I can't go anywhere. I can't even get into the cabin now he's taken my card. I glance around, faking interest in the wall art in an attempt at distraction. Rough seas, calm seas, ships by night, ships by day. Finally, Captain whatever-his-name-is turns and walks back to where I'm sitting.

"We're going to have to ask you to wait in the security office Mrs Rhodes."

"Why?" And why does he keep saying *going to have to ask you...*

"Just whilst we perform a search of the ship. It would appear, at first glance, that your friend has not been picked up on any of the ship's CCTV in the obvious places since the first night of the cruise."

I raise my eyes to his, only fleetingly. I'm a specimen beneath his microscope. "She's not been well."

"But she isn't in your cabin."

It's more of a statement than a question.

"As I've said before, she was planning to get off here for the day."

"Well, as we very well know, she hasn't. Nor have we been able to reach her by telephone."

"She was definitely planning to get off."

"As we also very well know, you've got her cruise ID card. And now Miss Atkin's sister has been in touch expressing concern, which means we're concerned too. You must have some idea where we might find her?"

I shake my head. I need to keep my cool. "We'd arranged to meet right here and get off the boat together." I point back towards the exit.

"*Meet* here. Why?" He raises an eyebrow as he looks back at his colleague behind the desk. Now that the queue has almost vanished and it's quieter, he seems to be listening in. "If you'd been sharing a cabin, I mean?"

"I've stayed in someone else's cabin for the last couple of nights." I've already considered the alibi that meeting

Stephen has afforded me. Win-win. "I went straight for breakfast. Helen's been a bit sea-sick, you see, so when I checked in with her earlier, she still didn't want anything to eat." I astound myself with how fast I can think on my feet at times. "So I suggested we meet here instead."

"If that is the case, what is your reason for telling two of my staff *you* were Helen Atkins when they visited your cabin this morning?"

I feel myself colouring up which is not like me at all. "I didn't."

"Yes you did. One of them has made a full statement describing a woman matching your own appearance. Certainly not a description which could belong to your friend. He glances down at Helen's image."

"Your *member of staff* must be mistaken." I square up to him. He might be the captain of this poncey boat but he's not talking down to me.

"In addition to that, you've said you weren't at your cabin this morning. Yet clearly you were. Which is it?"

"Just for a few minutes, to pick something up."

"Like I said, Mrs Rhodes." He stares straight back at me and despite my dislike of him, I'm taken aback by how blue his eyes are. He has a gaze I fear can see right through me. "We're going to do a thorough search of the ship and of your cabin. If you'd like to step this way please."

DEAR DIARY
HELEN

Oh. My. God. Lou, my next door neighbour, Darren's ex-wife, is dead. Actually DEAD! I can't believe it.

I missed what happened - I must have been in the shower. I *never* miss anything that goes on around here. Not normally.

I'd noticed Lou sitting alone at her patio table, when I closed the blind in the back bedroom. She was nursing a glass of something, as though she was cradling an injured bird. She looked well pissed off. I assumed she must have fallen out with her boyfriend.

One minute she was alive and kicking, the next...

I had no idea anything was wrong until I heard sirens, then footsteps drumming up and down the drive. I dove into the back bedroom. Donna was weeping over a slumped shape beside Lou's shed. At first I thought Lou must be drunk. I couldn't tell what was going on at all. It was only when I went outside and leaned over the fence that I realised something was *badly* wrong. I can't imagine they'd put those white tents over someone that was still alive. They'd have been getting her into an ambulance if she still had a chance, not covering her up with a tent, surely?

All these years I've been jealous of everything about her. Who she's got, what she's got, how she looks, everything she does. And now, what's there to be jealous of? Oh. My. God.

The police wouldn't tell me anything. Not a thing. Even though, living next door to her might be a risk for me. They weren't even giving anything away when they came to take a statement.

They've only just gone. I could tell them a few bits and pieces, but not much. I told them about that dreadful man at Lou's door late yesterday morning. I caught bits of what he was saying to Lou; but his gripe seemed to be about Donna.

Scott and Donna left a short time after him, and there was something odd about it all. Especially since they'd left at the same time. It was as though there'd been an argument. Then later on, Lou seemed upset as she left the house. I tried to talk to her but she completely blanked me. Even more than usual. When I gave my statement, I also told them how she looked to be alone in the garden, upset even, and the next thing I saw was Donna bent over her.

I wonder what the hell's happened over there. Right now, I'd say it all points to that man in the Mercedes, the one who was carrying on with her this morning.

It's one o'clock in the morning and I'm absolutely wired. I don't think I'll get a moment of sleep tonight. Poor Charlie. I can't stop thinking about what will become of her now. Maybe Darren will come back and look after her? My chest twists into itself at the prospect. Only now I know about him being married to Liz, it's not with excitement. Perhaps she'll go to live with Lou's Mum. I could even end up with new neighbours. Ones who might want to be friends with me?

I told the police before they left that I don't feel safe after what's happened to Lou. After all, it's only next door, and for all I know, whoever's done it might be targeting women around here who live on their own. But the policewoman told me I've nothing to worry about. She assured me there's enough police personnel coming in and out of next door to patrol a football match.

It's all horrible, but just a tiny bit exciting. Nothing interesting ever happens around here.

CHAPTER 16

IT's like waiting to be hung, drawn and quartered. At least that captain hasn't taken my phone away. There's no phone signal here, where they're forcing me to wait, so I've been staring at the same page in an eBook - reading and re-reading the same paragraph for who knows how long. That man would have no right to confiscate my phone anyway.

However, I'm beyond thankful that I had the sense to chuck Helen's phone overboard when I did. There lay the proof in that stupid note she'd typed about me.

The bottom line I must keep hanging onto is, they won't be finding Helen on this ship... but nor can they prove my involvement in where she might or might not be. I sigh, perhaps too loudly. The man behind the desk looks up from his computer screen. At least it's respite from the constant click, click, click, tap, tap, tap that's been irritating the crap out of me.

"Can I have something to drink please?" Since I've got his attention, I might as well use it.

He points at the water cooler in the corner without speaking. Ignorant sod. I'll be complaining about him after this. As I get to it, I turn back. He's not taking his eyes from me. I imagine if I tried to leave here now, he'd have me chased down in five seconds flat. I fill my cup, before drinking deeply, the chill of the water sliding straight into my empty stomach. I lied when I said I'd had breakfast. I haven't eaten a thing yet today; the nerves have been getting to me. Something that isn't the norm. Since I helped Helen on her way, I've known today would probably be the day questions would start to be asked. I've just got to get through it.

I watch the bubbles in the water barrel gurgle to the top, imagining the bubbles in the sea as Helen gurgled to the bottom. I thought my troubles had drowned with her. I didn't really count on every inch of this ship being combed in what will prove to be a fruitless search. Who cares anyway? What's she got to show for her life apart from a dilapidated house, a stinking dog-walking business, and a dog. Shovelling shit is all she was ever good for.

I've been waiting here for over an hour and I'm getting seriously pissed off. How long does it take to search a boat with all these staff? And all because her nosy sister has got in touch. I hope Stephen doesn't come back for a while. I'd hate him to get wind of my current predicament. By this evening, who knows what the situation will look like?

Eventually the captain looms in the doorway of the room that's become my prison. It's a good job, since my phone battery has given up the ghost, and I can't even stare at my screen anymore.

"Have you found her?" My voice is laced with hope, and my expression is one he'll surely construe as concern.

He hoists the creases in each leg of his trousers upwards as he sits facing me. His face isn't giving much away. "We've conducted a thorough search of the entire vessel and unfortunately have not been able to locate her." He surveys me over the top of his glasses.

The man comes out from behind the reception desk and speaks for the first time since I was ordered to wait in here. "I've done a search on the transactions Sir..." His voice is croaky after being silent for such a long time. "...as well as the camera footage you asked me to go through." For such a hefty bloke, his voice is more highly pitched than I would have expected.

"Very good." Though the captain's expression is strained. "Did you turn anything up?"

"Two things," he replies. "A bottle of wine on Tuesday night and a spa booking for a facial yesterday."

"Thank you. If you could look into those transactions, I'd appreciate that."

"Very well Sir."

Captain Devonshire turns his attention back to me. "And if you could continue to wait here Mrs Rhodes."

"This is getting beyond the joke now. You can't keep me here like this."

"Your friend is missing." His voice is cold. "Surely you want to help us find her."

I nod.

"We'll try not to keep you for longer than necessary."

He gets to his feet, and then disappears into the back room where I can see through the glass, that the other one is already on the phone.

I wait. And wait some more. I can't stand much more of this. Two pairs of eyes are on me as I walk the length of the room then back again. And again. Then I return to my seat and stare back at them.

Finally they emerge and sit facing me. I try to read their expressions. Do they suspect anything? Do they suspect me? The captain is silent for a few moments. All around is silent. There's none of the usual commotion I've grown accustomed to since boarding on Monday. Voices, laughter, music.

I imagine Stephen meeting whoever he's meeting, listening to whatever they say in that careful way he does, watching them intently, in the way I've come to enjoy. Then I imagine everyone else enjoying their day in Andalsnes, going from shop to shop, taking photos, eating lunch in a local cafe. Whilst I'm stuck in here like this.

"From the evidence we've gathered so far, it's looking like a person overboard event." The captain eventually says as he lifts his cap and rubs at the side of his head.

"No!" I hope the shock in my single word goes some way to alleviating the mental finger-pointing they're both probably doing.

"Mrs Rhodes." He replaces his cap. "I'm going to have to formally question you. Being that you're the last person to have seen Miss Atkins. If you'd like to come this way please."

CHAPTER 17

"Can I just get some more water please?"

Think, think, think, I say to myself as I watch the bubbles again. This time I've got two of them not taking their eyes off me. When I've spun out getting a drink for as long as I can, I follow him and his ignorant henchman through one door, and then another, along a corridor, and then finally to a polished wooden door, which looks exactly the same as the outside of my cabin.

"This way please." I'm led inside to a room which could have been a cabin. But instead of a bed, sofa, dresser and mini bar, it's plain and stark with just table and chairs in the centre. There's no patio door in here, just a porthole with the blind pulled over. It's maybe just as well. I can do without memories of the last time I saw Helen's face revisiting me. At least it looks like there's a toilet in here.

"May I?" I gesture at the door.

The henchman as I'm now calling him, waves his card in front of the door to open it. "We'll wait right here," he says.

"I should think so too," I reply, resisting the urge to invite him in to watch.

I take my time in the loo as I try to steady the chaos swirling around my mind. I've worked out what I'll say about those two transactions, so that's fine.

There's certainly no luxuries in here like there is in our en-suite. I'm still saying *our,* then I remember I killed her. Shower caps, soaps and soft, fluffy towels. Nor is there any means of escape. I'm just going to have to go out there and face this down. There's nothing else I can do. Face it. Get over it. Go home. Get on with the rest of my life. I hope they're not listening to me pee.

When I return to the room, the captain is already sitting at the table, the other bloke is hanging his jacket on the back of the door.

"OK, Mrs Rhodes, as I've already told you, my name is Captain Devonshire" He gestures to the seat opposite. "I'm speaking to you in my capacity as the captain in charge, not only of this vessel, but also of the wellbeing of everybody on board it." He clasps his hands on the table in front of him. "Therefore I need to ask some questions which *will* go on record." He looks at me, possibly to make sure I'm listening. "These questions concern the disappearance of your fellow cabin member, Miss Helen Atkins. My colleague here will take notes as we speak." He nods at him as he positions himself at a diagonal over the table from me.

I want to ask him if I'm being arrested here. It sounds very formal, but there's no recording equipment or anything. I'm not sure I understand what's going on. Can he even arrest me? It's not as if he's the police?

He must be able to read my thoughts. "At this stage you're simply assisting us with our enquiries Mrs Rhodes. You are free to leave at any time."

"And what if I did?" My voice sounds more defiant than I'd planned it to.

"If you decide to leave without answering my questions, I'd be forced to officially detain you."

It's a lose-lose as far as I can see. "But how can you arrest me? You're not even a police officer." It might be my imagination but his jaw appears to harden. "Forgive me for sounding flippant here. I'm just interested." Perhaps I should just shut up. Sweat drips from my armpit down the side of my body. It's like a furnace in this room. I wonder if they've turned the heat up on purpose to torture the truth out of me.

"Whilst we're at sea, yes - I, as the captain, have the authority to detain you."

"But we're not at sea, we're in a harbour." I look towards the porthole, longing to see beyond the still-closed blind.

"Perhaps you'd prefer it not to be me who speaks to you?" He raises an eyebrow and I wonder what he's getting at. I remain quiet. "Perhaps you'd prefer me to hand you over to the Norwegian authorities straightaway?"

He lets his question hang as he slips his jacket off and drapes it over the back of the chair. His shirt is pristine which reminds me that I didn't even get a shower this morning. I only turned it on, whilst pretending to have one so that the nosy crew member would piss off from outside the door. Self-care goes out of the window when your energy is going into how to get away with murdering someone.

"Believe me," Captain Devonshire continues. "If I'm not happy with the answers you're about to give me, that's exactly what I'll be doing."

I wonder then if I should be asking for legal representation here. I don't like the sound of *Norwegian authorities*. What if I'm chucked into some sort of foreign jail? They'll probably have totally different laws to what we have in the UK. Here, I imagine I'll be guilty until proven innocent. I've got to get myself out of this.

"I'll answer any questions you have." I do everything I can to soften my voice as I look from him to his colleague. "If it helps to find my friend."

An image of her face as I toppled her overboard emerges in my mind. Just before that I gave her that choice. Literally, *jump of your own volition or be forced over.* It's the first of the two which will ultimately form my defence here. Plan B. My Plan A of her disappearing whilst we've been docked here has been immediately scuppered. I honestly thought the turnstiles at the exit would operate like they do across the rest of the ship. Swipe your card. Access all areas.

"Thank you." The captains voice softens too. "That's all we're asking. Your help to find her. Right. I'll start by getting some basic information from you. If you could just confirm your name, address, date of birth and next of kin for me please?"

"Don't you already have all that?"

"Yes," he says slowly as though trying to keep annoyance from his voice. "But I'm asking you to confirm it."

"Elizabeth Rhodes. 30th November 1981. 7 Millfield Road, Farndale, Leeds."

"And your next of kin?"

I hesitate. There's only one name I can give. "Um, my husband. Darren Rhodes." I won't add that he's 'working away.' The less I say about him, the better. The less I say about *anything,* the better. If it does start getting sticky, I should probably ask about a solicitor. For the time being, I should just go along with this. To mention legal representation might be construed as an admission of guilt.

"And what about your travelling companion? Miss Helen Atkins."

'I don't know her exact date of birth. But she lives next

door to me. Her address is 9 Millfield Road. I guess her next of kin would be her sister Jenna."

"We've got her sister's details." He looks down at a notepad in front of him. His handwriting looks like spiders have crawled across the page. It would have been good to know some of what he's going to ask me ahead of time but no way can I decipher that lot. "How long have you and Helen been friends?"

"We go back years." A picture of Helen's pudgy fourteen-year-old face and bird's nest hair formulates within my mind. No one ever needs to know how much I despised her at school. There's probably only her sister who knows anyway. Jenna's becoming more of a thorn in my side than I first gave credence to. "Since we were at school."

"What made you decide to come on a cruise together?"

"I invited her. She never gets to go on holiday and I thought it would be nice." I'm not normally someone who uses words like *nice*. I'm also having to take great care to make sure I continue to speak about Helen in the present tense. One slip up and I'm history.

"You must be very good friends to share a cabin."

I'm not sure if this is a question or not, but I decide to answer anyway. "Yeah. I guess so. We see each other most days. And it was cheaper to share a cabin than get one each, obviously." *And far easier to carry out what I had in mind after reading her diary.*

"I see from our records that Helen's ticket was purchased with a debit card relating to a joint account in the name of D Rhodes on behalf of C Rhodes. Is this account your husband's?"

"Yes."

"Who is C Rhodes? What's that about?"

"Charlotte Rhodes. My stepdaughter." The word sticks in

my throat. "It's an account which has been set up since her Mum died. Darren and I are bringing her up, you see."

"And you're paying for cruises using that money?"

"Just until my new debit card comes through. My husband and I have access to each other's accounts."

Captain Devonshire looks puzzled and I can only hope he doesn't pursue this. What my payment methods have got to do with finding Helen, I don't know. "Did Helen pay you back for the purchase of her ticket?"

"No. It was a gift." I'm not sure what this has to do with anything but it's a line of questioning that's manageable, at least.

"Was your husband aware you were treating your friend to this cruise from this bank account in his name?"

"Of course."

"Did he not want to come on it himself?"

"He works away, like I said."

"What does he do?"

"He works for an offshore energy company. I often don't see him for weeks on end." It's an answer I've given more times than I can remember over the last six months. I hope he changes the subject now. And I hope to God that he doesn't ask for any more information about Darren's 'work.' This is getting uncomfortable.

DEAR DIARY
HELEN

Donna certainly didn't look like a typical murderer as she stood in the dock. There was once when Donna stared straight at me in the public gallery. I'm convinced it was a look as if to say *what the hell are you doing here?* Despite this, I was totally convinced the jury would find her not guilty.

I've never seen anyone look so terrified as Donna did when they came back in after only two hours. Clearly they'd made a quick decision. I'd be lying if I didn't admit to a small part of me wanting her to be found guilty. If only so she'd be taken out of the equation as far as Darren's concerned. The last time I slept with him was the night before Lou died. It's beyond weird to have him living next door again. First he was living with Donna which had me boiling over every time I saw one of them or heard them over the fence. Then, after she'd been locked up, Liz wasted no time in getting her feet back under the table. I was unsure how to handle it to begin with, but it's worked itself out. Darren generally blanks me, which hurts, but is probably for the best. Liz, on the other hand, has got friendlier and friendlier since she moved in. It's all so very weird. After many years of her being a bad school memory, to bumping into her at the supermarket, then having her as my new next door neighbour. It feels like some kind of strange fate. All I know is that if she was to ever find out about me and Darren, then God help me.

The other part of me didn't believe Donna could be guilty. Yes, she was one of the first on the scene. Then there were her bloodied clothes, an argument she'd had with Lou, as well as several other things going against her... but I'd seen and heard her and Lou together over the years. They were as close as me and Jenna. They even looked like sisters.

And Donna, no matter what preconceptions I had about her, wasn't actually too bad. When Lou went away for the weekend a few weeks before she died, Donna asked for the key to her house. She was charm personified and even invited herself in for a coffee. Out of curiosity I'd let her. Although I hated her because Darren preferred her to me, I couldn't help warming to her. She was nice to me that day, she was interested in my work and why I'd come to live here, in this area. In this house. In different circumstances, perhaps we'd have been friends. Or so I thought.

Then she came to pressure wash the patio next door. That must have been an awful job. The police had finished their searches and handed it over in that state. I tried to talk to Donna as she was going in, but she was really off with me. However, being rude does not make her a murderess and I'm still not sure if a mistake has been made.

But never mind what I think, or don't think. Today, Leeds Crown Court found Donna Meers guilty of murder. There were press *everywhere* as the security van left the holding area of the court. Her pretty face has been splashed all over the papers tonight with the headline *Frenemy*.

I still can't believe it happened. Or that I missed seeing what happened.

CHAPTER 18

"WHEN DID *YOU* LAST SEE HELEN?" Captain Devonshire cocks his head as he looks at me. *What to say. What to say.* I glance at my watch. It was actually two whole days ago. Well two and a half days now. It was at around half past eleven on Monday night. It's now nearly that same time, but Thursday morning. What's that, *sixty hours ago.* We've covered a lot of ground, well sea since then. I already told him when he first collared me that I haven't seen her this morning. But I've got to wriggle out of why I was pretending to be her to the cabin crew. I wish I hadn't now, but I wanted to throw them off looking for her. I really thought I could get away with explaining her disappearance as not returning from being docked.

I look him straight in the eye. "This is going to sound terrible but I've barely seen Helen for two days. She's been ill, like I said. And I've been with someone I've met."

"We'll need to get the details and cabin number of this *someone.*"

"I only know his first name. And that he's from Norfolk." OK, so this sounds terrible too. But who cares.

"If Helen was so poorly, why would she have used her

debit card for the purchase of wine and a spa treatment yesterday?"

"That was me." I knew this was coming. "Her paying for these treats for me was her way of saying thank you."

"Right you are. That's saved us lost time in finding the CCTV that backs that up then." He looks at his colleague as if to make sure he's logged this then turns his attention back to me. "Have you seen Helen this morning?"

"I dropped her a text when I was having breakfast. When I popped back to the cabin later, she'd already gone."

"And did she reply to your text?"

I shake my head as I swallow. "I should have checked on her sooner. In fact, I should never have left her like I have." I load as much anguish into my voice as I can muster. "I've been so selfish. I know now, I should never, ever have left her." It's not difficult since I do feel anguish. I don't want everything I've done to destroy what me and Stephen have started over the last couple of days. I'm normally such a lone wolf. Therefore, the feelings that are consuming me about him have come as a shock.

"What do you mean, *you should never have left her*?" It's so quiet in here, he's probably heard my stomach just rumble. And here's me going on about having eaten breakfast this morning. When really I was too wired to eat a thing and went straight from Stephen's cabin to mine.

"She's been down. I mean, really down."

"As in depressed?" The two men look at each other. So far, so good. "Why didn't you say anything about this earlier?"

"It's only when I've been sitting out there whilst you've been searching, that I've really started to consider it. Being here, on this cruise, I think, has highlighted how lonely and empty her life is. She was talking the other night about not being able to face returning home when the cruise is over."

"Go on." It might be my imagination but the captain

seems to sit up straighter in his seat. My mother always said I was a good liar when I was a kid. Another reason she despised me so much.

"And I've left her to it. I've never been much good with tea and sympathy but she seemed to prefer to be left alone anyway."

"Is her life really as *empty* as you describe? Her sister's quite worried about her." This is *definitely* going the way I want it to. I reckon they wouldn't suspect what I've done or what I'm capable of in a million years.

"Well, she's *never* had a proper relationship." I bite back the sudden fury that erupts in me at the memory that the only relationship she'd known was with Darren. I continue. "In fact she's *always* lived alone. And she hates it. Even her mum ignores her."

"Her parents are still living, are they? Her sister never mentioned them. Do you have their details?"

"I'm sorry. I don't." This time I load what I hope is genuine remorse into my voice. I need to be seen as a support in this investigation. Someone who's helped close the case for them. "Her mum's still around. Though they don't get along at all. I think she only sees her a couple of times a year and that's if she can't get out of it."

"What about her father?"

"He's dead."

The man taking notes stops scribbling and all is silent again. I must keep talking to fill it. If I'm talking, I'm in control here. "It was only last year when he died. They weren't close but it seemed to make her even more depressed than she already was. She's on two different types of tablets for it, you know."

"Has she told you this herself?"

"No. She seems ashamed of it. Tries to put a brave face on. But I've noticed them in her bathroom cabinet when I've been in her house." They're believing all this. I can tell. Keep talking. Keep talking. "Being here amongst all the enjoyment and togetherness of people has made her feel worse from what I can see. That might even be part of why she's preferred to hole herself up in the cabin. At least when she's in there she can't compare what she hasn't got to everything she sees around her."

The captain tugs at his beard as he looks at me. "But she's spent the *entire* time in her cabin."

"Not the first night. But then she started to feel really poorly too. She talked about travel sickness when I first mentioned the cruise, but I thought she was just trying to get out of coming. She's like that, you see. Really anxious about social situations."

"Sea sickness can certainly be an issue." This is good. His whole demeanour towards me has softened.

"That's why I booked a cabin in the middle. So she might not feel as sick as she was worried about." Hopefully I sound like an excellent friend here. Not only have I paid for a much-needed holiday for her, I've put care and consideration into making her more comfortable. It looks like the only thing I need to wriggle out of is why I pretended I was her when the cabin crew were knocking earlier. And it was only once. I didn't open the door to the first guy, so it could have been Helen.

"There's been no other purchases made from her card since she got here." He looks at me.

"Well that's another thing," I reply. "Another reason why I've paid for the trip. Helen's absolutely broke."

"Yet you accepted a bottle of wine and a facial from her?" He tugs at his beard again.

"She insisted. *Really* insisted. She reckoned it was money she'd have only been spending to live on if she'd still been at home."

"Is there a reason for her financial hardship? Other than running a house alone of course."

Looking at this man's round face and portly midriff, he doesn't appear to have known a day's hardship in his entire life.

"Helen's too introverted to hold down a job that involves regular hours and being around people, so she earns her living walking other peoples' dogs. But it's not really a good living." I shake my head. "She's been hand to mouth for as long as I've known her. I'm always helping her out."

There, another validation of my wonderful friendship. Blimey, if I go on here long enough, I'll start to believe my own tales. But I feel ten times better now than I did while I was waiting for them to finish their search.

"It really gets her down," I go on, filling the pause. If I stop talking for too long, he may ask another question which I don't want to answer. "Her lack of money is completely tied up with how she feels about herself. Which is ashamed and worthless most of the time."

"This still doesn't explain where she is now. Why a thorough search of this ship has not managed to locate her." The captain's henchman speaks now, his voice throaty after being quiet for a while.

Who rattled your cage? I feel like asking him.

"Don't you understand what I'm trying to tell you." Here. We. Go. I lower my gaze to the table then back up again. I look from one to the other. "I think she might have thrown herself over."

CHAPTER 19

THE CAPTAIN and I eyeball each other for what feels like an eternity. It's a contest I used to play at school - who can 'stare each other out' for the longest. I would always win. But I'm supposed to be Helen's friend and I've just voiced my concern that she might have topped herself. What I need at this moment are some tears. Quickly, I bring to mind everything that's ever hurt me. It's not often I cry, but when I do, they're never tears of sadness. Only ever fury. One thing I'm good at, however, is visualisation. Snapshots in time. The body of my mother, that bony hump beneath the covers. I lived with her body for nearly two full days before realising I needed to get some help. Not enough fury. I need more. There were the three days I was forced into isolation at the children's home. All I'd done was answered one of the staff back. After only two hours, I felt like I was going crazy in there. What other things evoke fury? Hiding from the landlord when I was in my twenties. Hiding from bailiffs. Being left out of everything from conversations to nights out with my so called colleagues. I was beyond relieved to be able to give up that horrendous job I had when I moved in next door to Helen. How I felt when I suspected Darren was sleeping with someone. Discovering it was Donna. Watching Darren going into Helen's house that night. Lou turning up at my door, looking down her nose at me. Making her threats. Being forced to live with Charlie for those endless months until she saw the light and cleared off to her grandma's house. Here they are. The tears. Rage. It burns at the back of my eyes like an old friend.

"Can I have a tissue please?" I squeeze another tear out as the Captain rises to his feet and strides towards the ensuite. If it can be called that.

"Had Helen given any direct indication that she might be suicidal?" He returns to his seat, holding a tissue towards me as he lowers onto it. He looks more sympathetic now, unlike the meathead sitting next to him. I keep catching him staring; there's a nasty look about him - a cross between sarcasm and arrogance. But I don't care what he thinks. It's unlikely he's the one I've to convince. I get the impression he's here merely as a witness to this conversation.

"Kind of. But I didn't take it seriously." I sniff as I dab at my eyes. Oscar winning performance here Liz. "I couldn't feel more guilty than I already do. I should never have left her." My words wobble as they leave me.

"What do you mean *kind of?*"

"Just that... she's said a few things. Things I should have taken more notice of, I mean."

"Can you be more specific?"

I pause, as though thinking. Really, I've had a lot of what I'm saying banked in my brain. I've laid awake the past couple of nights as Stephen has snored beside me, planning all this. "One thing she said is *no one would even notice she'd gone, if she was to die.* Oh, and the other thing she said, quite recently too, was that *if she was dead, at least her debts would get paid off.* But I thought she was being daft. If I'd thought for one minute that she meant it..."

"*How* recently did she say all this?"

"She's said stuff over the last week or two. But it's nothing new. She's always putting herself down, or talking about dying. I've just put it down to the depression, as well as maybe a touch of attention seeking. Obviously, I'm feeling pretty bad now - if I'd have known how bad it was, I'd have frogmarched her somewhere. Forced her to get some help." Oscar winning speech too. What they don't know here is that I frogmarched her somewhere alright. And definitely forced her into something.

"Right. Let's get back to more recently. Exactly when did you last see Helen Atkins?"

"Erm, I'm not sure. Yesterday, no, it might have been the day before."

"I need a specific answer if you don't mind."

"I'm sorry. When you're somewhere like this, on a cruise, I mean, the days seem to merge into each other. Plus I've been with Stephen - you know, the man I met on the first night." If I can fudge everything to point to me being with him right from Monday, that could make all the difference. Stephen noticed me on Monday, after all.

"But you must have been returning to the cabin, surely? For clothes? To check on your friend?"

"I went back after the first night I spent with him. Picked up a few things. She said she didn't mind me staying out. That's when she insisted on paying for my facial and the wine. She said she felt too crappy to be much company anyway."

"And where was she exactly? When you saw her." The captain nods at his colleague's notebook as though instructing him to keep writing.

"Still in bed. But like I told you, she was planning to get off here as soon as we docked. She reckoned getting onto dry land might do her some good."

"And she conveyed this... how, exactly?"

"When I spoke to her. I used Stephen's phone yesterday, as I'd left my charger in the cabin."

"I see." He looks thoughtful for a moment. "But you had her cruise ID card?"

"I didn't realise I'd picked it up, to be honest."

"And you went back to the cabin this morning? Surely you saw Helen again then? My staff member didn't bring the telephone message along until twenty-past nine."

We're going round and round in ever decreasing circles here. "I'd forgotten my purse. But when I went back, Helen wasn't there. I assumed she'd left to come up here already."

"What I still don't understand is why you would pretend to *be* Helen when my staff member came to your cabin." He looks like he'd happily allow the rest of what I'm saying to fall neatly into place, given a choice.

"Just to make things easier for her, especially with how unwell she's been lately." I've got an answer for this too. "She'd have only started panicking if I'd told her a telephone message had come through. It would have sent her into a right spiral. So by pretending to be her, I thought the message could be passed over to me, then her, straight away."

He frowns. But he's swallowed it, at least, I think he has. He tilts his watch towards his face and his frown deepens. "By not relaying your concerns sooner, Mrs Rhodes, if your friend *has* entered the water, the delay in searching for her means..." His voice trails off as looks at his colleague.

Entered the water. That's a rather genteel way of putting it.

"We need to alert the Norwegian coastguard." He turns to Mr Meathead. "It's likely to be a recovery, rather than a rescue operation." He glances back at me with an expression I can't read. "I'll relay what's happening to her sister."

"What about me?" My voice is a squeak, which takes me by surprise. "Is there anything I can do? I feel useless just waiting around. I want to help."

"You have done." He rises from his seat. "A little too late perhaps, but at least we know what we're dealing with now. Whilst the search for Helen gets underway, there'll be someone from the Norwegian police along to take a formal statement from you."

"The police? Will they speak to me here?"

"I'm not sure of their exact procedure but evidently you were the last one to see your friend alive. Also, if she *is* out there, she's in Norwegian waters."

"Then what?" I need to know what's coming. I always need to know.

But no matter what, I'm dead proud of myself today. I've gone and bloody got away with it. Again. I'm sure of it. I may well be able to pursue things with Stephen after all.

DEAR DIARY
HELEN

Today my dad died. I've had a strange sort of feeling in my gut since I found out, but it's not grief. I don't even think it's shock. I felt more shock when Lou died, if I'm honest. When Mum rang, I knew it must be something like this. She only ever rings me when she has to. Even *she* didn't sound upset. She was straight to the point - more so than usual. Anyone would think she'd been expecting it to happen.

"I'm ringing to let you know your father's passed away." Her voice was matter of fact, as though she was cancelling an arrangement, or letting me know she was going to be late.

"Passed away? As in *died*? How? When?"

I was curious about what had happened, definitely taken aback, but neither is the same as grief.

"Heart attack. It was quick. Nothing could be done."

It was on the edge of my tongue to ask her if she'd even tried. All that was going through my mind was that it sounded better than being beaten to death with a hammer like poor Lou and Darren. And at least Dad would get a proper send off, and not end up being flopped into a hole hidden beneath a pond.

"Did it happen at home?"

"Yes. Right in front of me."

"How awful. How are you doing?" I'm not sure I particularly cared, but my asking her would probably be expected.

"He came into my room in the early hours." She didn't even answer my question. "Said he didn't feel too good. Then he collapsed. He was dead before the paramedics even got here."

The question on the tip of my tongue was one I'd never have voiced in a million years - not even to Jenna. *How long did you leave it before you rang for an ambulance?*

Mum's always been cold. Ice cold. But there was an edge to her voice. It didn't sound like shock, and certainly not grief. Relief, maybe. It's not as if they were happily married. Ever. He was never at home to be happily *anything*. And for as long as I can remember they'd never even shared a bedroom. It's no wonder I never made it to marriage. There again, all I seemed to be worth was someone who wanted a bit on the side when there was no one else available for him to jump into bed with.

As I got older, my parents were barely even in the same air space for more than five minutes. As for me, I couldn't leave home fast enough. It was worth leaving school as soon as I could even after I'd discovered Liz, Sally and the rest of the bitches were going off to college, rather than staying on in sixth form. But I left anyway. Got myself a job. Then a room in a shared house. I don't think my parents have ever visited me once since I left home. Even as an adult, I've barely seen them, especially Dad. Christmas. Father's Day. His birthday. But that's it. I could do the perfunctory daughter thing alright. Even though he felt like a stranger. Both my parents have always been strangers.

I was relieved to get off the phone to Mum. She said she'd let me know of *the arrangements*.

After I'd hung up, I sat for a long time. Wondering why everyone around me seemed to be dying. One of my customers, Lou next door, Darren, and now my dad. I tried to squeeze a tear out. But nothing came. So I took out my photo album. Not that I had many pictures in there. Mum had given me the photos she had of me, when I'd left home. As if she'd wanted no trace of me remaining in the house. As I stared at my father's image, I tried to feel a sense of loss for one of the two people who had given me life. But it didn't come. I tried to conjure some sympathy for him. After all, he hadn't even got to sixty. That didn't come either.

Apparently Dad was the one who named me when I was born. Helen Veronica. Once, whilst he was drunk, he told me that he and my mother had struggled to come up with ideas for girl's names. They'd been so convinced I was going to be a boy. He admitted that he'd named me after two of his ex-girlfriends, Helen and Veronica. I wonder if Mum ever knew this. Without him I wouldn't have a name. I guess I wouldn't have a life either. It's debatable whether that's something I should be grateful for. Why couldn't I have had a mother like Lou's? I used to feel crippled with envy when I heard them enjoying each other's company in her garden.

I didn't know what to do with myself after hearing about Dad so I rang Jenna. She seemed *slightly* more moved about it all than me. But not that much more.

"Maybe we'll get upset when it's sunk in," she said. "No matter what, he was still our dad. We wouldn't exist without him."

"I was more upset when Oscar died." My little Westie was my wonderful companion, by my side from the moment I left home and moved into my bedsit, until five years ago. He lived until he was fourteen and was my thick and thin through money worries, loneliness and depression. Other than Jenna and now Coco, he's the only living thing I've truly loved.

"I couldn't stop crying when he had to be put to sleep."

"I do remember." Jenna's tone was dry. "But there's a bit of a difference between a dad and a dog."

"Oscar loved me."

When I got off the phone to Jenna, I went for a long walk down to the park. As I walked, I definitely missed Oscar more than Dad. I'm not sure if I could go through that pain of loss again with Coco. I slumped to a bench, and looked into the sky, making shapes in the clouds. I wonder if Dad and Oscar have found each other up there. Nah. They didn't even know each other. And Dad certainly didn't know me.

I sat for ages on that bench, watching life go on around me. People as they hurried past. All with point and purpose. If someone had sat next to me on the bench and we'd got talking, I could have said, *my dad's just died. Last night. Heart attack.* They'd have said, *oh, you poor thing* or *I'm so sorry to hear that.*

But I'd have been a fraud. I'm not sad. Nor am I grieving. I'm not anything. I don't even know if I want to go to the funeral. The part of the dutiful daughter doesn't feel like mine to play. After the life I've lived, both as a teenager, and the shitty time as an adult so far, I'm just numb. Perhaps I'll be without feeling for the rest of my life? Maybe the only time I'll ever talk properly is like this, writing in my diary?

CHAPTER 20

I STARE at Helen's house as the taxi pulls up. Everything looks the same as when we left it. Tatty curtains. Paint peeling off the door. It would look the same, I suppose. That might change if the police were to search it. There's time yet. If they go beyond accepting what's happened to her is suicide. That they don't seem to have been here so far is reassuring. I could well be in the clear.

After I was interviewed by the Norwegian police, I asked if I could bring Helen's stuff back with me - well the interpreter did - I don't speak a word of Norwegian. But I was told they could only release her belongings to her next of kin. There'd be only one person she'd have stated on her passport and cruise check-in - Jenna. So *she's* now going to be able to get inside the house - the main thing I was trying to prevent.

Helen's told me that Jenna's repeatedly asked for a key since she moved back to Yorkshire. She always managed to deflect her. And clearly Helen wasn't aware of me still having the key that Lou must have once kept for her. It was a good thing too. I'd have never known the extent of her intentions without being able to get in there and get my hands on that damn diary. Even before I picked it up, I knew I was going to find something I really didn't like in there.

I'm tempted to get the locks changed before Jenna has the chance to turn up, but someone's bound to notice a locksmith there. Once word of Helen's death gets out, my changing the locks would look pretty suspicious. And Jenna is bound to pursue things if Helen's key suddenly doesn't work.

One of my first jobs, as soon as I'm certain it's safe - after dark, is to get myself in there and find that diary. When I last let myself in, it was nowhere to be found. I've already been through her stuff in the cabin. So it's got to be in that house somewhere - in the crap she spilled into the notes on her phone, she'd explicitly said she'd chosen to leave it at home. *Because of me.* The thing needs bloody burning and I'll be only too happy to oversee that. I really should have burnt it before now. But, in the few minutes I spent flicking through, it was evident that she wrote in it most days. She'd have quickly noticed if it were to have gone missing. Plus, over the last month, I've been more concerned with my plan to take Helen completely out of the equation; more concerned than setting fire to her diary. I was lenient with her really. Compared to her two predecessors, she had it quick and easy at the end. All I need to do now is hold my nerve - this, like everything, will eventually pass.

I tip the driver generously. Now I've got money, I do enjoy spending it. And he's been pretty perceptive of my mood. At first he tried making polite conversation when he picked me up at the airport. But he seemed to realise I wanted to be left alone. As I wheel my case up the drive, I can hardly believe I've made it home.

When the captain and his assistant were questioning me in that cabin, they definitely suspected me of some wrongdoing. At least to begin with. The captain seemed almost relieved when I spouted off about Helen's depressive tendencies. Less paperwork to do, not to mention less bad vibes and negative publicity for the ship. I just have to keep telling myself. *No body. No evidence.*

I let myself into the house, sighing deeply as I close the door behind me. I've lived here for well over a year and it *smells* like home now. A combination of new carpet, coffee and leather. As I look around the hallway I decorated with Darren, it feels like an eternity since I locked up on Monday - much longer than four days. It's bloody good to be back. To close the door on it all and breathe again. I kick my shoes off, collect the gathered post from the mat and head to the kitchen. Coffee and food is in order. Then I'm desperate for some sleep. It feels like I've only had a few hours this week.

As I wait for the kettle, I throw the patio doors open. I like to air the house, especially when I've been away. The garden changes all the time and the spring bulbs have been doing their thing in the short time I've not been here. More crocuses have opened up and the daffodils won't be far behind. I might be as hard as nails in a lot of respects; my life up to press has made me that way, but like most people, I still enjoy the signs that winter is nearly over and spring is on its way. Metaphorically as well as literally.

The statement the Norwegian police took from me seemed like more of a formality than anything to worry about. If I was truly suspected of anything, I'd have never been offered the opportunity to get back on the cruise. Like I'd have been able to do that. It would have looked dreadful. *Yeah my friend's probably gone overboard but I'll just get back on board and back in the spa and into Stephen's bed, shall I?* Much as I'd have loved to have returned to him, there was no way. I found out his line of work in Norfolk, so he shouldn't be too hard to track down once all this has blown over. He'll have probably heard about the woman who's jumped overboard and put my sudden departure down to my grief. Eventually I'll get in touch with him and hopefully we can pick up where we left off.

The only thing I could do after what happened was to fly home. Another marker of how much life has improved for me. Once upon a time, there's no way I'd have had money available to book a flight on a whim. I told the police via the interpreter that not only did I need to be back home to come to terms with my friend's presumed death, but I'd also need to get back and support Helen's sister through it all. They've actually used the words *presumed dead* over and over now, even without having found her body. So I figured I was safe to do an internet search on this, after all, I'm only searching on something that's really happening in my life if it comes out. Apparently, if a body is going to wash up at shore, this would happen within two or three days. We're on three days now. Often, in deep and cold water, the body is never found. Result.

CHAPTER 21

I SLIDE my feet into the slippers I've left by the patio door and head outside. I've changed it a lot out here since it was Lou's garden. My gardener has re-landscaped, there's new patio furniture, pots and baskets, and Darren painted the shed not long before he died. *Darren*. Now I'm back home, back to reality, the cruise ship almost feels like a distant memory. I stride over to the fence and step onto a crate to look over. All is as it should be next door. Helen's crocuses are coming up too. The water fountain thing which was her pride and joy is still merrily flowing away. I can't imagine there's a lot left of Darren beneath that pond now, and we dug far enough down that even if the house gets sold, he's unlikely to ever be found. If anything's unearthed in the future, hopefully it will be well beyond my lifetime.

Another thing in my favour is that it will take months and months for that place to sell - both because of all the legal stuff, and because it needs absolutely gutting inside. I'd rip the kitchen and bathroom out for starters, they look to have been in there since the eighties. There's artex on the walls and polystyrene tiles on most of the ceilings. I reckon

Jenna will get the money out of it, that said, I can't imagine there's much to be had. Helen mentioned mortgage arrears when I first suggested the cruise. Plus, I know she's re-mortgaged more than once. And then there'll be all her debts to pay from it. Thank God I don't have to live like that any more.

As I continue to stare at Darren's final resting place, my attention's averted to movement by Helen's back door. Then a whimper. Helen's dog stands and arches her back. I check down the drive, bracing myself to have to deal with Jenna. There's just a couple of elderly ladies walking by. The dog whimpers again. I wonder if she's been here since Jenna's text came through the morning after. It must have got in through the bottom of the garden, which is a worry.

"Coco. Come here." I make clicking noises with my tongue. I expect her to come bounding over, after all, she must be starving by now. But she just glances at me and then lies down again. It's as if she knows what I've done. I stare at her. Now I am being ridiculous. After all, the dog's *never* liked me. Nor has that one she looks after for her sister. They'd both probably maul me to death given half a chance. I'd have thought this house would be the first place Jenna should have checked for Helen's missing dog. Anyway, it doesn't want to come to me. Nor is it my problem. I've had enough going on. And still have.

As I sip my coffee, I sift through my post. Bill. Statement. Renewal Notice. At least I don't have to be scared of these things anymore. Then a handwritten note.

I've been here several times now. Getting pissed off.

Who the hell's left this? I turn it over. There's a number on the back. It must be Charlie again. It could even be Jenna. *Getting pissed off.* They can do one. I reach for my phone and call the number, withholding mine first. I wouldn't want either Charlie or Jenna being able to reach me whenever they feel like it. It's more likely to be Charlie looking for her dad. I can't believe she hasn't taken the hint yet. Darren's not interested in contacting her. He never will be. And she'll never know why. The number I've called goes to voicemail. It's a standard network recording so I'm still none the wiser.

I rub at my hair as I step from the ensuite. This is one of the best things about having this house now. The only time I've *ever* had the use of an ensuite is when I've stayed in a hotel. Until moving in here after Donna was remanded, I could barely afford a night in a budget bed and breakfast, let alone an ensuite in my very own bedroom. I say *very own.* There's still the danger that Charlie will crawl out from under her rock, at least eventually, and try to oust me from here. But I'll stamp on her when the need arises. I've proved I'm not scared of dealing with whatever needs to be dealt with. Particularly when my home and security is threatened. But whilst this insect of a chance is still miles away from me, there's no need to seek it out.

Wrapping my dressing gown around me, it feels good to have washed the journey away, but I've also washed away Stephen's scent. A sudden need to sleep consumes me. I'll have a glass or two of something and then I'll get my head down. I'll get a few hours in and then I'm off to find that diary. I haven't slept properly since Helen died and it's not just because of Stephen. *Died* does sound better than *launched over the balcony railing.* I never do sleep properly, not for weeks, after ending someone's life. Which makes me sound like a true serial killer. And I'm not, not really.

Deep down, I want a normal, drama-free existence. To be finally living the life I've always deserved - hopefully with Stephen, or someone just like him, in it.

What I can't have, is anyone threatening that.

DEAR DIARY

HELEN

Last night was the worst night I've ever lived through. *Ever.* I've written words like this so many times but last night truly was. Whilst I was letting Coco out for a wee, Liz started yelling my name. I knew something was badly wrong. Her voice was strangled, desperate. She wouldn't come out of the house at first, but in the light from the patio doors, I saw that she was splattered with blood. Knowing Liz as I do, I immediately suspected it wouldn't be her own.

"It was self defence." She repeated these words over and over again after I'd gone round. Usually, we go straight into her kitchen, but today the door was shut. She shepherded me straight into the lounge. "It was either him, or me," she screeched as I sat down. I had to sit. I was shaking like a shitting dog.

Darren was dead. Liz had killed him. And there was only her version of events to hear. It was ages before I managed to cut in between her gabbling. "If you just tell the police the truth," I said. "That it came down to you or him. I'll back you up."

"I'm not risking that. No chance. We need to get rid of him. I've had all day to think about what we're going to do."

"I'll tell them I heard you screaming."

It's not as though I owe Darren any loyalty. Not after how he's treated me over the years. Obviously she doesn't know any of that.

"We can't just get rid of him. How can we? Where? We need to call the police."

Her face hardened. "Don't be such an idiot."

"I'm sorry, it's just..."

"Give it a rest Helen. Look I'll cut to the chase here."

"What?"

"We can do this the easy way or the hard way." Her tone had changed massively from when I first arrived. Desperation had become authority.

"*We?*" I finally cottoned on to the fact she was involving me in her shit. She'd summoned me for much more than I could have ever bargained for. I should have ignored her shouting. I should have gone back inside my own house and locked myself in. The house next door is cursed. I should have been nowhere near.

"You either help me get rid of him, or I'll say it was you who did this."

I laughed. After all, it was Liz who had Darren's blood dried onto her cheeks and matted into her hair. She grabbed me by the arm, making me regret my laughter. "You're coming with me." Suddenly I was a petrified teenager again.

"No... let go... I'm not-" I tried to tug away, but as she always had been, she was too strong for me. My arms were certainly accustomed to the imprint of her fingers boring into them over the years.

She marched me towards the kitchen door. And I'd never be able to unsee what lay beyond it.

Darren was curled into what can only be described as the foetal position, on his side, but his arms were raised in what might have been a final attempt at protecting himself. I've never seen so much blood in my life. More than in the garden after Lou died. One of his eyes looked like it had half popped from its socket and his forehead was dented inwards. If I was identifying him in a morgue, I don't think I'd have recognised him. Bile rose in my throat and I twisted my head away from him.

Liz. Had. Done. This. *Why?*

"How?" The word somehow formed itself at my lips as I turned to her. I searched her face for guilt, for regret, anything. A glimmer of accomplishment at what she had single-handedly achieved, was all I could find.

I followed her gaze to a hammer which lay in a pool of blood at the other side of him.

What a twist of fate that Darren died in exactly the same way as Donna had murdered Lou. Once husband and wife; they'd died in exactly the same way, on exactly the same date, a year apart. Both at the hands of women who were supposed to love them. It was the second dead body I'd ever seen. The first being Lou, albeit at a distance over the fence. Always, always at a distance. I don't know where that thought came from. None of it mattered. Not anymore.

"Take a good look Helen. This could have been you." Liz's voice bore the faked joviality of a game show host.

"What the hell are you talking about?"

"Go on. Look closer."

"I don't want to. I'm going home. I'm having no part of whatever's gone on here."

As I turned towards the door, her hands gripped either side of my arm then she shoved me from behind. It all happened far too fast for me to prevent where I was heading. Squarely on the top of Darren's body.

Recoiling against the stiffness and bloodied chill of what

had become of him, I screamed and sprang back, struggling to return to my feet. Liz was now not the only one covered in his blood. As I staggered back, trying to get my breath, and hold down the vomit, I realised the entire kitchen resembled something from a horror movie. As I looked down at myself, I saw that I did too. One minute I'd been watching my dog run around the garden, the next I was trapped in the middle of a complete nightmare.

"Now we really *are* in it together." She smiled. "I'm so glad you agree the easy way is the best way of dealing with this."

As I listened to what she had in mind, it was evident she'd already planned it in meticulous detail. Perhaps even before she killed him.

It had been a scorching summer and the pond at the end of my garden was bone dry. Water was being piped through the water fountain, one of my few tiny indulgences in life. Somewhere I used to enjoy sitting with a glass of wine or a cup of coffee, listening to the sounds of people living their lives swirling all around me. Jenna had bought the fountain as a gift for my thirtieth birthday. She'd wanted to give me something I could enjoy, rather than money she knew I would only blow on bills.

"It's nearly dark." Liz looked out of the window. Perhaps somewhere, from out there, Darren was watching us now. How could Liz be so blasé about this? Perhaps she would fall apart later. I knew I would.

"We can dig your pond deeper, get him in into the hole, and then cover him over. You've got a pond liner, haven't you?"

"We'd never get away with it."

"*We.*" Liz reached for my arm, softly this time, approval evident in her voice. "Oh yes *we* will."

A dead body weighed more than I could ever have imagined. And if it wasn't for the slotted fence panels, we'd have had to have dragged him through my house. I don't think I could have slept in here again if that had been the case. It's dreadful enough him being out in my garden, though at least he's at a distance. A few feet away. If we'd had to drag his body across the front of our two houses, even under the cover of darkness, anyone could have seen us. Thankfully, the neighbours to my left were away - I heard the taxi come for them at three in the morning last week. And the garden backing onto mine is well covered with the conifers they planted when they first moved in. At first I was miffed. It was as though they didn't want me seeing in and talking to them. But now, I couldn't be any more relieved.

We covered Darren over in the tarpaulin from the pond whilst we took it in turns to dig. I've never been so knackered. Ever. Adrenaline can only last for so long. Midnight came and went. One o'clock. Two o'clock. I used to enjoy the sound of an owl hooting in the distance. I'd found it almost ethereal, but now it sounded as spooky as hell. Darren, by this time, had been dead for over twelve hours. I don't know how Liz could have stayed in the house for so long, alone with his body. Death has always frightened me. I've no idea what she might have been doing between killing him and shouting for me. She hadn't even washed the blood from herself.

Today I ache in places I didn't know it was possible to ache. I still don't know where last night's energy came from. Perhaps Liz's threat of how she'd tell the police it had been *me*. She'd say I'd killed Darren in a fit of jealousy after he'd turned my advances down. I'd stared at her, wondering how she could have concocted such a story. God help me if she ever finds out how near the knuckle that scenario really is. I'd scanned her face for a sign she could know that I've slept with him, but there didn't seem to be anything. She went on to say it would be my word against hers, and that there were people she'd be able to 'persuade' into acting as 'witnesses.' The past became the present as I turned into fourteen-year-old Helen again, and obeyed her every command. I needed to move her away from any thoughts or notions of Darren *turning me down.* Or I might end up joining him in that hole.

I stand at my kitchen window, staring down the garden. The pond is now filled with water I've hosed in. Beneath it, a grave. Darren's body, curled in death as it would have been at birth. Possibly as defenceless at the end as in the beginning.

I'm not convinced Liz acted in self defence. Not after how she's acted towards me. She's always been the aggressor, never the victim. The anger that ignites all drama. And I fear her as much as I ever have done. I had no choice other than to do what she demanded of me.

CHAPTER 22

THERE'S that moment between sleep and wakefulness when you don't know what's real. First I hear Helen's scream. Next that splash. Then, what can only be described as whimpering. A dog. *That stupid dog must still be out there.* My next thought is Stephen. Word will have spread through the ship about the search for someone 'overboard.' He and I didn't swap numbers, and he knows nothing about me apart from being called Liz, and being from Yorkshire. I guess that's the way I wanted it. With things being this way, when I get in touch with him again, I am a blank sheet. I can portray myself as anyone I want.

I sit bolt upright on the bed and shiver. I've dropped off to sleep without pulling the duvet over, and despite still being wrapped in my dressing gown, it's freezing in here. I switched the heating off on Monday and was too tired before my shower to think about putting it on. I squint in the darkness at the clock at the side of the bed. 9:54. It must be night time. At least I've had a few hours, though I feel groggier for them. Really I'd planned to be in that house next door earlier than this. The sooner I get hold of that diary, the sooner I remove any possibility of someone finding evidence against me.

Swinging my legs over the side of the bed, my feet connect with the soft pile of the new carpet. I head across to the window. Sure enough, still by Helen's back door, is Coco. I'm going to have to do something. After I've got hold of the diary, I'll try contacting her sister through social media. Until then, I'd better get the dog inside here, and try to stop her whimpering before people start paying attention.

I jump as the doorbell echoes through the house. It's probably something to do with the dog. Someone seeing if I know where the owner is. *Funny you should ask that but...*

I point my feet into joggers and tug a hoody over my head, before twisting my hair into a bun on the top of my head. Whoever it is can wait. Damn dog. The whimpering is louder than earlier. Sound carries more at night, especially around here. I know that better than anybody. Where I used to live it was all screeching cars, music and raised voices. A place that never seemed to sleep. Around here, there's a quiet like nothing I've ever known. At times, eerie. By the time I get to the door, whoever it was has gone. I'm glad. I'm too knackered to be arsed with dealing with anyone tonight. Besides, I've got an important job to do. An engine dies away along the street and tail lights disappear around the corner. I wonder if that was my caller? If so, it can't have been a complaining neighbour. I close the door, noticing a scrap of paper poking from the letterbox. It's the same handwriting as before.

I'll be back again tomorrow and I'll keep coming back. I'm not going away. No matter how much you'll want me to.

Puzzled, I head to the kitchen. Who the hell is it? The dog will have to wait for a few minutes. There's no number on the note but I'll still have it in my recent calls list. I hit call. This time it's answered. No one speaks. But someone is definitely there. I can hear breathing. "Hello?" I eventually say. The line goes dead. It will be some crank, I'm sure of it. However, I'm uneasy. I try the number again. It goes straight to the stock voicemail message.

I push my arms into my coat and my feet into wellies. I'd better get round there. Stop that dog and find that diary. The last thing I need is anyone poking around in the garden. I have visions of someone getting in there with a dog of their own and it picking up a scent. Apparently this has happened with some of the dogs Helen's looked after, especially at first when the smell of Darren's decaying body would have been at its worst - even more so in the hot weather. But police dogs are trained to pick up the scent of death months, even years later. I yank Helen's key from the hook and dart to the door. I wouldn't normally check, and re-check that I've locked my door but after that note... If it's Charlie, as I still suspect, I can't risk her getting inside the house - I might never get her out again. Legally, I couldn't. But of course there are other ways.

Helen's gate is padlocked. I forgot she'd got it all locked up to protect our little secret. Her dog has *definitely* found its way through all the bushes and trees at the bottom of the garden. Behind the pond. If Coco has got through, other dogs and wildlife will be able to. Though I'm certain any digging up would have happened well before now, if it was going to, I'm not taking any risks. I'll find a way to plug any gaps later. I exhale a long breath. Thirty minutes ago I was sound asleep, and now it's all coming at me.

I glance around as I head towards the door, raising my hand to my neck in response to a prickling sensation. It's the prospect of being alone in that house, late at night. It's unnerving me, which is weird - nothing usually unsettles me. It's that note that's done it. And I think I've gone a bit soft since meeting Stephen. It's unsettled my focus.

Right. Through the house. Move it. I'm shocked none of the neighbours have been to investigate this whimpering already. They're either deaf, or they've got their TVs on full blast.

With fumbling fingers, I unlock the door and step into Helen's hallway. Or what *was* Helen's hallway. I bury my nose in my jumper. It's never stunk this badly of dog in here. It must be worse because of the house standing uninhabited and cold for so many days. Most houses have an identifying smell when you enter them, but this one's dire - it's not only dog, it's foisty washing. It's mould, the stench of despair. I've never known how Helen could live as she did. No wonder she dragged her chin along the floor most of the time.

I jump as the door slams after me. It doesn't normally do that - the wind must have caught it. Those two notes have really creeped me out - especially with one of them being from such a late-night caller. Instinctively, I reach towards the light switch but immediately think better of it. I don't want anyone finding out I've got a key to get in here - it might get taken from me, something I can't risk. Not only is there the diary to find, Helen might have other stuff written down to incriminate me. Then obviously, there's the garden to protect.

At least word doesn't seem to have got out yet of what's happened to her. Not as far as I know. There would be flowers at the gate if any of the neighbours knew she was *presumed dead* - the official line now, which will hit the news at some point - I just haven't checked since I got home. The cruise company can't keep it under wraps forever, no matter how much they might want to. Helen was only in her thirties, so no doubt there'll be an outpouring of false grief over a person nobody knew or wanted to know. Then the headlines will turn to something else for them to gossip about.

I grapple my way through the darkness towards the kitchen. The back door key had better be where she normally keeps it. Since I've got back here, I'm thinking of Helen more in the present tense, which is strange since I was there at her end. What happened to her was all my doing. Despite this, I keep expecting her to turn up at the door saying *Boo.* Being in her house on my own is seriously giving me the jitters.

I fumble around in the cutlery drawer, irritation rising as the dog's whimpering becomes a full on howl. *Ouch. Shit.* I jump back at the sharp pain to my finger. Fuck! It stings like one of those cuts that's unlikely to stop bleeding for the rest of the night. I bring it to my mouth, my tongue filling with the metallic taste. This is all I need when I've got that diary to find. I can't exactly be leaving a trail of blood behind me. And this could be my only chance to look for it.

CHAPTER 23

Kicking the kitchen door shut, I flick the light switch beneath the cooker hood. I need to see what I'm doing. The light in here is concealed enough that it shouldn't draw attention from any of the surrounding houses. If I don't find the diary in the kitchen, I'll have to use my phone torch to go through the rest of the house. It will probably be well hidden, with the crap she's been writing.

I'm more than wide awake, wired even, after that note, then whoever it was on the end of that phone not speaking. I might as well channel this new-found energy in to finding the one thing that can bring me down if it's discovered. If I can stop my finger from bleeding all over the place, that is. I rip at the kitchen roll and twist a piece around my finger, pressing down on the cut. I scan around where I've been, checking for blood spots. That would look great, my blood on the floor of someone who's just died. And in what could be construed as mysterious circumstances too. I press onto the cut as hard as I can. *The bloody dog!* She must think Helen's back. Finally, I wrench the key from the drawer using my good hand and leap towards the door.

Coco cowers as my shadow looms over her in the doorway. Then she slinks past my legs, as a frightened insect might, as though I'm the scariest thing she's ever encountered. This makes me sad. Yes, I've definitely gone soft. Looking at the state of her and her protruding ribs, I realise she needs feeding. I'm not a dog person in the slightest, but I'm not completely heartless either. I reach for a can of food from the top of the fridge and do my best to open it - albeit one-handedly.

I stab a fork into the congealed meat, the stench turning my stomach. As I place a dish on the floor in front of her, she just stares at me. "What is it with you..." My voice is deafening in the silence of the house. "Am I so terrible you won't even accept food from me?"

I fill a dish with water. "Suit yourself. It's there if you want it. Though I wouldn't eat it either if I was you." At least her racket has stopped. I'll probably leave her in here for tonight then get in touch with Helen's sister in the morning.

But first, the diary. Tonight really could be my only chance, especially when Helen's keys and possessions get passed on to Jenna. I imagine she'll be straight round here.

Every drawer and cupboard in this kitchen is stuffed to the brim with crap. Papers, magazines, letters - there's far too much to go though. The cover of her diary is red, so shouldn't be too hard to find. I always suspected Helen would be some weirdo hoarder but the amount of clutter surpasses all my expectations. And everything's so grubby - I'll need another shower when I get home. The last thing I want to do as I sift through it all, is to drop traces of my blood behind. So as I go, I'm keeping my eyes peeled for a plaster. Even if they would have been too much of a luxury for Helen. I'm surprised she even had kitchen roll. I open the tallest of the cupboards in here and loads more random things fall out. Nothing with a crimson-red cover though. That diary is somewhere in this house. And I'll comb every inch of the place until I find the thing.

To say the front door scares me is an understatement. Even the dog startles as it bangs, jumping from her basket and rushing to the kitchen door. She'll definitely think it's Helen, and for a moment, part of me wonders whether it could be. But no. A person can't fall into the North Sea at nearly midnight on an early March night and wash up alive. Can they?

"Coco!" There's a shriek as the door into the kitchen slams against the fridge. "Thank God you're here!" Coco leaps from her basket as though royalty has entered the house.

"What the..." I turn from my search and my eyes meet Jenna's.

"What are *you* doing in my sister's house?" She's not her usual perfect polished self. Her hair is scragged into a bun. Her eyes are dark and ringed.

"I'm just..."

My hesitation gives her an entry point. "You're *just* rifling through her stuff, that's what. What is it Liz? Are you looking for her will? Life insurance? She didn't have a pot to piss in as you very well know." She stands, hands on hips, like she owns the place. Perhaps she will, now Helen's gone. But at least she's speaking about her in the past tense. Meaning things may well blow over faster.

"How did you know where to find the dog?"

"I got a message from - what's it to *you* anyway? You don't give a shit about anyone but yourself. How did you get in here?"

I snatch the key from the worktop and drop it into my

pocket. I can't risk Jenna getting hold of that. "Helen gave me a spare."

"Bollocks. As if. She didn't even give me a key, so she's hardly likely to let you loose with one."

"Maybe she trusted me more than you."

"And look where that's got her." Jenna's eyes fill with tears. The eyes are the only similarity between the two sisters. Eyes that bore into me, needing answers she's never going to get. "What I want to know is... what the *hell* did you do to my sister?" She takes a step closer, pointing towards my chest as she does. She doesn't seem able to even look me in the eye.

"What are you talking about, *what did I do?* I gave Helen the chance of a holiday. I didn't see *you* , her so-called sister, shelling out to take her on a cruise."

"Helen might have been gullible and naive, but I'm not. Why, *her* of all people? That you'd invite to go away with you?"

"We'd sorted things out. We'd become friends. Things change. People change."

"You'll never change." Jenna's face hardens as she leans forward to pet Coco. "You've bullied the poor lass for as long as I can remember. She was barmy to have anything at all to do with you after how you treated her."

"That's between me and Helen. It's got sod all to do with you."

"It's got *everything* to do with me." Her voice rises, somewhat manically. "I'm the one who spent years holding her together when we were young. Of all the people for her to end up living next door to... I've begged her not to go within spitting distance of you. Why didn't she listen to me? Look what's happened to her." Her voice fades into the silence.

Jenna's hands curl into fists at her sides but at least she's stopped ranting.

It's a good job as fury's begun to snake its way up my

spine. Right. OK. Breathe. The woman's just *tragically* lost her sister, after all. I'm going to *try* to be reasonable. At least she didn't pursue her initial line of questioning about what I might be hunting through the kitchen for. "Look Jenna. Why don't we calm down here. I know you're devastated about Helen. We both are."

"Don't make me laugh." Her eyes bulge and for a moment she looks like she might fly at me. I'd like to see her try. "You've got what you always wanted now."

"What I wanted was to get her better." The more lies I tell, the more even I believe them. "Have you any idea how depressed she was? I took her away, *me,* I thought a change of scenery..."

Jenna cuts in again. "I don't believe any of that shit about suicide. I want to know what happened. The truth."

If she's using the word *suicide*, that must be the official line she's been fed. She'll probably have been told far more than I will. Being next of kin and all that.

"The only answers," she continues as she draws air quotes with her fingers as she says the word *answers.* "I've had so far, are that cruise ships are a common place to end it all." She folds her arms. "They must think I'm stupid. *You* must think I'm stupid. I want the truth and I won't rest until I get it." She glares at me now, straight in the eye, her eyes protruding from their sockets even more than they were before.

"I wasn't actually there when she fell into the water." I try to replace my fury with melancholy. "I feel bad enough as it is for not being there when it happened. Or seeing how low she'd got leading up to that point."

"*You! Feeling bad!*" She's screeching so loudly now, they'll be able to hear her three doors down the street. She, herself, is sailing on very choppy waters here. "You couldn't feel *bad* if your life depended on it. You're an absolute bitch Liz. The worst I've ever come across. You're capable of anything as far as I'm concerned."

She's brave, I'll give her that. Standing not even a foot away from me, spouting her venom. If she doesn't shut her mouth, she'll find out exactly what my capabilities are.

"I've told the police as well." She juts her chin out as she watches me, seemingly for my reaction. A certain light has returned to her gaze. She's evidently pleased with herself for doing something for her waste of space sister.

"You've told the police *what?*" I lean towards her, ready to shut her up, once and for all.

"What I think you've done. What I *know.*"

"You've *what?*" I lean closer still. I always knew there was something of a snake inside this one. And now she's gone too far.

DEAR DIARY
HELEN

It's nearly four in the morning. I wish I could stop my mind whirring round and round like a cement mixer. I can't bear how I'm feeling and really don't know if I can go on living with the guilt. I'd be the first to acknowledge that Darren treated me like shit when he was alive, but even he deserves better than this. And his daughter definitely does. In a strange way, I'm missing him too. He was the only man who ever showed an interest in me. I really think I'm going to have to tell someone the truth. Do *something*. Even prison has to be better than living under this weight.

I keep telling myself that the guilt belongs to Liz. She killed him, not me. But as much as I tell myself this, I helped with what came next, and it's my garden he's rotting in. It's only a matter of time before he's found there. Before someone realises something. Charlie's not going to give up trying to get in touch with him.

Last week a letter came through saying he was Darren's brother. I didn't even know he had a brother. Liz obviously opened it. He reckons to have been trying to ring, then email, and having gotten no answer, had written. Liz has got back in touch, telling him the same thing as everything else. *He's working away.* But, eventually his brother will take it further - he's bound to. Or Charlie will. One of them will look into where he's supposed to be working away. All it takes is for them to start looking deeper at Liz's house. There's bound to be traces of blood. It was the biggest bloodbath I've ever seen. No way could she have completely bleached that lot away. Or when they look into bank accounts and all that. I'm pretty certain when that happens, Liz will have no hesitation in taking me down with her.

If I get in there first, tell the truth... surely I'll get recognition for that. Telling the truth could keep me out of prison, or at least not for as long. I already feel as though I'm living in prison anyway.

So I know what I've got to do.

CHAPTER 24

"I THOUGHT I HEARD SHOUTING. Is everything OK?" Some man wearing a dressing gown curls himself around the kitchen door. Evidently Jenna's left the front door wide open. He's wearing slippers. Who really ventures into the street looking like that?

"No. Everything's far from OK." Jenna swings round to face him then looks him up and down, probably thinking the same as me. "Who are you anyway?"

"We live next door but one. It was us who let the police know about the dog." He looks from her to me. "At least they've done something about it at last. The bloody thing was driving us mad." He shakes his head.

"Haven't you heard about my sister?" Jenna's tone is etched with fury.

"Your sister? Why? What should I have heard?" As the man moves closer, I get a whiff of lager from him. That's the first thing I'll be doing when I get back home. Pouring a well-deserved drink.

"Helen." Jenna's voice wobbles as she says her name. "Who lives here."

"Well, *used to* live here?" I regret my words as soon as I say them. Maybe I should be trying to form an ally in Jenna - it would serve me better than being at each other's throats. Like it did with Helen, at least for a time.

"You're a heartless cow, you are-"

The man cuts in. "You mean, the woman who walks the dogs?"

Jenna leans against the counter, her previous anger seeming to drain from her. "She's dead."

"Dead. But she was only..." The man narrows his eyes as though he's trying to think.

"She jumped from a cruise ship just outside Norway," I tell him. I'm alright saying this. After all, it will soon be common knowledge.

"No, she did not jump. There's no proof of that whatsoever."

"There's every proof. If you'd ever bothered to-"

"It wouldn't surprise me if you pushed her over."

"Oh, don't start with me again." Any previous notions of an allegiance fly out of my mind. Though we're getting dangerously close to the bone, I need to keep my cool. Especially with a witness watching on now. At least he'll have some juicy gossip when he returns to his pipe and armchair.

"Blimey," he finally says. "Now you mention it, there has been something on the news." His voice is filled with curiosity. Then, he seems to check himself. "I'm so sorry." Sympathy floods his expression. "They did say, on the report, that the woman who'd died was from Farndale. But didn't name names or streets."

"Well now you know, don't you?"

"We heard barking. Then all this shouting." The man reverts to his initial reason for calling around. "My wife and I. Is there anything we can do to help?"

"Wave a magic wand," I reply. Probably a tad crass in the

circumstances. What would I do with a magic wand anyway? Would I change anything I've done so far? I guess I'd add to my hit-list anyone who wants to threaten the life I've carved out for myself. Such as Jenna. Then there's Charlie. And Donna when she gets out. Though that won't be for years. I read in the news that's she's appealing her sentence, but I can't imagine that will go anywhere. It never does. Lou's mum could be an obstacle too. Oh, and there's Darren's brother if he were to ever think of looking more closely for him, or coming back from wherever he is. It's not as if they were close. Him getting in touch before Christmas was the first time I've spoken to him since Darren and I got together. He didn't even know Darren had got remarried, but then, it was the most low-key of weddings. Just me, Darren, two witnesses and a registry office. The story of my life.

"Why don't you just piss off Liz?" Jenna's voice pierces my thoughts. "To be honest, I can't stand being in the same room as you."

"Then *you* piss off. I came round to sort Coco out." I reach to pat her but she springs back and darts to Jenna. "Since you haven't done a very good job of it so far."

"The dog's evidently a good judge of character." Coco nestles at her feet. "I'm taking her home with me."

Still Jenna doesn't move. We continue to eyeball each other. It's like pistols at dawn.

"Well off *you* go then. I can lock up here." I probably shouldn't have mentioned *locking up* anywhere. It will only draw her attention back to the fact I've got a key. If I can just get her to leave, I can find this wretched diary. I won't rest until the thing is a pile of ash.

"I'm going nowhere just yet. I've got things to take care of here." She doesn't take her eyes off me.

"Like what?"

The man's head twists from side to side as though he's watching a tennis match between us.

"None of your damn business," Jenna replies. "But I'll have that key back." Shit. I knew I should have kept my mouth shut.

That's my cue to leave. I'll just have to come back the moment she's cleared off. Even if I have to wait half the night. "No chance." I flounce out of the kitchen, slamming the door after me and dashing straight for the lounge. I flick the light switch and stride towards the coffee table, hoping for a glimpse of that bright red cover. If I see it, I'll pretend it's something I've lent to her. Jenna would have to wrestle me for it if I do find it. But there's no sign. Nothing.

"What do you think you're doing in here?" She's framed in the lounge doorway, and the neighbour's standing behind her. "I thought you were leaving."

"Helen borrowed something from me. I'm looking for it." Like I'm even bothering to explain. Jenna's beyond having a civilised conversation with me.

"Get the hell out of my sister's house. Now!"

I push past them both into the hallway. Back to the original plan. I'll just have to watch for her leaving.

"I want that key," she shrieks after me.

CHAPTER 25

I WAKE with a start to the rattle of the letterbox, wondering for a moment, why I'm waking to a crick in my neck after dropping off on the sofa, rather than in my top of the range bed upstairs. It's the bed that was Lou's - one of the few things I didn't see the point in changing.

Darkness has given way to daylight which is streaming around the edges of the curtains. I glance at my phone, surprised to see that it's gone nine. After storming back from next door last night, I'd watched for what felt like forever, waiting for Jenna to get into her car and bugger off. But midnight came and went, then one o'clock. Finally, I was forced to accept that she wasn't going anywhere. Then I had to practically knock myself out with wine to get a wink of sleep. I've been even more wired coming back home than I was when I set off from here on Monday, knowing what was ahead of me.

The few hours I slept for yesterday didn't do me any favours either. But sleep's a good escape right now when it does grant itself to me. A way to allow time to elapse more quickly. The more minutes that turn into hours into days, the more this situation is moving on. It's highly unlikely Helen's body will wash up somewhere now, not after all these days. And the police haven't asked any more questions so far. Which means I'm probably in the clear. I'm sure there will have to be some sort of inquest, but am confident there will be a verdict of suicide. No matter how much Jenna tries to blacken my name. After all, there's proof of Helen being depressed and riddled with anxiety. Yet there's no proof of the altercation between us on Monday night. Stephen approaching me that Tuesday morning, the morning after, was a pure stroke of luck. It's given me an alibi. I'd have probably had to report Helen missing sooner without that and there'd have been an increased risk of them finding her body then.

I shuffle barefoot across the carpet and throw the curtains back. Jenna's Fiat is *still* parked outside. Who the hell would want to stay in that house? Her being there is making me panic, especially with that diary being in there somewhere. My saving grace is that it seems to be well hidden. The second she's out of the way, I'll be back in there. And I won't give up until I've found it this time. I imagine Helen would have either written it at the end of the day whilst in bed, or maybe in the lounge before going to bed. The bedroom's the first place I'm going to take apart until I find it, followed by the lounge. The minute that car moves. But in the meantime, I need coffee.

Whilst I wait for the kettle, I down a pint of water and some paracetamol. I started on a second bottle of wine last night. On an empty stomach too. I pace the length of the kitchen and back again. I can't settle. Not yet. I'm still not out of the woods. Then I remember the letterbox rattle which woke me up.

I locate my slippers by the back door and head through the hallway, feeling grubby as I realise I'm still wearing yesterday's clothes. I was so intent on watching for Jenna leaving that I never did get a shower to wash the stench of Helen's house away.

My stomach twists as I realise it's another note.

Came early doors. You can't avoid me forever. I'll be back.

Just as I'm contemplating where I left my phone to try that number again, there's a knock at the door. Thank God the door is filled with frosted glass. Even though Jenna is not who I'd particularly want to see silhouetted through it, she's better than the possible alternatives. Shall I answer it? My head's banging so I don't need any more shit right now. But she might know something or have heard from the police. Forewarned is definitely forearmed. I should probably get a bag of stuff together. Be ready to take off from here. But first, that diary.

"What do you want?" I peer through the crack in the door. I wouldn't put it past her to come steaming in here. I'm not giving her the chance.

"I want the key to my sister's house."

"The police gave you her keys. You don't need mine."

'It's not *yours*. I don't want you being able to get in whilst I'm not there."

"Look you." I widen the door slightly. "What *is* your

bloody problem with me? Helen and I were friends in the end. What happened at school is ancient history."

"My problem is *you* Liz. I've never trusted you and I never will. So I want that key. Right now." She holds her palm towards me.

"Piss off Jenna." As I start to shut the door she jams her foot in it.

"Not until I've got that..." Her words fade into a gasp as a police car pulls up in between her car and mine. Normally I'd be pissed off at someone parking across my drive but this.... Well, I'm both worried and curious in equal measure. Worried mainly. They're either here to say their investigation's concluded. That Jenna can do whatever it is you do when someone's presumed dead. Or they're here with news I'd rather not hear. I try to keep my expression nonchalant as one of the police officers approaches the gate. My gate. They're coming to see me, rather than Jenna by the looks of it.

"Elizabeth Rhodes?" The policewoman says as she pushes the gate open. A male copper gets out of the passenger side before hurrying behind her.

"Yes, that's me? Why?"

"I'm DI Susan Macron and this is my colleague, Sergeant Robin Wilson." She gestures towards him as he catches her up. "Can we come in please?"

"Erm, yes, but..."

"Is this about my sister?" Jenna folds her arms as she steps in front of them, blocking any passage they have to the door.

"And you are?" The man's radio crackles and beeps as he looks at Jenna. I glance across the road. There are curtains twitching in both houses facing us. At least they're less obvious about being nosy pillocks around here. Where I used to live, they'd have been hanging out of their windows, or out in the street.

"Jenna Atkins. Helen's sister."

Both sets of eyes turn to me. A flicker of recognition crosses DI Macron's face. "Have we met before?

I shrug. "I don't think so." I know full well we have, but if I can avoid her making the connection between me and Lou....

She keeps her gaze fixed on me, which is unnerving. "I know where from now." She slaps her hand against her folder as though she's just recalled a winning answer. She turns back to Jenna. "If you'd like to return home Miss Atkins. There's a unit on the way to speak to you."

"What do you mean, *home?* I'm *here* now."

"You left details where you were to be contacted. And it wasn't here."

"What's it about please? I need to know."

"We'll radio through - let our colleagues know you're here." She nods at the sergeant. "If you could sort that. Rob."

"Right you are ma'am."

"Can't you just tell me what's going on?" Her voice is wobbly again. Sometimes I wish I'd had a sister. Maybe things wouldn't have been so bad then.

"I'm sorry. We're here to see Mrs Rhodes. But I promise, there will be someone along to speak to you very soon."

Jenna doesn't move. "Anything you've got to say to *her...* " She jerks a thumb in my direction. "Well, I should hear it too. Helen was my sister. I've got a right to know what's going on."

"If you could just listen to DI Macron." Sergeant Wilson turns towards her. "Our colleagues will be with you soon." He turns his attention back to me.

"What's going on?" I scrunch the note within my palm. I've evidently got bigger things to worry about than some crank posting bits of paper through my letterbox.

"If we could just come in please." It seems they don't want to talk to me in front of Jenna.

I widen the door and they step inside, her first, him following. Jenna looks on wide-eyed from where she stands on the drive. The only silver lining in this particular cloud is being able to close the door on her.

She probably wouldn't be able to hear our conversation through a closed exterior door, but I step away from it anyway. "So how can I help you?" I turn to face them, hoping my expression and voice isn't portraying the anxiety swirling around inside me.

"We interviewed you, then reinterviewed you after the murder of Louisa Rhodes, didn't we? You and your husband?"

"That's right. The murder Donna Meers was found guilty of." The less I have to remember *that* night the better. I really was living at the edge of my nerves from the moment I turned up here when Lou was still alive and kicking, sitting in her garden. Somehow I managed to give her what she deserved, get out of here and then pull off what needed to be done at Donna's to make things stick.

DI Macron nods, looking uncertain. "How come you're here, in what was Louisa's house? Are you actually living in it?" Her elevated tone suggests that to live in the house of someone's ex-wife is unthinkable. Perhaps, to some, it is.

"It was once my husband's house as well. He's moved back in to take care of his daughter."

"So where are they now?" She seems to look beyond me, curiosity written all over her face.

"Darren's working away."

"Oh? What about your stepdaughter?"

I hate it when Charlie is referred to as *my stepdaughter*. Probably because it's a title that attempts to connect us. She's the last person I would want to be connected to.

"She's staying at her grandma's. Whilst her dad is away." I add the last bit as an afterthought. It sounds good, anyway.

A flicker of recognition enters her eyes. "Ah yes, Carole. How is she?"

I relax. If they were here to arrest me, she wouldn't be

standing here enquiring about the wellbeing of someone else. "She's not great as far as I know. She's better when Charlie's around her. I think it gives her a sense of purpose." Gosh, I actually sound like I give a toss, when really, I couldn't care less.

"I have to say, I'm surprised to find *you* living here. When I heard the name Rhodes, I don't know..." Her voice trails off.

"You still haven't told me why you're here." If that sounds rude, I don't really care. I want them to say what they've got to say and then piss off. Small talk isn't moving things forward.

DI Macron looks at her colleague who clears his throat. Evidently he's going to be the one to impart whatever it is they've got to tell me.

It could be my imagination but his chest appears to swell, perhaps with the idea of his own self importance at being the one in charge of their visit's main purpose. Finally he gets over himself and speaks. "The body of Helen Atkins was discovered by a jogger, washed up on Alnwick beach earlier this morning."

"Alnwick beach," I echo, frantically trying to compute what this actually means. I told them I last saw her on Tuesday morning, at least I think I did. I can't remember. Would we have cleared the UK by that time? They didn't start looking for her until we'd docked in Norway. Shit. I've *got* to calm down. I was mostly with Stephen, after all. I've got an explanation. I'd go as far as calling it an alibi as I'm certain he'll vouch for me if need be. That's if I can get in touch with him and get him to understand why I suddenly disappeared. I was in shock and I was grieving. Or so he'll think. Shit. I can't believe her body's washed up. I really thought I was in the clear there. Yet I've a feeling that the location of it will only be a part of the problems I will need to face. After the scuffle we had, it's going to be a battered body. And once they start looking closely, they will know someone else was around before she died.

"Are you OK?" DI Macron's voice is gentle. If she thought I was anything to do with Helen's death, I'm sure she'd be more cutting with me. She wouldn't be asking if I'm OK. Hopefully she's taking my pause from the conversation as my shocked reaction to the news.

"We'll need to ask you a few more questions Elizabeth. Being that you're the last person who saw Helen alive."

"Call me Liz. I hate being called Elizabeth." Like that really matters in the scheme of things.

"We'd like you to come with us please Liz. Just so we get what you say on record."

"Come with you?" I'm sounding like a parrot. "Where?" What a stupid question. There's only one place they're taking me.

DEAR DIARY
HELEN

I'm depressed. I've got tablets for it. And I'm anxious - beyond anxious. I've got tablets for that too. But what I'm struggling with most is this horrendous sense of foreboding. I can't shake it, no matter what I do. Usually when I feel like this, it's a sign. Jenna's always commented on how intuitive I am. She once said I could make a living out of being a fortune teller, rather than being a dog sitter. So what's my gut trying to tell me here?

Perhaps Darren's remains will get discovered in my garden. Dug up by wildlife. Or something bad is going to happen to Coco, or Jenna. Or me. An illness. A terrible accident.

The feeling intensifies every day. Sometimes when I'm out with the dogs I get a sense of being followed. In a way I am - the shadow of guilt pursues me everywhere, even into the shower. But it's more than that. It's something more concrete. I'm absolutely certain I'm being watched. There's a car, tatty looking. It stands out like a horse at a dog show. Especially around here. It's been parked over the road nearly every day for the last week. And it's not just parked there. Someone's sitting inside it. I wondered at first if it was someone from the tax office checking I'm being truthful about my earnings, and my depression, to claim the benefits I get. I mustered every ounce of courage I had this morning to walk up close to the car - see if I could recognise who was sitting in it. But the windows are tinted, so I had no chance.

It was back again this afternoon. I'm certain someone's watching me. I'm going to have to warn Liz. I can't shake this hunch I've got... A hunch that perhaps Donna's been sent to prison by mistake. That maybe it was *someone else* who murdered Lou. And now whoever it is has come back for me, or Liz, or both of us. I'm scared. Really scared.

CHAPTER 26

"SORRY TO KEEP you waiting Liz. We had a couple of things to attend to. Some more information coming in."

"About Helen?" I look up from where I've been sitting for what feels like an eternity. The metal seat in the waiting room is not designed for a long stay. My bum's numb and I can only be thankful that I've got my phone with me. If I'd been arrested it would have been taken, and I'd have been locked in some stinking cell. So far, I've never been formally arrested, but I've sure as hell been questioned several times.

"I'm afraid I'm not able to answer that Liz, but we'll see what information emerges when we talk." She nods towards a room, presumably an interview room.

Whilst waiting, I've been nosing about on social media - and have visited Helen's page. It's the least interesting page I've ever seen. Photos of her dog, an inspirational quote and then there's been no post since a couple of *Happy Birthdays* last year. But now it's become more interesting with the sudden flurry of ghouls and their *gone too soon* comments and *heaven has gained another angel*. Yeah right. I've been particularly shocked to see a comment posted by Sally from school. *Sorry - on so many levels. RIP.* She's clearly feeling guilty for her part in our long term feud with Helen.

I'd recognise Sally, my former co-conspirator, anywhere, even twenty years on. We were eighteen when we last saw each other. In her profile picture she looks to have exactly the same hairstyle she did back then, a jaw skimming bob. She now wears glasses and looks like the Maths teacher we used to have.

Whilst I've been waiting, I've also looked at the local neighbourhood page where a picture of Helen has been posted. There are comments such as *I never knew you but I wish I had.* Then one I liked, *Hopefully you're at peace now.* The word on the street is definitely suicide, which puts me in a stronger position for what I'm now facing.

As I walk behind the DI and Sergeant towards the interview room, I tell myself that public opinion is what I'll hang onto as I get through the questions about to be thrown at me. I take my seat where the Sergeant points. I'm certain it's the same room I spent hours in when I was quizzed over Lou's death.

It's like deja-vu firstly as I'm cautioned and secondly, as I reel off my information *for the benefit of the recording.* First with the cruise ship, then the Norwegian police, now here. This is hopefully for the final time. I listen peripherally as DI Macron and Sergeant Wilson do the same.

"As already mentioned Liz, you are not under arrest at this stage, you are free to leave the interview, and you may seek legal advice at any time."

"Is this a formal interview?" I thought that they were just asking me a few questions. Shit.

"You've been asked here today to assist with an ongoing

inquiry into the unexplained death of Helen Atkins. So this is known as an interview under caution. Do you understand this?"

"Yes. Might I need legal advice here? Even though I'm not under arrest?" Something about the demeanour of these officers since we've arrived at the station tells me they don't like me one bit. Especially *her.* She was a right cow when I was interviewed the first time around. Perhaps she sensed something about me, or maybe I'm just being paranoid. Luckily I'd stitched Donna up like an old postbag.

"Only you can decide that. Perhaps we could go ahead with the questions, but you can stop us at any time if you feel you need to. Then we can get someone here for you. Does that sound OK?"

"Yes. Go ahead." The quicker she asks what she's got to ask, the faster I can get out of here. I've still got to find that diary.

"I'd like you to firstly describe your relationship with the deceased."

The deceased. I take a deep breath, hoping we're not going to be long in this room, tainted by the whiff of feet and stale chewing gum. I look her straight in the eye and hope my voice comes out steadier than it's feeling. I still can't believe that her body has washed up. "Helen and I were friends. And obviously next door neighbours."

Sergeant Wilson writes something.

"But you weren't always friends, were you?" DI Macron arches a perfectly-shaped eyebrow. Clearly, like me, she's got plenty of money to spend on herself. I can tell by her perfectly manicured nails. She won't have as much time at her disposal as I have though.

There are no prizes for guessing who they've got this information from. "No, not always. We went to school together and didn't get on back then."

DI Macron tips her head to the side. "It was worse than *not getting on*, wasn't it? You bullied Helen. You and another girl. " She glances down at her notes. "Sally Hughes?"

"That's all well in the past now. We grew up. And Helen had forgiven me."

"According to Captain Devonshire, the purpose of your cruise together was to *atone* for the past? Isn't that right?" Her eyebrow rises again with her voice, an emphasis on the word *atone*. She's kind of irritating. So is the current pen-clicking activity of her sidekick.

"I suppose so."

"To make up for your former behaviour. That would suggest it wasn't quite as *well in the past* as you make it out to be?"

"That didn't mean it was front and central. I used what once happened between us more as an excuse to persuade her to say yes to coming with me."

"Why did she need persuading? Especially if you were such good friends in the end."

"It was all to do with money. She couldn't afford it. And I could, and I wanted company on the cruise. Helen looked as though she could badly do with a holiday." So far so good. Sergeant Wilson hasn't said a word yet. In my experience, one of them seems to do all the talking whilst the other one makes notes. I've never seen the point of that, not when what I'm saying is being recorded.

"What happened to Helen? What *really* happened?" Her tone is suddenly friendly as though she's suggesting that anything I say is in confidence. When we both very well know that *anything I say might be used as evidence.*

"Like I've already said, I don't know for sure. I wish I did." I gear up for another outstanding performance. "It makes what I did look terrible now."

"What *did* you do?" The expression on her face reminds me of a dog waiting for a biscuit.

I swallow and attempt to muster as much guilt as humanly possible into my voice. "I met someone on the first night."

"This will be the man," she looks down at her notes again, "Stephen, that you mentioned in your statement to the Norwegian police?"

"Yes. Helen had been exhausted, and on the first night she left me in the bar to go to bed early. Anyway, we got talking. Me and Stephen, I mean. We really hit it off." I'm not completely lying here. Even if it was actually the next morning when we'd got talking. Stephen said he'd *noticed* me on the Monday night, so only a minor technicality that won't even get flagged up.

"Then what happened?"

"Well, I'm ashamed to say, I neglected Helen after that, preferring to spend time with Stephen. She was ill, not just with seasickness, but her mental health seemed to have taken a turn for the worse as well. She wasn't much fun to be around, and I know that makes me sound heartless, but nothing I seemed to say or do was making any difference."

"What makes you say her mental health had deteriorated?"

"The things she was saying."

'Such as?"

"She told me she wanted to be dead. Or at best, she wanted to be someone else. She was going on and on about money on that first day too. Or lack of it - it was as though she was trying to make me feel bad for being able to afford things. I know it sounds selfish but I'd wanted some fun on the cruise. Which is why I jumped at spending time with Stephen."

"But what about your husband? You're married, aren't you?"

"I know." I hang my head in mock-shame. "I was lonely. Hopefully he never has to find out."

She pulls a face as though to say *unlikely.* We then go round and round the houses, answering questions I've already answered to other people. This is all a formality. It's all going to be fine.

Then, just as I'm beginning to relax, comes the killer punch.

CHAPTER 27

"THE BODY DISCOVERED at Alnwick was formally identified by Helen's sister a short time ago. It *is* Helen Atkins. What we need to do next is ascertain the reason behind some injuries she's sustained. Injuries which have been discovered throughout the early stages of the post mortem."

"Injuries?" Hopefully the high-pitch of my voice conveys innocence. "What do you mean?"

"An initial examination has found contusions on the body in several locations"

"Contusions?" What does she think I am - a scientist?

"Bruising."

"But isn't that to be expected? Our cabin balcony was quite high up. It would have been a long way down." Like I don't know. I watched her go. I heard the splash.

"Not in the areas she sustained them." She looks at me pointedly. Whether she suspects me, it's hard to tell.

"Between her legs, around the tops of her arms, the back of her neck and her lower back."

Whilst she's speaking, Sergeant Wilson pushes a sheet of paper across the table. There's the outline of a person with crosses marked as DI Macron describes. He points the nib of his pen in turn at them as she lists each injury, one at a time.

"Bloody hell." I sit up straighter in my seat and look from one to the other, trying to read their expressions.

"Are we to understand from your reaction, that you have no idea of how Helen came to suffer these injuries before her death?"

"None whatsoever. Of course I don't." I raise my voice more as if I'm incredulous that they could even suggest it. "Look I know we used to scrap at school, but we'd become friends since then." I lower my voice. "I wouldn't have hurt a hair on her head."

"The condition of Helen's body and the location in which it was discovered would place her time of death late Monday night, or the very early hours of Tuesday morning. What have you got to say about that?"

I'm aware of my gaping mouth as I shake my head at them. "I don't know."

They look at each other, as though they're exchanging an unspoken knowing that makes me wonder what is coming next.

"Liz can you tell us why it would appear that your *friend* Helen Atkins entered the water more than *two days* before you acknowledged her absence? And even then, it was *by chance* that her absence was discovered by the crew."

"I wasn't there. In the cabin, I mean. I know it sounds really, *really* bad but I didn't even go back to the cabin. Helen was ill, like I've told you. She wanted leaving alone. I thought she was safe in there. But maybe someone got in? Have you looked into that?"

"You've been picked up on the ship's cameras in several locations close to your cabin on Monday night. And then leaving again early on Tuesday morning?"

"I'd probably have been going for breakfast. I met Stephen

again. But Monday night?" I pause, as if remembering. "I was really drunk that night - mainly through being tired and not having eaten much. I really thought she was there, in bed when I got back. To be honest, the cabin was dark. I didn't look properly and didn't put the light on so as not to wake her."

"You seem to remember a lot about it to say you were drunk."

"I never have any problem remembering things. I swear to you. I thought she was there. In fact, I'm still sure she was there." My voice cracks. I'm on seriously shaky ground here. If this gets any worse, I'm going to be forced to request a solicitor. Maybe I shouldn't be saying anything at all. I've seen *no comment* interviews on the TV, but I feel like giving one of those would be prolonging the agony. It would no doubt make me look guiltier than they might already think I am.

"Our colleagues in Norfolk are in the process of speaking to the man you claim to have spent your time with on the cruise," she continues. "And obviously, the post mortem and investigation is proceeding. We'll know more when we've had a full report back from the lab."

I'm surprised this matters to me, but I hope they're not saying damning remarks about me to Stephen. What others think of me has never bothered me one iota before, but he's had a strange effect on me. What *he* thinks of me does matter. A lot.

"In the meantime..." DI Macron's mouth and eyes seem marble hard, probably because I haven't given them a lot with my answers. "Is there anything else you can tell us? Anything at all that can help us to piece together what happened to Helen before she died?"

"Nothing more. I'm so sorry - I wish there was. One minute we were having drinks and planning to get something to eat. The next she felt like she was going to puke, and as far as I knew, she was holing herself up in our cabin."

"Why didn't you go back with her?" Something in her tone suggests that's what *she'd* have done, if she'd been in my shoes.

"I was more than a bit fed up. Helen was depressed, granted, however I wasn't looking forward to spending the cruise alone if she didn't sort herself out. I was glad when I met Stephen, if the truth be known."

"There's another question I need to ask." She glances down at her notes, her hair bobbing with the movement. "How could you have arranged to meet her at the ship's exit point when you docked at Norway?" They both look at me now.

I don't speak - I think I know what they're getting at. This might be a good time to say *no comment*.

"You told the captain when you were in the line that you were meeting her? But she'd been dead for over two days by then."

I swallow. Then pause for as long as possible to cobble an answer together. I just want to get out of here. "Visiting Andalsnes had been the thing Helen was most looking forward to about the cruise. Whenever we discussed it in advance, she was always going to get off there. I guess I just assumed."

"But you were in the queue with her cruise ID card?" The look on her face tells me there isn't a molecule of her that believes a word I'm saying. But so far, she clearly doesn't have enough evidence to arrest me. Not yet, anyway. It's starting to look like I might need to do a runner before she does.

"Like I've already said in the other interviews, I'd picked Helen's card up by mistake." I shrug, a little too nonchalantly perhaps. "Easy done. And obviously because she was ill in her cabin, she didn't ask for it back."

"She didn't ask for it back...' Sergeant Wilson speaks now, his tone sharp, "because she was dead in the water."

"I didn't know that, did I? Of course I didn't know that. If I had, I'd have done something about it." I need to change tack here. I scrunch my eyes together for a moment. I'm probably coming across as cold and calculated, going on about her being poor company and preferring to be elsewhere.

It's time to do what always works to evoke a tear or two. Like I did in front of Captain Devonshire. It worked then, and it can work now. I'll awaken that angry, emotive side by conjuring images of my mother, Darren's ex wife, Helen, Jenna, Charlie and Donna, all swirling and merging inside my mind as one huge and threatening monster, capable of bringing me down and threatening my very existence.

I've risked too much this time. I've not considered the whole of it and given it enough thought. I should have thrown Helen straight over. Instead I gave her a choice - the opportunity to jump, and therefore the chance to wrestle with me first. She was warned what was coming. She had the chance to fight. And, I could have reported her overboard soon after she went. It would have looked more like a suicide. Maybe keeping quiet has worsened things for me.

"We'll need to have a look at your phone Liz." DI Macron's voice is soft.

"Why?"

"Just to check a few things. We'll let you have it back as quickly as possible." Despite the fact they're taking my phone, this is actually starting to sound positive. Like they're maybe going to let me go.

"Are you absolutely sure there isn't anything else you can tell us?" Sergeant Wilson says, like I've even told them *anything* whilst they've been questioning me. In another job, Sergeant Wilson would be a very good-looking man. But I've never liked coppers so he isn't for me. Besides, one of my first jobs when I get out of here will be to try and find Stephen. Find out what the police have been asking him.

I shake my head. "I'm sorry. There isn't. Only that she was depressed and I should have realised how much, sooner." I emit the biggest sigh I'm capable of. "I should have been able to stop her."

They both stare at me with blank eyes. There's silence for a few moments, as though they're considering the next move. It's eventually broken by DI Macron saying, "we're going to bail you, pending further investigation Liz. Clearly there are still many unanswered questions. And with Helen's body only just being formally identified, many more questions are bound to emerge as the inquiry continues."

"We'll be in touch," Sergeant Wilson adds.

The walk home takes forever. But it helps clear my head and clear the Sergeant's words *don't go far* which have been ringing in my ears since I left. I can't believe the pillocks have taken my phone from me. I feel lost without it; I can't even use it to make contact with Stephen. I hope to God his alibi for me was sound. From what's just happened in there, it seems I've got an answer for everything - they might not believe me, but they can't prove otherwise either. Yet.

Eventually I round the corner of my street, now home to me. When the police drove me away earlier, part of me wondered how soon I'd see this place again. I've spent so many hours watching this street, that house. Needing to know what Darren was really up to when he told lie after lie to me. I always knew when he was lying. When his lips moved really, but there was a twitch in his eye. I knew him well enough to catch it every single time. He deserved everything he got after how he treated me.

As I get closer to the house my breath catches. Jenna's car

isn't there. Finally, she's gone. She's probably unable to face being at the house now that she's identified Helen's body. Some things can never be unseen.

I let myself in, and slip the key to next door from the hook. I'll double lock the door from the inside this time. And I'm not leaving that house without that diary, even if I have to tear the place apart looking for it. I dart down my drive and up Helen's, checking around the whole time to make sure no one's watching. There's a car parked at the other side of the road. One that doesn't look as though it belongs around here. Someone's sitting in it but I can't worry about that now. I slide the key into the lock. It doesn't budge. I turn it the other way up. It won't even go in that way. I give the door a shake. Try the key again. It's no good. Today's just getting better. The bitch has changed the lock.

DEAR DIARY
HELEN

If I had the money I would just disappear. Get away - miles from here - perhaps abroad. There's only Coco and Jenna that I care about enough to not want to leave behind. But they could both come with me. At times I get carried away with the idea and plan where I'll go and what I'll do. Cyprus would be amazing, but what if I couldn't take the dog with me? I could move to Ireland, or Cornwall instead. I would occupy a little corner of the property I'd buy myself and the rest would operate as a bed and breakfast. If I had a new life, I'd have the confidence to face people. All three are places I'd love to visit. I've never been anywhere. Looking at my bank balance, I never will either. I'll be stuck in this house with that rotting body in my garden forever. And whatever weirdo who's been parked up outside, watching. I haven't seen the car for a couple of days though. Thank God.

The money I get for the dogs each month only seems to service my overdraft and credit card. At this time of year, none of the dogs are boarding for holidays so I've even less money than usual. I don't know how much longer I can keep going like this.

Also, it might be just my imagination, but the lower I get, the more often Liz seems to come round here. All that time when Lou lived next door and I was yearning to make friends with her. And I've ended up with Liz of all people. She keeps asking if she can trust me. She keeps going on about the past, asking if I've forgiven her. But the main thing she's quizzing me about is whether I can remember what she said when she was drunk. She's asked me over and over again. I've told her that my brain feels so fuzzy I can barely remember yesterday, let alone several days ago when we were getting hammered. I'm going to have to make an appointment with the doctor tomorrow. See about getting some stronger tablets. I've got to sort myself out.

CHAPTER 28

No sooner have I poured a much-needed glass of wine than the doorbell goes again. Much as I want to pretend I'm not in, I need to know. It might be Jenna. It's looking like I'm going to have to break in and find Helen's diary before Jenna does. Either that or I'll get a ladder up to the bathroom window. I can't imagine Helen's fixed the dodgy catch she's sometimes moaned about.

The shape of someone wavers behind the frosted glass. I pause for a moment, trying to work out who it is. I'll have to answer it - this could even be where I discover who's behind those notes. Whoever it is takes a step back as I reach the door. At least they're alone. Two people standing there could mean the police. It's maybe too soon to be worrying about that as it's only a couple of hours since I spoke to them.

As I inch the door open, I immediately regret not following my hunch to ignore it. For it's none other than bloody Charlie. It's been weeks since she called round. And if it were years, it wouldn't be too soon. After the day I've had up to now, she's the last person I want to see.

"What do you want?" I peer through the crack in the door,

holding it ajar just enough so she can see my face. Part of me wonders whether I should be sliding the chain across. But that would be a little extreme with a fifteen-year-old at the other side, even by my standards.

"Can I come in please?" There's something in her face that's less bolshy than usual. Normally she stands right up to the door with a look about her as though she owns the place. Which really, she does. Not that she's ever going to get it. Over my dead body.

"You haven't answered my question. I said, what do you want?"

"To talk to you." God, she reminds me of Darren. More and more as she grows into adulthood. It's in her eyes. And it's very unnerving. This girl has needled at me for as long as I can remember. I wish she'd leave me alone.

"As far as I'm concerned, we've got nothing to say to each other."

Charlie steps forward whilst reaching towards the door handle. She's no idea how foolish it would be to attempt to force her way in. Only I know what I'm capable of. I might have always detested her, but even I would hope to draw the line at being forced to shut her up completely. She's only fifteen, after all. But if I have to, I will.

"Please Liz. I just need some answers."

"Does your grandma know you're here?" I step through the door and close it behind me, shivering as the chill envelops my bare arms. I can't help but notice the car, from earlier, is *still* there, parked in the same place. It has darkened windows, I can just about make out the shape of someone behind them. Not so long ago, Helen thought our houses might be being watched. In the same breath, she suggested Donna's sentence could have been a *miscarriage of justice*, her words, not mine. She'd said, *Donna could be serving a sentence which should rightly belong to the occupant of that car. One of us could be next on their hit list.* I'd laughed at her 'overactive imagination.' But now, noticing that car parked there for the third time since I got back, along with the notes that have been coming through, to say I'm unsettled is an understatement.

"Do you know anything about notes I've been getting?" I look straight at Charlie, something I've never often done. I once overheard her whining to Darren. *Why does Liz hate me so much? She can't even bring herself to look me in the eye.* But I do now, and find myself envying her youth, the blank sheet of life she's yet to walk on. I wish I'd had her chances, her safety net. The only thing we've got in common is I had no parents either, at her age. But I certainly wasn't born with the silver spoon in my gob that she's always had.

"What notes?" Charlie might have her dad's eyes, but she sounds exactly like Lou as soon as she opens her mouth. She's a reminder of everything I want to get beyond. Other than the police getting hold of any damming evidence to pin Helen's death on me, Charlie poses the second biggest threat. To my home, security and lifestyle. She'd do well to cut her losses and stay well away from me.

"Handwritten notes. Through the letterbox. Looking for me."

"That's not my style." Her voice is quiet. She's become more assured in herself in the time that's elapsed since I last saw her. She stands back and looks up at the house. "I hate coming back here. It makes me miss my mother."

"Well that's easily solved." If she's here for tea and sympathy, she's very much in the wrong place. "Don't come back here."

"What happened to Helen?" She jerks her head to the right. "You were with her, weren't you?"

"Not at the time it-"

"Did she really *mean* to fall in? She didn't seem the type

who'd do something like that on purpose. Not that I knew her all that well."

As if we're having a nearly-civil conversation. "Why, what does someone who's so depressed they don't want to live anymore look like?" By taking the moral high ground, hopefully I can throw her off course. With her grammar school education and her posh grandma, she should know enough about being politically correct and not generalising.

"Helen always seemed alright to me." She averts her gaze from next door, back to me. "Anyway, I'm here about my dad. I really need to see him."

"He's not here. How many times do I have to tell you?" My own mother's in my voice as I say *how many times do I have to tell you?* It really takes me aback. That woman is the last person I want in my head.

"Still? Have you split up or something?"

"As I've told you - numerous times now - he's working away."

"You must have a number for him." Her eyes don't leave mine. "I've been ringing his mobile several times a day. All I ever get is *Sorry I can't take your call right now.* I don't just want to hear my dad's voice through an answering service. I'm sick of him ignoring me."

"If it's any consolation, I haven't heard from him for ages either." My voice is close to sympathetic. But she looks like she believes me. When Lou was alive, she used to berate Darren over his lack of commitment towards Charlie. At least it will have stood her in good stead to believe this.

"But I'm his daughter. He can't just bugger off and ignore me."

"I'm his wife. And he's buggered off and is ignoring me."

We stand for a few moments, just eyeballing each other.

"Was there something else?" I eventually say, folding my arms.

"I need some help with my grandma. She's not well. I'm worried she'll go the same way as Helen," she glances towards her house, "if I don't get her some help. That's why I'm here."

"You've come to *me* for help?" I resist the urge to laugh.

"I've come to my *dad*. I know I'm the last person *you'd* want him to help. But he's my dad. And there's nothing you can do to change that."

"Well, he's not here, is he? So I'm going back inside. Sorry, I can't help you."

"Not as sorry as you're going to be." But her actions and voice don't match her words. For as she speaks, she steps back, her voice wobbling as her gaze falls. Evidently, she can no longer meet my eye. "This is my mother's house. *You* shouldn't even be here."

So finally, we've come around to this. I wondered how long it would take. At the very earliest, I thought she'd get to sixteen. Eighteen really. Someone must have put her up to it. "I'm Darren's wife whether *you* like it or not. " I waggle my ring finger in the air. "So I've every right to be here."

"Not if he's not."

"Who says he isn't?"

"I don't believe a word you say. I *know* he doesn't live here."

"How do you *know?* "

She taps the side of her nose. "I'm not stupid. *Of course* I know. And you might think you've got rid of me, but..."

Fear crosses her face as I step forwards, closing the gap between us. Then my attention's averted to the slow pulling away of the car across the road. Maybe it's my imagination. I'm as jumpy as a hammered reflex right now, and until I've got a few more days under my belt, I'm fearing the worst. *Fear the worst and you're never disappointed,* my mother used to say. Why the hell am I thinking about her again.

Charlie follows my gaze. "Why won't you tell me where my dad is? If you won't tell me, I'll..."

Then we both look as another car pulls up by the gate. It's a CID looking car. A cold hand of fear clutches at my chest. I wouldn't even be out here if it wasn't for *her* banging on my door. I could have hid inside, plus I wouldn't have known about that car over the road being back. If it is the police, that could be Charlie's 'in.' I can hardly refuse her getting into the house in front of them.

As my brain goes into catastrophe mode, the car door slams. The late afternoon sun blurs my vision as I watch to see who's opening the gate.

CHAPTER 29

IT'S...OH MY GOD. "STEPHEN!" I call out. "How did you know where I live?"

"You won't live here for much longer." Charlie spins on her heel and stamps up the drive, almost knocking into him as he steps through the gate. "I'll be back," she shouts over her shoulder. "You haven't heard the last from me."

"I'll let you know if I hear anything." My voice is probably the most pleasant she's ever heard from me. She stops and gives me what can only be described as a look of astonishment.

"All those flowers piled up there are a bit of a give-away." Stephen jerks his thumb in the direction of Helen's garden wall, where a shrine of flowers and fluffy bears has accumulated. I knew it was Farndale from the news - so a bit of driving around, and hey, it's good to see you again." He stops in front of me, grinning. I smile back, whilst wanting the ground to swallow me up at how bad I must look. I haven't showered since going into Helen's house last night and am wearing the joggers and hoody I fell asleep in. I haven't even brushed my hair. Or teeth. I was too busy at the bloody police station. As he has been, by the sounds of it, but I'll get to the bottom of that shortly.

"You never mentioned having kids?" Stephen turns from watching Charlie as she shuffles further along the road, back to me.

"No. She's my stepdaughter. She lives with her grandma."

"Oh right."

"She was seeing if I'd heard from her dad."

"And have you?" He raises an eyebrow. "You've been really evasive when this topic of conversation has come up so far."

"He's still away. And what's wrong with being *evasive*. We all have pasts, don't we?"

"So he's definitely consigned to your *past*, is he?"

"Sure is. Anyway, let's not talk about him. I'm so glad to see you."

"You too." His appraising look offers assurance that his attraction hasn't waned since I abruptly left the ship. This is hugely reassuring - it means he's probably been questioned without anyone saying something that could have incriminated me, or put me in a bad light - yet.

"You're looking way better than I expected." His eyes continue to roam up and down me. How anyone could fancy me when I look like this is beyond my comprehension. But I'll take it.

"What do you mean?"

"With what happened to your friend, Helen, wasn't it? I couldn't believe it when I found out."

"Do you want to come in?" The last thing I want is Jenna turning up, all guns blazing whilst Stephen's on my doorstep.

"I thought you'd never ask."

"Nice place." I put my hand out for his coat and hang it up. Stephen's an odd sight in the hallway, the first man to enter this house since Darren. Apart from Sergeant Wilson, that is.

"Shall I take my shoes off?"

I glance down at his polished shoes. They look so expensive, they're probably handmade. I forgot how minted he is. But even without all his money, I'm interested in *him*. He's the first person in a long, long time, perhaps *ever*, whose opinion of me actually matters. He makes me want to be a better person, something I can hardly believe I'm considering. But people *can* change, even after doing terrible things. Even I can change. Can't I?

"No, you're alright, I've got wooden floors, you can keep them on?" Although Charlie's visit has made me realise they're not actually *my* wooden floors. But I'll deal with all that later. Including getting to the bottom of the threat she made as she was leaving.

"I'll put the kettle on. Come through."

"I was sorry to hear about your friend." He follows me. "What a terrible business. "I gather from the news that they've found her."

"Yeah." I busy myself in filling the kettle, avoiding his gaze. I suppose he feels he needs to talk about that first, no matter how much I'd prefer to avoid it. "Have a seat."

"The police wanted to speak to *me* about it, you know."

"So I've heard. I answered a few more of their questions not long ago. I've only been back here for a couple of hours." I tug the packet of coffee from the cupboard. "Is that what's brought you up here? Speaking to the police?"

"Well, they did offer to get someone to speak to me down in Norfolk." He pulls a chair from beneath the table with a scrape. "But I decided coming up here would give me a good excuse to look you up."

"I'm glad you did," I turn from scooping coffee into the cafetière. "I'm sorry I look such a mess today."

"You don't at all." He smiles again. "But even if you did, you could hardly be blamed for it. I mean, your best friend's just *committed suicide*." His eyes crinkle in the corners as his face breaks into a smile. "So go easy on yourself."

I place a mug before him then sit with him, sidewards on. I can't sit face to face. We became that close during the time in his cabin that I worry he'll sense things about me. Things which no one else has. No one's ever been able to read me before, but I really think he can. That both scares and excites me.

"So how are you doing Liz? I mean *really* doing, behind that lovely smile?"

"Ah, you know." I stare into my coffee. "I expect it'll get easier. I just hope she's at peace now."

"I can't imagine what you must have been going through. And then there's the police, with their interrogations and their fact checking."

"Is that why they wanted to see you? To check things?" I've probably asked this question too quickly. But if he thinks this too, his face isn't giving anything away.

"Pretty much." He wraps his fingers around his mug. "Anyway, at least I was able to give you a solid alibi." He must sense me stiffen for he immediately says. "Sorry. That sounded crass. I didn't mean..."

"Hey, it's fine. I'm just glad you decided to come up here - I wasn't sure if I'd ever see you again after my sudden disappearance." I want to ask him if he's given Monday or Tuesday as the day of meeting me to the police, but decide to keep quiet.

"I do understand. Why you had to leave." He sips his coffee. "Of course I do. You make a damn good brew Liz. Perhaps I'll be visiting Yorkshire more often."

"How long are you here for?"

"Well, I've got a big meeting first thing tomorrow. But I could head off at the crack of dawn when the motorway's quiet if you want me to stick around?"

Something flips within me. There's nothing I want more. I pray with every fibre of my being, the police don't come back today. Or anyone else for that matter. Namely Charlie or Jenna. The most sensible thing would probably be to get out of here. "Do you fancy going out," I ask. "I'll need to get a shower and a change first." I gesture down at myself.

"I know what I fancy more than *going out*." He winks at me. "How about I join you in that shower, then we'll work up an appetite. After that you can show me this Yorkshire of yours."

DEAR DIARY
HELEN

Oh. Bloody. Hell. No.

I have to write this down before I go mad. It's all probably come bubbling to the surface because Liz's constant questioning has brought it to the forefront of my subconscious. Last night when I was lying awake, at about two o'clock in the morning, I suddenly remembered what Liz said to me when we were drinking wine the other night.

"It was me who killed Lou with that hammer."

No wonder she's been grilling me to find out what I could remember.

I'd stared at her for a few moments, wondering whether she was joking.

"Don't be daft," I eventually said. "Donna did it."

"So everyone thinks." She smirked. She actually smirked. Oh God, it's all coming back.

"But she got sent down for it."

"That's because she was sleeping with my husband whilst he was married to me."

Oh God. I don't want to remember this conversation. And God help me if she ever finds out about the times I've slept with Darren. It happened several times, even after he and Lou had split, so he could even have been with Liz by then. Then there was the time I *knew* he was with her. I'm in it up to my neck in so many ways.

"But *why*? Why would you do that? I know Lou was married to your husband *before* you but that's hardly..."

"She was a right bitch to me Helen. She lorded it over me the whole time. Just because she'd had the house and kid. And the money. She even said she could click her fingers at a moment's notice and Darren would go running back to her."

"That's hardly a reason to kill her." The vision of Lou's slumped body by the shed returned to me. It's an image that doesn't visit me as often as it did in the beginning but it still appears far too often for my liking.

"She turned up at my house that day. I've told you about this already, haven't I?"

"Kind of. You told me about her threatening Darren with the Child Support Agency over Charlie."

"Bloody Charlie." She spits her name out like a fish bone. "I'm sick of the sound of her name. And I was sick of the way Lou looked at me, spoke to me. She made me feel like a piece of shit on my own doorstep that day."

"But that still isn't a reason to *kill her*." Like there ever would be a reason to kill anybody. As I sat facing her, I pinched the skin on the back of my hand. I wanted it to be a bad dream.

I should have known it wouldn't have been Donna who took a hammer to her best friend. They'd been friends for years and I used to listen to them over the fence together. Hearing their conversation and laughter would make me feel lonelier than ever, partly why I haven't turned down emulating what they had with Liz. Well, kind of. We'll always be *pretend friends*. Stuck together because there's no one else.

"Two birds with one stone." Liz had smiled. I knew she

248

was warped when we were at school but I honestly thought she'd changed.

"What do you mean by that?"

"Well. Not that I'm blowing my own trumpet here but I'm not too dissimilar to Donna in looks, am I?"

I stared at her. She was clearly about to tell me that not only had she beaten Lou to death with a hammer in her own back garden, but she'd also set Donna up to take the blame for it.

She's right though. I saw the CCTV stills in the news reports in the early days, just after Lou's body was found. It *could* have been Donna.

"I really thought you *knew* it was me Helen. You're always looking out of your window."

"I wasn't then though. Not until Lou's boyfriend showed up and all the commotion started."

"You *really* didn't know it was me who'd killed her? I honestly thought it had become something we weren't to talk about. The elephant in the room. Like what happened with Darren."

She uses the words *what happened* as though he merely had an accident.

"No. I didn't know. How could I have done?" I cast my mind back again. "They'd found Lou's blood in Donna's shower, clothes, trainers..."

"Who do you think put them there?"

"Why are you telling me all this? Why now?"

And more importantly, *what was I going to do with it*. When the conversation had revolved enough times to make my head spin, she wanted the answer to this too.

"So what are you going to do Helen? Now you know for sure what I've done."

"You mean, am I going to tell anyone? I don't know. This is a biggie, isn't it?"

"We're friends, aren't we? Remember what I said, *a true friend will help you hide a body.*" She'd laughed then. Actually laughed. I couldn't believe it.

"I'm not sure how you live with yourself," I eventually said to her. "I'm not sure how you ever have."

I lie on the sofa, resting my diary on my chest. I feel better for pouring the conversation out. It's not just trapped within me now. It's penned in my diary, as good as out in the world. Unleashed to a darkness which doesn't just live in me anymore - I've been able to release it. My subconscious has buried what Liz told me for two days. OK, so it has come bubbling up but there's no reason why it shouldn't simmer back down again. I want a friend. I want a normal life. But I'm not sure I want to go on this cruise.

CHAPTER 30

EACH DAY that passes without any developments is an absolute relief. Not only are the police leaving me alone, but no more notes have been posted through for a couple of days. As well as that, miraculously, Jenna hasn't been back to the door... and neither has Charlie. Even that car with the darkened windows seems to have gone away. Yet I can't help but worry that this could be the calm before the storm.

After hiring a ladder yesterday, I managed to get into Helen's house. I'm knackered today, after being up nearly all night. It was nearly four in the morning when I got into bed and after what I'd been doing, I was too wired to sleep.

I check out of the window now, to see if the hire company have arrived to collect the ladder from my drive yet. No - it's still there. Hopefully they'll come and go without any of the neighbours noticing. Although whether or not I hire a ladder and for what purpose, is my business. If anyone asks, I'll say I needed to clean out the gutters or something. Whilst I'm standing here, I check up and down the street, feeding my obsession with looking for cars. Namely police cars, Jenna's car or cars with darkened windows. Nothing.

Getting through Helen's bathroom window had to wait until most normal people are asleep. Thankfully the window is at the back of the house and I was able to get through the fence panels in the same way as when we dragged Darren from my house to Helen's.

Luckily, Jenna hadn't noticed that the handle of the bathroom window still needs fixing. It would have been worth the bumps and scrapes I gave myself squeezing through that tiny space if I'd managed to find that wretched diary.

I went through that house like a forensic examiner so if it was there, I would have found it. I came across other diaries, ones Helen must have kept over previous years, full of page after scrawled page of her never-ending misery. But absolutely nothing from either last year, or this one. Perhaps she decided to get rid of it; she could have been worried about leaving it lying around whilst she was away on the cruise.

I've never understood the warped practice of keeping a diary. The very existence of them is to expose information that should never see the light of day when someone finds it. And someone always does. More often than not, it's *after* someone has died, like it would be in Helen's case.

But there is nowhere in that house I haven't searched, short of ripping up the floor boards. I even went through her crap in the loft. So no, if I haven't found it after searching all night, no one else is going to find it either.

Stephen wanted to drive back up to see me tonight. It took every ounce of self restraint to give him the brush off, but I have to keep my distance until I know, for sure, this is over. He seemed to accept my need for space to 'come to terms with Helen's suicide,' as I put it. Until I'm as certain as I can be that I'm in the clear, I can't have him around. There'd be nothing worse than him watching me being handcuffed and led away. Right now, he represents the only hope I have of escaping everything, especially myself. Who I've been, and all the people I've been forced to end. With Stephen, I sense a chance for something else, something different, a life which I've never dared consider mine for the taking. For now, I'll be content with his messages, after this, who knows? Hearing from him as often as I do, whilst it is keeping me positive, I also wish, in some ways, that he hadn't come into my life. Getting involved like this is a distraction; the whole thing is clouding my judgement. In other ways, I can't imagine going back to life before I met him. I barely go five minutes without thinking about him, therefore I will do whatever it takes to prevent him from finding out what I'm capable of. What I've *been* capable of.

I *am* going to change.

I'm so deep in thought that a letter dropping on the doormat startles me. I've changed most things since I took over here but the mat was Lou's. *Welcome. I hope you brought wine,* it says.

I wonder how different things might have been if I hadn't killed her. Darren would probably still be alive for starters. It was only when I saw his reaction to the fact I'd killed Lou that I realised what needed to be done. I don't think about the night with Lou very often, but for some reason, an image of the blood splattering from her head after the third hammer blow enters my mind. I blink it away and bend to the mat, exhaling in relief when I see there isn't a note nestling alongside the letter. Those notes are really unnerving me - it's the not knowing. I like to know what I'm dealing with. I *need to know* what I'm dealing with.

I turn the envelope over, scrutinising the writing. Though really, there's only one person who could be writing to me with an envelope postmarked Newpark Prison. Donna Meers. What the hell would she be writing to me for?

I tear it open. Four sides of a double sided sheet are available to be written on, but she's only written on the front page. Most prisoners would probably utilise the entire space, filling it with everything they want to say to their partner, or friend. Everything they're unable to say in person because they're incarcerated. Yet there's just a few words.

I need to speak to you ASAP.

And a visiting order. I turn it over, looking for a phone number of the booking line. It's valid for a month but I'll go as soon as they can book me in. The *not knowing* will plague me otherwise. After all, Donna's serving a sentence that would have been mine had things not gone so beautifully to plan. And some. Everything just seemed to align for me that night, unlike it has with Helen's demise.

What the hell does *she* want to see me for anyway? Why couldn't she have just written about it, instead of dragging me into a bloody prison of all places. Just as I'm about to call, I remember the police have got my phone. Shit. And we took the landline out. With payphones few and far between these days - I could ask at the gym or the salon to make a call, but booking a prison visit is hardly something I'd want people to eavesdrop on.

In the end, I manage it over the internet. Feeling pretty pleased with myself for working out how to make a voice call using my computer, I book it for the day after tomorrow. What she could possibly want from me, I've no idea.

. . .

I jump again as the doorbell goes. I've never been as nervy at I am at the moment. So much for me basking in the calm. I should've known it wouldn't last long. Perhaps it's Stephen, unable to stay away. Part of me hopes it is. He's my solace right now. Perhaps if he'd come along sooner... no, I can't think like that. What's done is done.

For a split second, I stand before the glass, trying to work out who it is. It's not Stephen. Nor is it the police. It's too tall to be Charlie and doesn't look in the slightest like Jenna. I inch the door open. "Can I help you?" I ask the woman standing there. There's a familiarity about her which I'm struggling to place.

"Long time, no see." She steps closer to the door and stretches her arms out. "Bloody hell Liz. It might have been twenty years but I'd recognise you anywhere."

No sooner has she grabbed me, than I pull back. I don't do hugs - I never have. And definitely not with people I don't recognise. I stare at her some more, trying to work it out. Then I realise. Even without the help of social media filters and skin smoothing enhancement tools, it's none other than Sally. She must have an old picture online - she certainly looks more haggard and chubby in the flesh.

"Well, I certainly wasn't expecting to see you." I'm unsure how to react other than this. I don't want her here. This is someone who knows me. *Really* knows me. All I want to do is to put everything behind me.

Her smile doesn't waver as she stands there, evidently waiting to be invited in.

"How did you know where to find me?" I fold my arms, not budging.

"It's amazing what can be found out through social media. Especially with all the bad news that's been happening around *you* lately." Sounding as though she's stifling laughter, she steps towards me. "I thought I'd pay you a visit."

"What's that supposed to mean?"

The widening of her eyes conveys *'work it out,'* but the smile remains fixed on her face. "Are you going to ask me in, or what?" Something in her face dares me not to. Suddenly, we're sixteen again and she's got me over the same barrel she always had. I'd like to shove her inside one and send it to where Helen was supposed to end up.

Partly through curiosity, and partly through fear at what trouble she might be capable of causing, I open the door and step to the side. Hopefully it's just a social call but something suggests it very much isn't.

"Coffee, tea, or something stronger?" I smile too, trying to load my voice with a friendliness I'm not feeling. Not one bit.

"Well, I know it's early but it's not as if I'm driving. Let's have a glass of wine, shall we? After all, it's been ages since we've been together."

Even if she hadn't chosen wine, I'd have had one on my own, the way I'm feeling. My nerves are shot through; I can do without her showing her face around here. She knows too much. She's almost as much of a threat to me as Jenna.

We sit, facing each other over the kitchen table as I pour the wine. The first glass slips down as we exchange false pleasantries. She imparts where she's living, who she's divorced from and what she does these days. I tell her nothing of my own circumstances. She's probably worked much of it out for herself already, knowing her. She'll have stalked me in every which way.

"I couldn't believe it when I heard about Helen." She holds her glass out as my hand rests alongside the bottle. "Don't mind if I do."

"I know. Tragic, isn't it?"

"As if the two of you ended up as neighbours." She gives me a knowing look. "Of all the people you could have ended up living next door to."

I laugh but Sally probably remembers me enough to tell it's forced.

"Tell me Liz." She takes a big gulp of her wine. "How did Helen *really* end up floating face down in the North Sea?" Her face relaxes into another smile. I want to wipe it clean off her face. This isn't going to end well.

"That's for the inquest to work out, isn't it?" I stare back at her.

"Will you be there? At the inquest, I mean?"

"Of course I will. According to the police, I'll be called as a witness."

"Yes. You'd have been the last person to see her, wouldn't you? Just like with your mother." Her smile broadens. Sally's exactly as she was when we were at school together. With her barbed comments and insinuations. But she's ventured onto very shaky ground, mentioning my mother.

"What are you getting at Sally?" I put my glass down. It seems as though I need to keep a clear head here. "I don't want to talk about my mother, have you got that?"

"Just saying." She clinks her glass onto the polished wooden surface as she looks around. "Nice place."

"I like it."

"I'm not sure I could live here after what's happened." She jerks her head toward the patio door. "How does Darren find it?" Her bobbed hair swings to one side as she tilts her head, waiting for my answer. "Living here, I mean?"

"How do you know what my husband's called?"

"Like I said, social media. Nice drop of wine, this. Was it expensive?" She's got an air of confidence far greater than she had when we were at school. Or should I say, arrogance.

"I hardly ever post on social media. You can't have found much about me that way."

"You'd be surprised." She taps the side of her nose. "Funny. Now you mention it, Darren's not been active for quite some time either. What's the story there then?"

"He's working away."

"Oh? Where exactly?"

"On the rigs."

"Interesting." She pulls a face.

"Look. I'm not being funny Sal, but I feel like I'm in a police interview here. What's your game?"

"You've been no stranger to those lately from what I've been gathering."

"Why, what have you been gathering?" I suddenly wonder if it's been *her* sitting outside in the car, watching. But she's already claimed to not be driving today so I can't check right now. But I could get her to write something down - maybe her address. Check her handwriting against those notes.

"You've certainly become a beacon for death and disappearance." She reaches for the bottle and drains it into her glass. "It's going down a treat this." She's got the start of a red wine moustache and I've got the start of a plan formulating.

"I'll open another, shall I?" I push my chair back and stride across the kitchen. This will be my course of action. Another glass or two should really loosen her inhibitions and get her talking. "Shall we take these through to the lounge?"

"Sounds like a plan." She picks up her glass as I grab a bottle from the rack.

"Come through."

CHAPTER 31

"Whoa. You've done alright for yourself." She looks around before sinking into the armchair nearest the fireplace.

"I'll leave this here shall I?" I slide the coffee table in front of her and place the bottle on it. "And there's plenty more where that came from." I need to get to the bottom of exactly what her motive is for being here, and then get her drunk enough so I can deal with it. *My way.* I sip from my own glass to maintain the impression that we're getting drunk *together.* She's going to regret ever casting her shadow over my doorstep.

"Gosh, is it warm in here, or is it me?" She slides her cardigan off and drapes it over the chair arm. "Maybe I'm getting to that age."

"You've years before all that," I reply, whilst knowing she actually hasn't. We sit quietly for a moment. As well as loosening her tongue, it's time to lull her into a false sense of security. I wonder when she's going to let me know why she's really here. "Shall I find the photos from that French exchange we went on?" I load as much enthusiasm into my voice as I can muster. "I haven't looked at those for years." I stride over to the sideboard without waiting for her reply. I need to keep her occupied whilst I get as much of this wine as possible down her neck. She doesn't know what she's kicked off in me by mentioning my mother.

"What, from when we were fifteen, you mean? I've never seen them."

"Well, you're in for a treat then." I pull the sideboard door open. There are hardly any photos of me from when I was younger, only a few pre-school ones, before Mum really got off her head on smack. After that she was too out of it to even feed and clothe me, let alone take photographs. The care home I was in footed the bill for me to go on the French trip.

In the thirty minutes or so that follows, I almost let myself relax into Sally's company. Her purpose for visiting me seems to be momentarily sidelined. We discuss the people we used to know in the photos - who's doing what now, and where? She's kept in touch with quite a few people. Unlike me.

By now we're well onto the third bottle. Or should I say *she* is. I'm taking tiny sips, and only when she's looking. I wouldn't be surprised if she's developed a drink problem over the years. She can certainly put it away. However, what she doesn't know is she's now putting away some home-made stuff, brewed by Darren a couple of years ago, and once famed for its potency. He proclaimed it to become even more lethal over the passage of time. That said, she could be drinking Strychnine right now and I doubt she'd notice the difference.

"Some people would kill to live in a house like this." She's slurring her words. We're on our way. "But then, you probably have."

"Right, I've had enough." I slam the package of photographs onto the coffee table. "You and your snide remarks. Whatever it is you've come here to say, spit it out."

She's drunk enough. Things might as well get moving. She pauses - and the only sound that passes in or around us is the boiler firing up from the kitchen. "Do you know there's a Facebook group been set up to support Donna?"

"What?" I wasn't expecting to start up a conversation about Donna. We all went to the same school back in the day but her and Lou were above us by at least a couple of years.

"Yeah. In support of her appeal."

"If a Crown Court has found her guilty once, I can't see how..."

"She doesn't look the sort if you ask me," Sally cuts in. "Which is why that public gallery's going to be full to bursting. And I'm going to be sitting at the front of it."

"Why would you all waste your time?"

"I wouldn't miss it for the world."

"She was found guilty by a bloody jury of ten people! Isn't that good enough for you?"

"Not unanimously though. Plus she's got cast-iron grounds for appeal, according to what's been leaked from her legal team." She places her glass onto the coffee table, slopping wine over the side. "Right from the start. I thought it was all very odd."

"Who cares what you think?" I imagine she's going to tell me what's *odd* anyway. I hope I'm nothing like her when I'm drunk, with her wine-stained lips and her bloodshot eyes.

"But what's really odd is that you're living in the house of Donna's best friend, whilst *she's* serving time for-"

"I married Lou's ex, didn't I? This was *his* house too."

"So where is he then? No one's seen him since last August. His daughter's been all over social media, looking for him."

"I've already bloody told you where he is."

"And now, your neighbour is dead too. The one you nearly bullied to death at school. What's the story, Liz? You know more than you're letting on."

"You bullied her just as much as I did."

"I bloody well didn't. I just tagged along." She jabs a finger in my direction. "*You* were the one who made her life a misery."

"So, why did you carry on hanging around with me? You can't deny you took more than your share of the money I got out of her."

"Because *you* wouldn't let me out of your sight." Her jaw tenses as she points again. "After you'd told me your sick secret."

"You're the last person I should have told anything." I point at her. "I'll never know why I did."

"Well I for one, wish you hadn't." Sally reaches for her glass again. "Do you know how much of a burden that was for me back then? Knowing what you'd done and not being able to tell anyone?"

"So why are you here now? We lost touch for very good reason. We never had to have anything to do with one another again, yet here you are. I don't want you here."

"Have you ever told anyone else what you did to your Mum, Liz?"

"Why do you keep banging on about that? It's ancient history."

"For you it might be."

"I was just a kid. It's dead and buried now."

"I thought it was dead and buried too, which is why I've never said anything. But then all this has happened." She sweeps her hand in front of herself. "With you smack bang at the centre of it. Two people dead. Another in prison when any idiot can tell she shouldn't be there. And one more who hasn't been seen since last summer."

My fists bunch in my lap. "You ought to mind your own business Sally. You've always been good at sticking your beak in."

She swallows more wine. "Perhaps my conscience won't allow me just to stand back any longer."

"Conscience. *You?* You don't know the meaning of the word."

"Of course," she pauses. "I could be persuaded to keep quiet. Similar arrangement to before?" She looks around again. "You're clearly good for it, looking at the set up you've got here and the life I've been watching you lead. Whilst I've got more than a few debts that need to be settled."

"Ahhh." I guessed as much. "You're here to blackmail me." Yet she's so *nice* with it. Exactly as she was at school. Pretending to be my friend, extracting everything she could, whilst using her knowledge of the truth as a stick to beat me with.

"I've never liked the word *blackmail*. A better word would be *compensation.*"

"Compensation! For what?"

"The guilt. *Your* guilt, yet you've forced *me* to live with it. I've known all along I should be doing something... getting justice for what you've done, yet not being able to - all to save your sorry arse."

"You can't prove a thing Sally."

"I can tell them everything I know. And I mean, *Everything.*" She empties the contents of her glass into her mouth and slams it down. "That would certainly be enough to kick things off."

"Why would you want to do this to me? You come to my house, drink my wine, pretend to be my friend, yet all the while, you're stabbing me in the back."

"Don't take it personally Liz." A ghost of a smile crosses her face. "Only, desperate times call for desperate measures." She reaches for what's left of the third bottle of wine and drains it into her glass.

A silence descends between us. I wrack my brains, searching for my next move. I can't throw her out of here. Not with a gob like that on her. No, I need to lighten things here.

Throw her off guard, then I'll have her. "OK. Perhaps we can come to an arrangement. But you've got me all wrong Sally. I'm not that thirteen year old girl anymore."

"Nope. I know. You've gone bigger." Then as though she's talking to no one in particular, she adds, "Darker. Cleverer. Or so you think."

"Before passing your judgement on me Sally, you should try considering a few things. You've got no idea what it's like to have a mother who cares about her next fix instead of you. Not to know where your next meal is coming from or whether some weirdo man coming through the door is going to rape you as well as your mother. I did the woman a favour. I put her out of her misery. And me out of mine." I run out of breath as the words leave me. My chest is tight. She's absolutely forced me into a corner where there is only one outcome. I didn't want this, not anymore.

After a few moments, she jumps up, muttering something about needing the bathroom, before staggering to the door. I wouldn't be surprised if she's off to throw up.

She bangs around for a while, then my bedroom door squeaks. She's clearly nosing around. I hope she's not sobering up. I resist the urge to go up there and 'catch' her. That isn't part of my plan.

Eventually she returns, looking sheepish. Then drops back onto the armchair like a rock into the sea. She actually looks drunker now than when she headed upstairs, so I don't bother asking her what she's been hoping to find up there. I wonder what she'd say. *A body? A stash of money?*

Getting to my feet, I nod towards the empty bottle and say, "I'll get some more wine, shall I?"

"I think I'd better have coffee actually." She can barely articulate the words. She's not sobering up. All is as I need it to be. Good. That wine hasn't let me down. It's the same batch I drunk when I let it be known to Helen what I'd done to Lou. I know better than anyone how lethal it is.

Whilst the kettle is boiling, I rummage around in the kitchen drawers. Finally, I lay my hands on the plastic box I always knew would come in useful one day. Lou's B12 injection kit, containing a dozen or so syringes. She certainly has no use for them anymore. I, however, have.

What I've got planned might not work, but I've sure as hell got to try it. If that bitch thinks she can waltz in here and blackmail me *again*... Well, I'm going to be the last person she blackmails. Ever. I've come too far for anyone to threaten everything I've had to strive for.

When we were kids, I had to resort to robbing from people like Helen to satisfy Sally's demands for money, not that I didn't benefit from the money. But it's not just that. She's sniffing around far too closely to the rest of it for my liking. Asking questions about Lou, Darren and Helen. I've got much more to lose these days, having just met Stephen. I've got a chance with him, a big chance, I need to keep a lid on everything. Therefore Sally's got to go. Permanently.

I reckon she's drunk enough for me to get away with what I'm about to do. As long as I can persuade her that having a lie down in the guest room and sleeping it off might be a good idea.

There's no need. I can't help but smile to myself as I push open the door into the lounge. I sit in the armchair, watching her for a moment. Her slack-jawed face is bathed in the mid-afternoon sun, her drool glistening in its rays. She's well gone. However, I'll wait a little while longer. Just to make sure.

Half an hour passes. She hasn't moved a muscle. In fact, she's so completely still that occasionally my vigilance travels to her sternum, watching for movement, checking that she's even breathing. If she wasn't, that would certainly simplify the situation.

Thirty-five minutes. I need to get this over with. Shuffling along the carpet, I peel back a plaster and lay it on the coffee table. Then I pluck two syringes from the pocket of my jumper. Turning up the heating whilst we were in the kitchen has done the trick - it forced her to keep her cardigan off.

The arm I'm after hangs over the side of the chair. This is it. It's almost too easy. I know only too well I've got just one chance of getting this right. Straight in, straight out. Clean as cut glass.

I pull back the syringe as far as it will go. To steady myself, I take a deep breath as I lower myself beside her. Here we go again. Suddenly I'm thirteen again, kneeling beside my stupefied mother, forced to do something desperate. Back then, it felt like the only way to save myself. I study Sally's arm, choosing the best vein.

Having done this before, I know what I'm looking for. Only that time, the syringe I clutched contained enough heroin to kill a horse, let alone my mother. This time, nothing is needed. Just fresh air. *The best medicine,* my mother used to say when she locked me out of the house as a kid. And of course, the other thing that's going to be required, again, are my stage-worthy acting skills.

There's hardly a tremor in my hand as I bring the syringe to Sally's arm. Gently, so gently, the needle pierces her skin. I should have been a surgeon. She doesn't even flinch as I push it forward. Whether the air bubble will really be enough to cause a stroke or cardiac arrest, like I've heard it should, remains to be seen. But I've got another syringe ready just in case. Slowly, I withdraw it, dab the blood away and smooth the plaster over. If it's noted at the post mortem, they'll just conclude she's had a blood test or something.

I retreat to the kitchen. Put the kettle on. Then watch the syringe dance around in a jug of boiling water. Eventually, I replace it in the box. Put it away.

I glance around the kitchen, at the life I've painstakingly carved out for myself. I might have allowed Sally to have one over on me when we were young, but she was right. I've upped my game since then. She might have suspected my involvement in the deaths of the others, but I doubt she'd have known the extent to which I was involved. If she'd known what I'm *really* capable of, I doubt she'd be sitting where she is right now.

Another half an hour passes. I fold some laundry. Wonder if Stephen is thinking about me. He mentioned being in a meeting all afternoon. I'll send him a message from the computer later.

All is quiet. How long will it take to work? Will it have worked by now? As I head back towards the lounge, I realise that I've never felt so peaceful at the end of someone's life. The very first time, with my mother, it was the last thing I wanted to do. Not really. But I had no choice. She was dragging me down with her. Then with Lou, Darren and Helen, the end was violent and unsavoury.

Here, with Sally, it's totally different. Which is the least I can do for a person I used to be such good friends with.

DEAR DIARY
HELEN

I wonder if a person can actually die from not sleeping. Sometimes I drop off for a few minutes but I'm quickly awake again, my mind going around and around like a fairground ride. No, fairground rides are happy. My life has *never* been happy. Perhaps it never will be.

When I'm lying here in the darkness, I remember how Liz, Sally, and the others, used to bully me at school. It was hell. They were *all* as nasty as alleycats but Liz and Sally were the worst. However I can't imagine Sally would have bullied me on her own. She was more Liz's sidekick.

Miraculously, I didn't see Sally ever again after leaving school, or Liz, despite us all living only several miles apart - as I found out later. But suddenly, we were 'bumping into each other' all the time. Every time I saw Liz, I couldn't shake the sense that she'd deliberately sought me out. She had no reason to be in the initial meeting place; there would have been a dozen supermarkets closer to her home. Knowing what I know now, it's possible that as well as spying on Lou, Liz was spying on me. I hope to hell she never saw the occasions Darren came and went from here. They were few and far between, but she found out about Donna in the end, so why not me? I've wrestled with this scenario repeatedly and have come to the conclusion she'd have said something or done something to me by now if she'd any inkling whatsoever I was once sleeping with her husband.

She invited me for a coffee a couple of times. I didn't really want to go but felt too scared to say no to her. I'd morphed into the Helen of old, petrified of what Liz Welsh might to do me. Once, as I faced her over the table, I remember thinking *what the hell am I doing here? With you of all people.*

She would pummel me for information. Who was Lou's new boyfriend? How often was Donna round there? Had I seen anything of Darren? Was he collecting Charlie on the occasions when he'd said he was working? Whenever she said his name, there was a tremor to her voice and a darkness seemed to enter her eyes. It was enough to make me wonder if she knew about me and him already. Perhaps, once she'd got her claws into that house and the lifestyle she enjoys now, she'd always intended to get Charlie out of the picture. Followed by Darren. I can't deny he was a complete arsehole to me - I was to him, as he told me the last time he came to my house, nothing better but a *posh wank*. He did nothing but use me, however I never got even a whiff of a violent side to him.

Therefore, I should have known right away the night Liz dragged me into all her shit that the necessity for her to have acted in self-defence against Darren was a complete load of crap.

The more I think about it all, the more 'convenient' it all seems. I'm certain I was targeted all along. As Liz's new sidekick to take Sally's place. But then, how did she find out I was Lou's next door neighbour in the first place? And am I just being paranoid? As usual? All I do know is that I'm driving myself demented. And I'd give *anything* for a proper night's sleep.

CHAPTER 32

I STARE at the imposing building before me. This is where I could end up if things don't go my way. Porridge and mail bags. I seem to have been sailing closer and closer to the wind just lately. Perhaps I should be giving things more thought. When I'm plotting out what I'm going to do to someone, I don't tend to think beyond the deed itself - instead I'm totally fixated on just getting the person in question out of the picture. The consequences come later, as they are at risk of doing this time.

I was exactly the same as a child. *Act first, think later,* my mother used to parrot at me. When she could actually speak, that is. Before whatever she could shoot up her veins became more important than my behaviour.

Still, she schooled me well in the deft usage of a syringe. It certainly brought it all back the other day. And it wasn't the first time Sally had attempted to use something I'd done as her weapon of mass destruction. Given the circumstances, it was fitting that I used exactly the same method she'd blackmailed me about to shut her up once and for all. Albeit this time the syringe was filled with fresh air instead of heroin.

Perhaps I've been fooling myself, believing I can reform. If I could, I would have done by now. But no, I didn't invite Sally to my door, I didn't ask her to blackmail me. She might have got away with it once upon a time. But when she sat across the table from me, smirking, whilst hinting that I could somehow be involved in the deaths of Lou, Darren and Helen, I realised I had to swat her off once and for all.

Even with what she was saying, surely there's no way she would *really* believe I would be *entirely* responsible. The more I think about it, the more I doubt she'd have even risked being alone with me. Not if she'd known what I'm really capable of.

I thought Helen would be the last life I'd ever be taking - I'd certainly never planned what happened with Sally. But she's been the most straightforward one of them all, well, other than my mother. If I ever have to take care of a situation with anyone in the future, it seems a syringe of none other than fresh air is the way to go.

I lock the car up, wondering if it will be safe left in this car park. Who knows what sort of people will be parking around me? However, there are cameras everywhere, so it should be OK. And according to the information sheet that came with the visiting order, I can lock things like my handbag in a locker. Fury rises in me at the reminder that my phone should be going in there as well, but the police still haven't returned it. I can't imagine what they can still be looking at.

Even with no sat nav on my phone to guide me here, I've managed to get here early. Prisons always seem to be well signposted. I lower myself onto a wall to wait for two o'clock to come around so I can check myself in at the visitor's centre.

As I stare into space, I'm unable to stop replaying the events of the other afternoon, after I'd rung for 'help' for Sally. As far as I'm concerned, I gave a sterling performance.

"Come quickly," I'd screeched into Sally's phone. "It's my friend. I've just found her like this. I don't think she's breathing." I'd left it a good twenty minutes before calling an ambulance. Just to be on the safe side.

The operator talked me through CPR. *Breathe into her mouth. Chest compressions.* I got her onto the floor. I did everything they said. To the letter. Crying the whole time into the phone that *it was useless, nothing I was doing was working.*

When the paramedics eventually turned up, I was exhausted. Not only from my exertions onto Sally's lifeless chest, but the pretence of keeping up the hysterical friend façade.

They confirmed almost straight away there was nothing they could do. Pronounced her dead there and then.

"Was it all the wine she'd drunk?" I sank to a chair, my head in my hands. "I should never have let her drink so much."

"At this stage, It's looking like she's suffered a cardiac arrest." The paramedic was kind. "A post mortem will be able to tell us more."

"A cardiac arrest? God, to think I was only in the kitchen when it happened. Tidying up, and sorting out laundry, instead of saving my friend's life."

"You mustn't blame yourself. We tend to find in Sally's age group that there was something underlying. A condition she wouldn't have even known about."

"So there's nothing I could have done? Is that what you're saying?"

She nodded, looking sad as she looked from me back to Sally, laid out on my carpet in front of the window. "You shouldn't be on your own. Is there anyone you can call to be with you?"

I could hardly tell her my phone had been confiscated as part of an investigation into the death of another of my 'friends.'

"I'll be OK," I replied. "I'll maybe go to my boyfriend's place." I knew I wouldn't really turn up out of nowhere in Stephen's neck of the woods, much as I'd have liked to have done. And, I knew I had this visit with Donna looming.

"If you could wait here, at home, for now please." The paramedic got to his feet from where he was crouched beside Sally. "With Sally's death being so sudden, the police will need to ask you a few questions."

My face must have given a hint of something. There was something far more abrupt in the voice of the male paramedic than that of his colleague. I didn't like the way he was looking at me, even if that was my imagination.

"Don't worry." The female paramedic rested a hand on my shoulder. "It's just a formality."

It took two hours for the undertakers to come for her. The neighbours were agog at their windows. Yet again, we'd given them something to talk about. Surprisingly, the police didn't turn up until first thing yesterday morning. They can't have been all that concerned initially, that Sally's sudden demise was anything more sinister than a cardiac arrest. It was a different police officer, so DI Macron and Sergeant Wilson can't have been on duty. The fact that Sergeant Kathleen

Johnson was on her own also reassured me. The stars had aligned for me once again.

Sally was 'in line' for a post mortem, she told me. Like someone can be *in line* for anything after they're dead. But in light of Sally's age and the unexpected nature of her death, they needed to look closer. Thankfully the questions Sergeant Johnson asked were as quick and painless as Sally's death had been. Easy to dutifully answer, whilst pausing and allowing myself to become choked up in all the right places. *How long had I known Sally? Was I ever aware of any underlying heart or circulation issue? What time had Sally arrived? What was the nature of her visit? How much wine had she drunk? What had actually happened?*

Sergeant Johnson truly seemed to be swallowing my version of events. That Sally had fallen asleep whilst I was in the loo. I'd left her whilst tidying around in the kitchen, then I'd realised a while later that she didn't seem to be breathing. She'd been unresponsive, to use their lingo, so I'd called an ambulance. The rest, as they say, is history. It was just questions, then answers. She didn't even take a statement.

"I'm really sorry for your loss," she said as I showed her out. "We'll be in touch if we need to know anything else." I thanked her as I brushed a tear away.

A queue into the visitor centre is forming. I rummage in my bag for the visiting order and my ID.

It takes an eternity to get in. The endless waiting and the feeling of being trapped has echoes of when the cruise ship was being searched for Helen. I pass through three different desks, six sets of doors, a walk through a yard where prisoners are heckling from behind the barred windows. Then a scanner search, a dog search, a photograph, fingerprints.

Bloody hell. By the time I get to the final door I feel like one of the inmates myself. The only thing they seem to have fallen short of is a strip search.

There's only so long I can stare at the yellow brick wall in front of me, waiting for them to call out my name and number. For the first time since arriving, I study my fellow visitors. There seems to be a dress code of hoodies, joggers and trainers around here, even for the women. I look out of place in my designer jeans, knee length boots and knitted jumper.

It's like waiting in a bingo hall for someone to call house as numbers and names continue to be called out, one by one. Just as I'm on the verge of complaining to one of the circling guards a sharp voice calls *Meers. Table thirteen.* Unlucky for some. Donna. But not me.

CHAPTER 33

As I HEAD GINGERLY towards table thirteen, I'm struck by how much Donna looks like she doesn't belong here. Sally was right.

I couldn't hate anyone more than I hate Donna after what she's done with *my* husband. Despite this, it's undeniable what men see in her. That air of girlish vulnerability has probably ensured they're drawn to her like flies to a corpse. She's kept her hair long in here, though it's scraped back and lifeless. A lot like she is. Her eyes look larger and somehow more green in her gaunt face. She didn't really have any weight to lose before all this, but she's certainly managed to drop even more in the time she's been locked up. Her clothes, prison issue, by the look of them, hang from her. They'd probably have more shape on a coat hanger.

A flicker of recognition crosses her face as our eyes meet. We've never actually faced each other, apart from at her trial, but I've stalked her enough on social media. It's bound to be the same the other way round. Especially since she continued to sleep with Darren, time and time again, even after he and I got married. She deserves to be here for that alone.

As I arrive at her table, my stomach twists with anxiety. Until I got inside the prison walls, I didn't feel nervous at all. I don't do nerves as a rule. However, the closer I've got here, to the visitor's hall, the more the nerves have intensified. After all, I've no idea what she wants from me? Or what she knows. I wonder if she has *any* idea that it should be me sitting in her place. The only thing that continues to ensure we're not swapping over is I'm ten times smarter than she is. But I had to know why she sent that visiting order. I only hope that curiosity doesn't kill this cat.

We're silent for a moment, as if daring the other to be the first to speak. We must be the only inmate and visitor in the vast room not pleased to be in each other's company. As I lower myself into the chair facing her, my eye falls on the drinks counter. Much as I could murder some coffee, I'll wait. I'll hear what she's got to say, then I'm out of here. She's the last person I want to sit having a coffee with.

"Thanks for coming," she eventually says. "I wasn't sure if you would." Her voice is as dead as her eyes.

"I was curious."

"I heard about Helen." She narrows her eyes. She certainly looks to have aged from the photos I've seen online. "What happened? You were with her, weren't you?"

"Not when she topped herself," I reply. The people at the next table stop their conversation and look at us. "She was depressed." I attempt to soften my tone. I can do without people listening in.

Donna pulls a face. "I didn't realise you and her were as pally as all that," she continues. "Not to go on a cruise, of all things." Her face hardens as she stares at me. "It had *better* not be my friend's money that paid for it."

My expression probably conveys what I'm thinking already. But I say what's on my mind anyway. "You're one to talk about spending your friend's money Donna. I was in court, remember? What was it again, oh yes, a loan, a car, her purse, her jewellery box."

"I don't know a thing about her purse or her jewellery. Not that I'm going to discuss any of that with you."

"So what do you want to discuss with me?" I just want to get out of here. There's an air of desperation everywhere I look. People trying to cram their relationships into a two hour visiting slot. What a miserable existence.

"Why was Helen so depressed? She's always seemed OK when I've spoken to her?"

Bloody hell. She's clearly not letting go of this.

"What's with the sudden concern for Helen? I'm not here to discuss *her.*"

"I was only asking. Unlike *you,* I care about people."

"Yeah right. Whatever you say Donna. I just want to know why you sent me that visiting order, then I'm out of here." What I don't add is that I'll be taking a long shower when I get home. Wash away the stench of this place. It's a mixture of unlaundered clothing combined with rancid vegetables. "I can't imagine you've asked me here to dig for the lowdown on the next door neighbour."

"Far from it. I want to talk about Charlie actually."

"Charlie? What about her?" I hope the relief isn't too evident in my voice. I don't know why but I've been worrying, if that's the right word, up until now, that Donna's on to me. But she's not.

"She's been in to see me."

"Here?"

"Well we didn't exactly meet at Starbucks, did we?"

I feel like telling her that sarcasm doesn't suit her but instead, I say. "How? Haven't visitors got to be eighteen?"

She glances over at the play area. Why someone would bring a small kid into a place like this is beyond me.

"Who brought her in?"

"You don't need to know that. But what you do need to know is how much you're wrecking Charlie's life Liz." It's the first time she's used my name and I don't like it. "As if she hasn't already suffered enough already?"

"*I'm* wrecking her life." I laugh. "Let's just refresh our memories, shall we. On where it is you're currently sitting, and why."

"I'll be out of here in the next couple of weeks." She dismisses my comment with a flip of her hand. "On appeal."

"That's what they all say in this place, I'm sure." I laugh harder. "Still, if it helps pass the time faster."

She fixes me with a stony stare. "There's new evidence actually. You'll see."

It's not just her words, but the confidence in her eyes which unnerves me.

"What evidence?"

"I don't know the details yet. Not that I'd be telling you even if I did." Something in her face tells me she *does* know the details. She clearly thinks she's got one over on me here.

"Have you got a date for it? Your so-called appeal?" Now this, I'm interested in. This affects me. I wonder if this supposed new evidence had anything to do with Charlie visiting her.

"All you need to know is that you'd better get your stuff packed. Whether I get out of here, or not." With her saying that, she can't possibly know of my implication in anything. Her only interest is wanting me to hand everything over. Good.

"What the hell are you on about?"

"That's Charlie's house you're squatting in. And she wants it back."

"You mean you want to believe *you're* going to be living there as part of this little pipe dream you've concocted. You're deluding yourself."

"I *am* going to be living there. With Charlie."

"She wouldn't live with you. Not after everything you've done."

"Charlie knows I'm not guilty. Do you think she'd have been in to see me if she thought I was *really* capable of killing her mother?"

Dodgy ground. I need to move the conversation back. "I'm going nowhere. My husband has rights too."

"Darren gave up any rights he might have had when he abandoned that girl seven months ago.

"Like I've told Charlie, Darren's working away."

"So why won't you tell her where he is?"

"You mean *you* want to know Donna? Don't think I don't know about you slagging it with him behind my back."

"That's all in the past. I won't be going anywhere near him when I get out, if that's what you're worried about."

Too right you won't. I fold my arms and wait for her to carry on as the hum of conversation rises and falls all around us. I hope to God I never end up in here.

In fact, I reckon I could be doing myself a favour by getting away from Yorkshire whilst the going's good. Whilst I've still got my passport.

"So, back to why I wanted to see you. Charlie."

"What about Charlie?"

"She's been round time and time again, and all you can do is slam the door in her face." Her voice softens slightly which takes me aback. I prefer the sarcastic, confrontational version of Donna. "You lost your Mum at a similar age, didn't you?"

I swallow. "That's got fuck all to do with you. I don't even know how you've heard about that." Darren must have told her. Bastard. He had no right discussing my life with anyone. Especially *her*.

"Why the hell can't you show Charlie even the slightest bit of sympathy?" She leans forward in her seat.

"Why the hell should I? She's not my bloody kid. I had her forced on me, remember. And I've been forced to put up with her for long enough." One of the prison officers is staring at us. I'd better tone it down.

"That house belongs to Charlie, Liz. So does that inheritance. Yet it's sitting, or at least I hope it's still sitting, in some bank account that Darren seems to have got his hands on." She drives her finger into the table as if to emphasise each point she's making.

"You should be speaking to him then, not me, shouldn't you? I can't believe you've dragged me all this way, into this *shithole* for this crap?"

"Since he's gone awol, I'm speaking to *you*." She points at me. "Charlie wants her money, and she wants her house."

"And you've appointed yourself to sort that out for her, have you? If she wants anything like that, she'll have to do something a bit more official than have the likes of you summon me for a prison visit." Laughter bubbles within me. "Do you seriously think you can order me here and I'll just roll over and die?"

Another plan is bubbling away in my mind. This visit probably wasn't a bad thing, not if it's forced me to take stock and take some action. Whether I leave Yorkshire, or not, that money's staying under my control. And even if I do leave, the only way they'll get into that house is to force their way in. I'll make it look as though I'm still there.

"Someone's got to stick up for Charlie. She's got rights you know. We can go down the official lines if you want to push it that far. It won't take long for us to get you out of there. You do know that, don't you?"

"Rights? Charlie's still a kid for God's sake. And she's fine living with her grandmother. I'm sick of saying this." I slap my hand onto the table. "Read my lips Donna. Charlie is not my problem."

"I agree completely. But what *is* a problem is that you won't let her into her house. You won't even allow her over the doorstep. *Her* house, not yours. She's lived there her whole life. You've got no right doing what you're doing."

"I'll remind you again, shall I? I'm Darren's *wife*. So I *have* got rights." I raise my eyes, blinking in the glare of the florescent lights. "Well this is fun, isn't it? Going round and round in ever decreasing circles."

"I'll cut to the chase. I don't want to sit here with you any more than you want to be here. I've got you in here to give you an ultimatum."

"*An ultimatum!* You don't scare me Donna." I shake my head. "Not one bit."

"You either do the right thing, or you'll be forced to. If you just leave quietly, you'll never hear from us again."

"Us? Who do you think you are? You're banged up in here." My voice rises so much that those at the neighbouring tables turn to look at us. "There's absolutely *nothing* you can do from inside a prison cell."

"Up to now, Charlie hasn't known what to do about you." Donna ignores what I've just said and steams ahead with her argument. "She hasn't wanted to load her Grandma up any more than she already is. Which is why I'm stepping in."

"You can't step anywhere Donna."

"There isn't just me involved in this. I'm warning you Liz. You've got seven days to get your stuff out of that house. All of it. You leave the keys at Carole's, along with any bank cards for her accounts. She also needs address details of the company Darren's working for." Donna's voice has a tremor to it. Is it fear, or is it anger? If what's she's saying about her appeal is true, and she ever encounters me on the outside, it won't just be fear she'll be shaking with.

"Or else?"

"Or we do it the hard way. We'll force you out through the court."

"Fine by me. It'll take months to do that." I shrug.

"Well, as long as you're not expecting any money in the meantime. The two bank accounts have been frozen."

"By who?"

"Never mind *by who?*" She pulls a face.

If it wasn't for where we're sitting, I'd have probably gone for her by now.

"I hope you've got enough in your personal account to cover your moving expenses." Her sarcastic tone is back.

I stare at her, hoping for a hint that she's lying about the accounts being frozen. I've been so preoccupied with meeting Stephen, hiding the truth about Helen and despatching Sally, that I've taken my hands off the wheel. It's been a couple of weeks since I looked at Darren's account. I made a transfer right before the cruise. I should have a reasonable chunk of it left, even after shelling out for the flight back from Norway.

"Seven days. Like I said."

"And like I said, I'm going *nowhere.*"

"You can piss off now anyway." She raises her hand. "I can't stand being anywhere near you." I look to where a prison officer is marching towards us.

"Visit over Meers?" She looks me up and down. "You've still got an hour."

"I don't want to spend another minute in her company."

"Fair enough." The officer nods towards me. "If you'd like to make your way towards the exit via the fingerprint machine."

"Again? Why?"

"It's procedure."

"Do you actually keep them? My fingerprints, I mean?" So far I've only *helped the police with their enquiries,* so my prints aren't on their system. And I'd like to keep it that way. I'd no idea they'd take them in here.

"Why?" You haven't got anything to hide, have you?" The officer's laughter rings in my ears. I walk away from the table without looking back, worried my expression might give something away.

"Seven days." Donna's voice echoes across the room as I reach the door.

DEAR DIARY
HELEN

This is the last time I'll be writing in my diary for a while. Instead, I'll have to use the notes app on my phone. Without being able to write at all, I would go completely mad. It releases some of the agony, not to mention the guilt.

I'm worried, well terrified, about leaving the house, especially the garden, unattended. I keep telling myself that if someone was to discover Darren's remains out there, it can happen as easily whilst I'm here as when I'm not.

But let's say something was to happen to me... I hope I'm not tempting fate by saying this, but if I was to have an accident, or worse... if the house was standing empty for a while, or for *ever*, I know I'd want the truth about everything that's happened to come out *somehow*. Much as I despise everything about her, Donna's serving a life sentence for a murder she didn't commit. But the person who is really playing on my conscience is Charlie. The poor lass has been through enough. And now she thinks her father has disappeared on his own volition, and believes he doesn't give a toss about her.

Whilst I've still got breath in my body, I want the truth to come from *me,* in my words, from my lips. I need to be able to explain how and why I got involved, and why I was too scared to speak out sooner. I can still do the right thing. I know I can.

But as I know only too well, it's impossible to know what's coming next in life. If the truth needs to come out some other way, I have to make sure there is a way for *someone* to be able to discover it apart from through me. Whilst I'm about to hide this diary well, it won't be hidden *too* well.

CHAPTER 34

I LET a long breath out as I pull up outside the house. Home. I can't really call it that anymore. I should have known it couldn't last. I'm going to miss this place.

"Now what?" My voice is loud in the silence of my car as I notice Jenna stride up the drive from Helen's house. "Do one." I slam the car door. "I've got nothing to say to you."

"I want to know the truth Liz. I'll never believe my sister's death was a suicide."

A neighbour gardening across the road turns to the sound of Jenna's elevated voice and rises to her feet to watch. She probably thinks she's living in the middle of a soap opera with the carryings on at this side of the street. And she doesn't know the half of it.

"They won't release her body. I can't even lay her to rest." Jenna looks like she's trying not to cry. Perhaps she thinks I'll feel sorry for her.

"Nothing to do with me."

I just want to get away from here, away from the threat of being locked up like Donna. Especially now I've seen how gruesome it is in there.

Jenna carries on. "You shouldn't have the right to go on enjoying your life after what you've done to my sister."

"I wasn't with her when she jumped. How many times do I have to tell you?"

"I don't believe she jumped. Not for a minute. Anyway, the police want to speak to you again. And it's about time you told them what *really* happened." She follows me down my drive. My temper's rising.

If she goes on much more at me... "Leave me alone, I'm warning you."

"I won't stop until I prove *you* had something to do with it."

"Get out of my garden. You're trespassing. Don't come near me again."

"Your garden!" Her voice is a shriek as she throws her head back in laughter. "You shouldn't even be here."

There's such a knowing in her voice that I wonder if she's somehow in league with Donna and Charlie.

I unlock the door, and slam it in her face as she continues to rant. Then I glance down to the doormat. Shit. She was right about the police. I bend to pick up the card, along with a letter beside it.

Yorkshire Police. DI Macron. Please contact us as soon as possible. It could simply be to get my phone back. But something in my gut says it's more likely to do with Sally. I haven't been properly questioned about it yet. Or it could be about Helen. They'll have done this forensic post mortem or whatever it is they were doing by now. She could even want to speak to me about this so-called new evidence Donna was banging on about. But one thing is for certain. I can't just wait around here like a sitting duck. No way.

I drop the card back onto the floor, then turn the envelope over, my breath quickening as I notice the stamp above the address. *Evans Thwaite Solicitors.* This isn't going to be anything good either. I scan the page, taking note of the more salient points. I don't believe this. That bitch said I had seven days before anything official happened. They've been instructed by Mrs Carole Banks. Acting on behalf of Charlotte Rhodes. The bottom line is the activity on the bank accounts, and the inability to make contact with Darren Rhodes. The accounts have been frozen, pending investigation.

I dash to the kitchen. Lift the laptop lid and log into the accounts one by one. Sure enough, I can no longer access Darren's personal account or our joint account. I've never been able to access the trust account directly but I've been able to use the debit card for it. That will have been stopped. The set of bastards. I plug in the numbers for my own account. I really am screwed if I can't get at that.

My heart feels like it's banging against my rib cage as the site loads. I wrench a glass from the cupboard and slop some wine into it. Then return to the screen. I'm in. My account is fine. And there's more than enough for me to get away from here. Whichever flight is available, I'm getting on it. If only I could be going to Norfolk now, to Stephen. I wish I'd met him sooner. Perhaps then, I'd only have my mother's death on my tally sheet. The thirteen-year-old me, living in the circumstances my mother forced on me would surely be forgiven for what I did that day.

I've not been arrested, so as yet there are no bail conditions to adhere to. No surrender of my passport. There's nothing to stop me leaving. Yet. As long as I do it now, without telling anyone. It means cutting my losses completely with Stephen but that will be a small price to pay for keeping my freedom. Wherever I end up, I'll live under my maiden name. I can use a different first name too. Mum used to call me Beth when she was coherent. I've never really been a *Beth* but it's something different.

Provided I can get a cheap enough flight, then there'll be enough left to buy new clothes when I get to wherever I'm going. And I'll get my hair cut short. Just in case.

There's no reason to stay and wait to be evicted. I'll be gone before the results of Sally's post mortem, which could be any minute. The first thing they'll be doing is looking into the puncture from the needle in her arm. And there's still the investigation into Helen's death. I got the impression from Jenna that something's about to blow up there too. Going abroad also means I'm well away from Darren's body, and from this so-called new evidence Donna's talking about. After all, if one card flips, the rest of the pack will come tumbling down. That's how secure my foundations have always been. Like a house of cards.

I book a taxi through the computer then delete the history. Twenty minutes. I'll sort a flight when I get to the airport. There's just enough time to pack the essentials and close the house up. I'm not going to make it easy for them. As far as anyone will know, I'm still here. I close the bedroom curtains, and set the timer switch on the bathroom light and the light to what used to be Charlie's room. My car's outside and no one's got a key to the new front door lock. If Charlie thinks she's just going to waltz in here and take over, she can think again. There'll be a procedure they'll have to follow to get me out, or think they're getting me out. The longer people are trying to get in here to get to me, the more time I have to get well away and do what I need to do.

· · ·

Soon, I'll be able to hit the reset button. Start again where nobody knows who I am, or about anything I've done. I've been a prisoner in these four walls for long enough - I deserve a life as much as anyone else. It's just a shame I've got to lose Stephen in the process. Maybe one day...

The taxi pulls up outside. I hurry to the door. The last thing I need is for the driver to beep the horn and for one of the neighbours to pay attention to my leaving. I look left, then right. No one seems to be watching. I pull the door behind me and rush to the taxi.

"Leeds Bradford Airport. I'm in a rush to catch a flight," I tell the driver, lowering my gaze as I sit behind his seat.

Then noticing a police car as it rounds the corner, I bend forward to adjust my shoe.

Finally, I'm on my way.

Before you go...

Thanks so much for reading The Fall Out - I really hope you enjoyed it!

Frenemy is the prequel to the book you've just read and Nemesis is the final part.

Join my 'keep in touch' list to receive a free book, and to be kept posted of other freebies, special offers and new releases.

One of the best things about being an author is being in touch with readers.

You can also join via https://www.mariafrankland.co.uk, and this is where you can also find out more about me, and my other domestic thrillers.

BOOK GROUP DISCUSSION QUESTIONS

1. Discuss the psychology around what makes a bully a bully.
2. What was life like for Helen as a child? What effect did this have on her into adulthood?
3. Could Jenna have done anything differently to help her sister?
4. In your opinion, could Helen have initially felt justified for helping Liz in what became of Darren, after how he'd made her feel over the years?
5. Discuss Helen's feelings of inferiority and inadequacy. What could she have done to change things?
6. Have you noticed any glimmers of a conscience emerging from Liz about the lives she ruined and ended? If so, has she sustained them?
7. If she's not stopped, who might be next on Liz's hit list?
8. Could a friendship built on foundations like Helen's and Liz's ever be successful?

9. How could Helen's relationship with her parents be impacting how she lives as an adult?

10. Talk about how the story could have gone in an alternate direction had Helen jumped when given the choice, rather than fighting against Liz and being pushed.

11. Thinking back to the characters from book one, give three possibilities about what could happen in book three.

12. Did you think the relationship between Liz and Stephen softened her in any way?

NEMESIS (PROLOGUE)

It's impossible to tell where the commotion is coming from. Some sort of fight. Women, by the sounds of it.

People surge into the lobby, craning their necks upwards to watch. At first, I wonder if I'm seeing things. If I'm not mistaken, one of them seems to be hanging over the ledge.

When I was heading to our room on the first night here, I commented to my wife about how low those ledges are. "If anyone was really drunk," I'd said, "and got into a scuffle, it could be lethal." She'd laughed at my overactive imagination.

I count the floors up: one, two, three, four, five. Easily thirty feet. If that woman...

Everything's gone into slow motion. All I can see is flailing legs. It's impossible to see whether she's being forced off that ledge. Or those other women are trying to pull her back up. My wife clutches my arm, boring her fingers into my skin.

There's a thundering of footsteps as police charge around the edges of where we're gathered, towards the lifts. They're pursued by what must be hotel staff. My gaze flits to them all, then back up again. Oh. My. God. I can't imagine they're going to get there in time.

Then, a collective gasp. Women screaming. Children being ushered back. Meanwhile, someone's turned the music off.

Then, a scream that overrides them all. Blood curdling. Spine tingling. A sound that will probably echo around my mind for the rest of my days.

I shouldn't be watching. I shouldn't even look at her. It's a sight I'll never be able to un-see. The women, whoever she is. *Was.* Hitting the floor with such force and speed, I can only hope her heart stopped on the way down.

Blood seeps from every angle of the crumpled body. People rush forward, police storm in, hold them back. Others don't move. In shock, probably.

I look upwards again. The other women have disappeared. After a few moments, voices begin to fill the silence.

"What happened? Did she fall? Was she pushed? Who is she?"

To find out more, visit Amazon.

ACKNOWLEDGMENTS

Thank you, as always, to my amazing husband, Michael. He's my first reader, and is vital with my editing process for each of my novels. His belief in me means more than I can say.

A special acknowledgement goes to my wonderful advance reader team, who took the time and trouble to read an advance copy of The Fall Out and offer feedback. They are a vital part of my author business too and I don't know what I would do without them.

I will always be grateful to Leeds Trinity University and my MA in Creative Writing Tutors there, Martyn, Amina and Oz. My Masters degree in 2015 was the springboard into being able to write as a profession.

And thanks especially, to you, the reader. Thank you for taking the time to read this story. I really hope you enjoyed it.

INTERVIEW WITH THE AUTHOR

Q: Where do your ideas come from?

A: I'm no stranger to turbulent times, and these provide lots of raw material. People, places, situations, experiences – they're all great novel fodder!

Q: Why do you write domestic thrillers?

A: I'm intrigued why people can be most at risk from someone who should love them. Novels are a safe place to explore the worst of toxic relationships.

Q: Does that mean you're a dark person?

A: We thriller writers pour our darkness into stories, so we're the nicest people you could meet – it's those romance writers you should watch...

Q: What do readers say?

A: That I write gripping stories with unexpected twists, about people you could know and situations that could happen to anyone. So beware...

Q: What's the best thing about being a writer?

A: You lovely readers. I read all my reviews, and answer all emails and social media comments. Hearing from readers absolutely makes my day, whether it's via email or through social media.

Q: Who are you and where are you from?

A: A born 'n' bred Yorkshire lass, getting over the shock of turning the ripe old age of 50, with two grown up sons and a Sproodle called Molly. (Springer/Poodle!) My 40's have been the best: I've done an MA in Creative Writing, made writing my full time job, and found the happy-ever-after that doesn't exist in my writing - after marrying for the second time just before the pandemic.

Q: Do you have a newsletter I could join?

A: I certainly do. Go to https://www.mariafrankland.co.uk or click here through your eBook to join my awesome community of readers. I'll send you a free novella – 'The Brother in Law.'

f facebook.com/writermariafrank

⊙ instagram.com/writermaria_f

♪ tiktok.com/@mariafranklandauthor

Printed in Great Britain
by Amazon